Tomorrow *in your* DREAMS

Part I: The Basics

Part II: The Freudian Interpretation

Part III: 101 more Dreams

Appendix: Lecture to Hypnotherapists

Kurt Forrer

Author of *Pregrams of Tomorrow* (1991)

Midorus House

Published by Kurt Forrer 2012

Published with the assistance of
Publicious Pty Ltd
www.publicious.com.au

Cataloguing-in-Publication Data available on request

ISBN: 978-0-9873645-0-0

Also available as an ebook
ebook ISBN: 978-0-9873645-1-7

Cover art by Lyndel Thomas
Cover and book layout design
by Publicious Pty Ltd
www.publicious.com.au

To my beloved wife, Lyndel

And you, my Wizard, are the key
To that which came to pass:
It's you who challenged me
The Whole beyond the Half to see,
As through a crystal glass.

You may, yourself, be unaware
Of what you did, and how
You touched a chord so rare
In me: I knew it slumbered there,
But sought in vain till now.

Eva

Table of Contents

Foreword

In 1970 I was terrorised by a series of horrific dreams. Because I feared that dreams might come true literally, my life turned into a living hell. It began to undermine my marriage and my career shifted onto shaky ground. There was no one I could turn to. So the question of how dreams might become reality began to usurp my thinking to such an extent that there was scarcely room for any other thought in my head. This was particularly so before going to sleep. I began to dread the nights. Their terror grew and soon I lived in constant fear of sleep.

The most horrific dream of all took me into a green field. In the middle of it stood, buried up to the buttocks, a black statue of what I later found to be a representation of Persephone. As I looked over to the dark Goddess I was suddenly whisked away into her womb, which felt like a pitch-black cellar. There I floated about in frozen angst. Suddenly a green fluorescent swastika* and a luminous disk* of the same colour began to spin before my eyes. A few moments later a TV screen lit up below me. On it appeared a cartoon-like figure on a throne. It reminded me of a painting of Daruma by an old Zen painter. His fierce eyes protruded from their sockets like a couple of tennis balls. In his raised hand he held a sceptre made from the wheel and axle of a railway car. There the memory of the dream broke off. I woke in a sweat gasping for air. The dream had been more real than waking. In fact as I slowly woke from this terrible vision I thought I was going to sleep.

The next morning I woke with the memory of a dream that played itself out at once and so clearly that it was as if a door between night and day, between the world of dreams and the reality of waking, had been flung wide open.

I

All my fear of dreams had instantly been wiped out. I felt I was given the key to the mystery of dreaming. For twenty years I used that key to unlock the secrets of the night. Then I wrote my first book to make public my findings.

Almost another decade later I was induced to write the present volume. By now all my observations had been verified thousands of times, not just by me, but also by my wife and the members of my regular dream workshops.

---

* It only occurred to me much later that the swastika and the disk were the emblems of the Sun and the Moon respectively. The two together suggest the transfer of the dreams of the night to the waking experiences of the day.

Consciousness is the *sine qua non* of existence.
It means that anything we think or do
Is subservient to consciousness.
Having no control over consciousness,
Where is our control over thoughts and deeds?

From 'Aphorisms' by Kurt Forrer

A Word of Warning

The popular saying, 'a dream come true', goes much deeper than commonly assumed. To most people it is little more than a way of saying that something they had wished for, yet believed to be unattainable, had been realised. In other words, the dream that had come true for them was in their mind not a dream of the night, but rather a reverie of the day.

Put another way, they would not see their 'dream come true' as being in any way associated with sleep, but rather with waking. They would say, if we asked them about it, that it was simply something they had thought of often and with special longing.

It would not occur to them that their phrase, 'a dream come true', might go deeper than that. They would find it ludicrous to think that their daydream might have sprung from a dream of the night. If we would put that possibility before them, they would probably just laugh or shrug their shoulders. And if we asked these same people if they dreamt at all, they would most likely say, 'I never do', or 'only very seldom'. Such people see themselves as non-dreamers.

If we put the same possibilities before the other part of humanity, the 'dreamers', they would be inclined to listen to us and consider our proposal as feasible. To me this idea that daydreams have their roots in night dreams is not just feasibility, but fact. As a consequence, this book about dreams and dreaming makes a case in favour of daydreams being rooted in night dreams. It goes even further than that. It purports that all our ideas, all our thinking and doing, in fact our entire existence, has its roots in our dreams.

When I tell people of this conviction of mine, they often respond with things like: "That is a frightening thought!" Because of such reactions I wrote this 'word of warning'.

It hopefully will serve to forestall some of the fears and anxieties that might otherwise arise due to my claim that our dreams of the night will manifest in our waking life. Although I have dealt with this in the main text of the book, I want to draw attention to it at the very start, so as to save you, the reader, unnecessary apprehension and angst.

The most common factor that causes such anxieties is the belief that dreams, should they come true, would manifest literally. In short, if we dream of the death of our best friend, we might fear that our friend will physically die. Whilst this is a very rare possibility, it is much more often than not a sign that our friendship is over. In other words, while the dream will portray the death of a person, waking reality will see the death of our interaction with that person. Such associative manifestations are far more common than literal ones.

Dreams are in the main allegories of things to come, rather than literal previews. If we read our dreams literally instead of allegorically, then we make the same mistake as taking the stories of the Greek gods, for instance, as physical fact. It would just be like believing that a physical Eros had actually flown into Psyche's bedroom to make love to her, when in reality that story wants to do nothing more than present the human susceptibility to love.

Introduction

Dreams love drama; they excel in theatre and they put us, the dreamers, centre stage. When they cast us as the main actor, we may often find that the role we had played on the nocturnal stage will, when the same plot is acted out on the waking stage, belong to someone else. We may for instance dream that we had a car crash. Then, on the dream day, that is after we have dreamt the accident, we will hear that a friend of ours had that very crash, or we will see a similar crash on TV, suffered by someone quite unknown to us. Or we might read of it in the paper accompanied by a startlingly accurate photo of the scene of the crash, or we might hear of it on the radio, or just receive the news from our neighbour. I call this shift from the dreamer to someone else ego-transference. It is so typical of dreams and occurs so frequently that ego-transference must be seen as a grammatical peculiarity of the dream.

Another characteristic of the dream is that its highly dramatic scenes portrayed in the most breathtaking and realistic manner will often get 'scaled down' in waking reality.

Instead of manifesting as live drama as we might expect, it will often turn out to be merely a bright tale told by a friend of ours. Looking back to our dream from such a verbal manifestation, it becomes evident that the dream will at times anticipate the spoken word in the same colourful and realistic way as the myth of Eros and Psyche portrays our susceptibility to love. The reason for doing so is brought to light by the very myth in question. And that reason is emotional involvement.

It is because of our emotional involvement that our dream of an accident will put us centre stage and cast us as the main actor. It is for that same reason that dreams will often anticipate a mere piece of conversation in the most realistic terms, with us right in the middle of it. It will picture the mundane contents of a letter, for instance, in the most realistic and exciting manner, with us as the star of the show, when in truth the letter may be about an ordinary experience one of our relatives or acquaintances might have had.

In other words the dream will do with the news from our sister for instance, something our brain is doing every time we are face to face with a dry piece of paper engraved with coded squiggles. Just as those squiggles spring to life in our mind as we scan them, taking on human and animal form set in natural surroundings, conjuring up deeds before our eyes and words in our ears, so will the dream portray the news contained in such a letter as if we were there where our sister was, and as if we experienced all the things she reported ourselves. (Ego-transference again). And, to make such magic even more miraculous, the dream will do all this long before we hold that letter in our hands. Indeed it is even possible that the dream will create such miracles even before our sister will think of writing to us!

In order to bring all this a little closer, I want to tell you just such a dream and how it became waking reality. First my dream: "My partner and I were travelling with a crowd of people by bus to a certain destination in Switzerland. Once there, we found out that we could also make independent excursions to destinations of our personal choice. I got really excited over this, telling my partner that I would take her to a favourite lake of mine, with no motorways on one side of it, thus making the place I wanted to show her, accessible only on foot or by boat."

On the second day after this dream, a letter from my sister who lives in Switzerland arrived. It told me that her daughter had come with her husband from Holland to spend a few days with her. (This corresponds, of course, with my dream-arrival in Switzerland in the company of my partner.) The letter went on to say that a couple of days after, another eight relatives arrived in order to take everyone on an outing to Lake Neuchatel - quite a crowd to be all travelling together. It is obvious that the dream prefigured this by 'the excursion of our own choice' that was to take us to a lake, albeit not to the one targeted in the dream. The reason for this change is to be found in my emotional attachment to the lake the dream had featured. The dream had also changed the fact of the crowd, featuring it in context of the bus trip to the holiday location, rather than in the excursion of personal choice. Such transference is quite common in dreams and is something that should be kept in mind at all times.

This shows quite clearly that reading a dream literally may lead us to utterly wrong conclusions. This should always be kept in mind when face to face with any dream. It should also be remembered that our dreams, because they love to highlight our emotions, might represent our impending anxieties as if they were physical fact.

One more word regarding death dreams. Children who are about to enter puberty will frequently have dreams that they have died or that the world blew up. In a sense this is true. They will die to their childhood, and their childish world will vanish forever. Please keep such transference or associative projections forever in mind!

P.S. Speaking of associative projection, I am compelled to report the following incident that took place just before this book went to press. My wife was holding a stall at the Saturday Market, collecting signatures in support of a more humane treatment of farm animals. On the table were photos of various animals, one of which was a pig. On the wall behind the stall were more such pictures with yet another pig. Next to her pamphlets lay a pile of my first book called '*DREAMS, Pregrams of Tomorrow*'. A woman came along, picked up one of the dream books and said: "Funny thing, this morning I had the weirdest dream of talking pigs!" Full of excitement my wife held up one of the flyers with a picture of a pig and pointed to the other photo of a pig behind her and I said: "I am here speaking on behalf of the pigs!" Before she could go any further, the woman burst out laughing: "You are not trying to tell me that my dream was about this!?" "Yes it was," replied my wife enthusiastically. The woman turned to walk away, still laughing as she disappeared behind the exit door.

Global Awakening

Thanks to the internet, a much broader view of the dream scene is unfolding. Sites like "Yahoo Dreams", for instance, offer a unique insight into the general attitude towards dreams. Like never before can we look at innumerable dreams of a wide cross section of the English speaking population. True, the querents that visit Yahoo Dreams are predominantly young people. The majority are seemingly of school age. I see this as a sign that the lore of dreams is entering a new phase: a phase of a deeper interest in the other, subtler, half of human existence.

But this group of youngsters also contributes considerable support to the idea that the dream can see the future. There is a steady trickle of observations passing through this site which underpins the notion that dreams do access the future. Currently it lists over twelve thousand dreams that clearly looked into the future.

At first many of these young witnesses are thoroughly confused about this. It is common for many of them to ask: "Is there something wrong with me?" or, "Am I going mad?" or, "Is it normal to dream the future?" or, "Do dreams really come true?" or, "How is this possible?" or, "Was it sheer coincidence?" It is to such questions that I respond with my 'standard reply' which is something like this:

Welcome to the most OPEN SECRET of life! Congratulations, you are waking up! Yes, the future is in our dreams, but most of the time it is presented metaphorically and only few people can read it correctly. I have a standard answer prepared for querents like you. It will give you an idea of what to expect when we start to observe our dreams seriously and keep a diary and scrutinise it on a regular basis. Many people are aware of déjà vus. The sceptics will say that déjà vu is coincidence or a trick of the brain. Apart from one exception, where there is a faulty neurological function, the déjà vu (which is French for having 'seen before') stems from a dream.

When we've had a déjà vu experience, realising that it stemmed from a dream, we may take it as a sign of psychic awakening. In time we will discover that dreams are the blueprint of our life and that everything is planned for us and that there is really nothing else to be done but to enjoy life. Many fail to discover this because they have been brought up in a society where this way of looking at life is anathema.

I have made a lifelong study of the future factor of dreams and found that ALL dreams are about the future. At the beginning of our awakening to this fact, we get a glimpse of this whenever a dream comes true literally, when it becomes a déjà vu.

As we focus more on this phenomenon, we will fully realise that dreams are the blueprint of life, exposing them as the basis not only of our usual waking experiences, but also of psychic perception. Indeed, they are the cause not only of déjà vu, but also of premonitions, of intuition, of instinct and all psychic phenomena as well. The difference between these and the déjà vu experience is that unlike with déjà vu, we have no recollection of the dream that told us what would happen, or where an idea or inspiration, or a premonition came from.

Once we have learnt the language of dreams, we will realise that we are in the hands of an energy that is much greater than our little selves. Once we have realised fully that dreams are our prompters at the footlights of the theatre of life, we will learn to yield to that all-encompassing energy.

Indeed, we will understand that we are not separate from that energy. We will also see that TIME IS AN ILLUSION. We will comprehend then that when we are awake, we are governed by that part of the brain that slows everything down to a 'step by step' perception of reality. As well as that, we will also learn that when we are asleep and dream, another part of the brain is at work. This is a part, or more precisely, a combination of parts, which allows us to see some distance into the future, a future where the barriers of time have broken down to a certain extent.

One of the best pieces of evidence that time is illusory and has different speeds is the Near Death Experience, NDE for short. During this traumatic time the dying persons see their whole life passing before their eyes. This happens at such a high speed that it only takes minutes to cover an entire life experience in the tiniest details.

With this in mind, we discover that THE BRAIN HAS THREE BASIC 'GEARS': The first 'gear' is the waking gear. There, things move slowly moment by moment with the future remaining totally hidden.

The second 'gear' is the dream gear. There, time and space are contracted like the information in a zip program for the computer. Once we wake up, this compressed information unscrambles itself like a zip program on the 'desktop' of our mind. We call it our waking experience. Dream interpretation is unzipping this program before it scrolls down as waking life.

The third gear is the 'fast-forward' gear, or more precisely, the 'fast-backwards' gear, which comes into action in some Near Death Experiences.

There is also a fourth slot for our gear stick: 'NEUTRAL'. This neutral position is the most difficult to grasp. Only the mystical experience will open up the brain to that most incomprehensible of all 'gears'. I called it 'neutral' because it is open to all directions simultaneously: we experience past, present and future ALL AT ONCE. It is the supreme evidence that time is an illusion. But it also shows that we, who have not had the experience of the 'open gear' yet, are 'split personalities'; split into dreamers and 'wakers'. One way of healing this rift between our two apparent halves is to observe our dreams and correlate them to their corresponding waking experiences. By doing so we are crossing the rainbow bridge to total integration with the SELF of selves.

Part I

The Basics

1. The three main phases of human consciousness.

The brain constantly produces electrical currents. They are known as brain waves. On the EEG (Electro-Encephalo-Graph) they show up as squiggly lines of varying design. The shape of these waves varies according to our state of mind. Each phase of consciousness has its own range of frequencies.

The waking brain: These frequencies of the waking brain range between 13-30 Hertz or 13-30 oscillations per second. They are called Beta waves. They are most common during everyday mental activity when we do complex thinking or fast mental work as, for instance, when we concentrate on solving a problem. The faster these waves vibrate, the less relaxed we are. Today's life in the fast lane produces all too many of these over-excited waves.

When we are in a calm and relaxed state the waking brain produces slower waves. They range between 8-12 Hertz. They are called Alpha waves. The brain also produces this kind of wave in a state of creative visualisation or the recalling of memories. So when we are remembering dreams, our brain is usually in this gear. It is a state of enhanced receptivity. Some scientists think this frequency is the bridge between the so-called conscious and subconscious mind. As you read on in this book, you will see that the term subconscious mind is really a misnomer. It should really be called dream memory. What nicely supports this contention of mine is the very fact that some scientists say that the Alpha state is not only the bridge between the 'subconscious' and the conscious mind, but also between the dream memory and the waking state.

The dreaming brain: When we are asleep and begin to dream, Theta waves take over from the Alpha and Beta frequencies. Theta waves have a frequency of 4-8 Hertz. This kind of frequency may also be induced during long and boring drives. On such occasions it often happens that we get sudden and unexpected ideas. We also may experience a heightened state of psychic perception. During deep day-dreaming Theta waves may also appear as is also the case in the state of deep hypnosis. This shows that the hypnotic state is closely related to dreaming. The earliest studies in dreaming concluded that dreaming was always accompanied by REM which means Rapid Eye Movement. Much later it was found that there is also dreaming without REM. Theta waves set in as soon as we are falling asleep. At that moment we see dream images or tiny dreamlets that last only for a very brief time before we sink into deep sleep. On occasions we can watch these images without completely losing waking consciousness. Then they are called hypnagogic visions. Although their structure is not like a fully-fledged dream plot, they are essentially dreams with the same qualities and capabilities as fully developed dreams.

The brain in deep sleep: In deep sleep there is no dreaming, no images to be perceived. In fact it is a state of light and bliss. Unfortunately most of us forget this boon as we wake up, because before we reach waking consciousness we go through a phase of turbulent and often bizarre and exciting dreaming. This erases all memory of the best phase of sleep. It can, however, happen that we slip into this state from a preceding dream. I say this because I have personally experienced it. But of that later. As is to be expected, this state produces very slow and calm brain waves of 0.5-4 Hertz or cycles per second. It is in this state that we recover from the toil of the day, stress and general turbulence.

The dream phases. When we go to sleep we briefly pass through a hypnagogic state. This is a Non-REM episode. It means that our eyes will not move rapidly to and fro as in REM sleep. At such times we see very short dreamlets before our inner eye. They reflect mainly past events and usually take place within a positive frame of mind. From there we dive directly into deep sleep. In that state we find rest and regeneration of our energies. Then, after a ninety-minute interval, we almost wake up. Our eyes flicker rapidly to and fro. This state is REM-sleep.

The earliest researchers thought that REM-sleep was the only time that produced dreams. Later studies found that NREM phases often contained fragmentary mentations of a subdued kind. The very latest research, however, has uncovered that these mentations are really fully fledged dreams, though of a short and retrospective character. When their retrospective tendencies were further examined it was discovered that these reviews of past events were in the service of improving future exploits.

REM dreams contrast sharply with the NREM kind since they are longer, livelier and more often than not filled with fear and anxiety. These apparently negative emotions, however, proved to be essential to the enhancement of our creativity. These discoveries suggest that nightmares are not totally negative experiences, but instead, helpful events in preparing us for subsequent adverse waking episodes. All in all these findings clearly support my contention that dreams are nothing less than the blueprints of the future.

In one night we pass through three or four sleep cycles that begin with NREM dreams from whence we drop into Delta sleep with its regenerative properties in order to return, after ninety minutes, to a REM dream phase. The first one of these is short, perhaps five minutes. Then we go back to deep sleep, but not quite to the same 'depth'. Once there, we stay in that state for yet another ninety minutes. Then we return again to the state of REM dreaming; this time for ten minutes or thereabouts.

With each cycle the REM dreams extend in time. The final REM phase may continue for twenty to forty minutes. It is this last act of our nocturnal theatre, which, like a drama on stage, pulls the scenes and acts of the whole nocturnal drama together and then recapitulates it all before bringing it to a climax.

Does everyone dream? Those who maintain that they do not dream are people who do not recall their dreams for one reason or another. Certain brain-lesions may prevent recall altogether, so that such patients will never be able to bring back a dream. Some will argue that these people do not dream at all. This is difficult to prove either way.

2. A few introductory examples of dreams and their later manifestations.

Dreams are chiefly allegories which are stories, situations or images that serve to symbolise a hidden and often deeper meaning behind it. When it used to be dangerous to criticise the king, writers would tell a fable or allegory about a lion. In other words the writers would substitute the king with a lion. This is an associative process, associative language, or as I call it, associative identification.

Because dreams are so allegorical and metaphorical, they are swarming with associative identifications. When the dream substitutes one person with another (the dreamer's ego with the ego of another) then associative identification becomes ego-transference. This is extremely common in dreams. It means that we may dream that we fell off a roof only to discover the next day that it was someone else who had this misfortune. In other words, we may discover that the dream had anticipated an accident that would happen to a neighbour, or that it had foreseen what we were to read later in the newspaper, hear on radio or watch on TV.

Dream A

'I went inside the little church with my bride. There was a mighty spread of fruits of the earth. They were displayed with great care on the altar. I thought it must be Thanksgiving Day.'

This man had been living alone for some considerable time. The dream announced a future relationship with an abundance of physical and emotional satisfaction. Once this became a living reality, he had reason indeed to celebrate a 'thanksgiving'. In some ways this dream came true literally, but not in others. He did get married, yet not in a church. Dreams often manifest in a mixture of ways: some parts may do so literally; others allegorically or metaphorically. (In this case the dream dramatised the couple's wedding in a church because this is a common social reality).

Dream B

'I have this recurring dream that I am in a hurry to catch the train. On the way I am dropping my briefcase and my personal effects spill all over the road. This forces me to waste time picking them up with the result that I always miss the train.'

Recurring dreams are a sure sign that we are stuck in a groove. It is more than likely that such dreams will continue to occur until we have resolved the issue that underlies them. Spilling all the personal effects means, of course, being in-effective. Since the effects are a very private possession, such accidents also see the dreamer spilling some of his most private matters of his life. Missing the train is a metaphor for missing a business opportunity or missing out on a job. While metaphors and allegories are quite naturally understood in everyday language, it seems to be a problem when they appear in dreams. It is for this reason that I often state the obvious.

Dream C

'I was driving along the road with my boys in the back seat. A whole lot of kangaroos started to hop past. Suddenly a big specimen jumped right in front of my car. The boys screamed: "Stop!" I hit the brakes, but it was too late. I hit the animal.'

Nine months later (protracted manifestation) this driver drove along a stretch of road with the very two boys of her dream in the back of her car. She came to an intersection where she had to give way. She stopped and waited for an opportunity to move ahead. There was a stream of cars zooming past. When she thought it was safe to go, she took off. Suddenly, and totally unexpectedly, a car came hurtling down the street from nowhere. The boys shouted, 'stop!' It was too late. There was a collision. The dream kangaroos turned out to be the cars of waking life. The big one of the dream was the unexpected car of waking reality. As is the habit of kangaroos, it 'leaped' from nowhere right in front of her car. The kangaroos were here a metaphor for the hazards of driving. Metaphors speak by associations. For this reason the dream kangaroos manifested associatively as cars in the waking world. They were an associative manifestation of the dream. This is a very common occurrence in realisations of dreams.

Dream D

'I was standing on a cliff by the sea. I looked to the horizon where I spotted a jet roaring towards me. Once it was overhead it stopped miraculously in mid-air. Its fuselage opened up and a shaft of light enveloped me. I was drawn upwards into the plane where I was thrust into the navigator's seat. A screen lit up before me with the map of Africa on it. That's when I woke up, unfortunately.'

This dreamer did go to Africa later on, although not in the navigator's seat and not in the curious way the dream had shown. All that is science fiction of the 1930's which today is taken seriously and experimented with. It is a splendid example that demonstrates how ideas come to us and how they eventually will find materialisation.

While such a dream might drive an inventor towards building an airship of this description, for this dreamer it was merely an expression of his burning desire to go to Africa there and then. Note the 'roaring towards me'. Standing by the cliff meant, of course, that for him the present lifestyle had come to an end. He was wishing to be lifted out of it so he could go on a new path of adventure. The dream showed him in the navigator's seat because he alone would be the one to resolve to go to Africa, instead of being inspired by anyone else. When we dream that we are driving a vehicle of any description, it means that we are in charge of a given situation. Obviously being in the backseat means the opposite. Being in a plane is a sure sign that we are in a hurry to get there. This is exemplified in the next dream:

Dream E

> 'My plane took off with a jerk. At the end of the runway there was a cemetery. I saw my mother's grave below. It was covered with pansies. To my dismay the plane gained height only very slowly.'

The word 'pansy' is derived from the French verb 'to think'. Pansies are flowers saying: 'Remember me?' It had to do with memories of his mother. Taking off with a jerk betrays the hurry of the dreamer to move on. His impatience is reflected in the fact that the plane is not gaining height soon enough. In this case it meant that he wanted to return to his homeland where his mother was buried.

Dream F

> 'I saw an alligator suspended in mid-air. It flashed its teeth at me. The creature reminded me of a colleague of mine.'

The colleague eventually got the dreamer's job. But it took a while. He lived in great suspense during that time. Time and time again it looked as if he could retain his position. In the end 'flashing teeth' got his job. Air is also spirit or an expression of thoughts, of our mind.

Dream G

> 'I hurried to the liquor shop to buy a bottle of gin. Just as I stepped towards the door, Lucy, the attendant, closed it in my face saying: "Sorry sir, I am closed!"'

This turned out to be a good description of lacking in spirit next day. So we need to watch the type of drink we will ask for in our dreams and how we will react to the attendant's refusal to serve it.

3. Why do we dream?

A contentious issue. Jung believed that our dreams were 'reconnaissance flights' for the purpose of scouting out future possibilities. Professor Jouvet*, a French investigator into dreams, thought they programmed our motor-sensory system. He came to this conclusion after countless experiments with cats. But he also pointed out that newborn babies seem to exercise their muscles while they were in the dream state. He explained that unlike adults, babies were much less 'anesthetised' in the dream state so that they could move their limbs much more freely than adults. *(Michel Valentin Marcel Jouvet, 1925 - Emeritus Professor of Experimental Medicine at the University of Lyon).

The dream as programmer. I believe Jouvet is right. But he does not go far enough. As I see it, the dream prepares not only our motor-sensory system or the body, but also the mind. Indeed, where are those hard and fast borders between mind and body?

The dream as problem solver. We don't have to look very far to find a plethora of evidence for this. There are innumerable reports that dreams will solve even the most complex problems. I have just mentioned that I believe that our mind is no less programmed by the dream than is our motor-sensory system. So it is of particular interest to know that the very mechanism with which the mind transmits its messages to the muscular system was discovered in a dream. The dreamer in question had been puzzled by this mystery for years. His name was Otto Loewi*. Long before Loewi was able to demonstrate this mechanism, he had a hunch that it was perhaps an electro-chemical process. But because he was unable to think of an experiment that would prove his speculations, he put the whole thing out of his mind. Then, one night, years later, he woke from a dream with the design for the definitive experiment. He went to the laboratory and performed the simple test required on a frog's heart. It worked. His nocturnal inspiration later became his theory of the electro-chemical transmission of the nervous impulse. *(Otto Loewi, German born pharmacologist, regarded as the Father of Neuroscience). Another German researcher before Loewi by the name of Kekulé* had also received in a dream the solution to a problem he was unable to solve. He had puzzled over the molecular arrangement of benzene. The result was the hexagonal benzene ring, which joins itself to other rings not unlike the cells of the honeycomb. The design was inspired by a dream he had during an afternoon nap. In it he saw a serpent that was biting its own tail while next to it circled a host of smaller snakes with their tails in their mouths. Of particular interest here is that while such a serpent has been an age-old symbol of eternal life, the benzene ring has become the symbol of biochemistry, which attempts to describe the perpetual self-propagation of life. *(Friedrich August Kekulé von Stradonitz, 1829-1896, German organic chemist, Principal Founder of the Theory of Chemical Structure).

There are many reports of mathematicians who have received the answers to their apparently insoluble problems in dreams. One famous man of figures was the Indian mathematician Srinivasa Ramanujan *. When he emigrated to Britain, the mathematicians there soon found that he was well ahead of the mathematical knowledge of the day. When asked how he accomplished his feats, he always said that the goddess he worshipped sent him the formulas in his dreams. He often found that the theorems given to him in his dreams were well ahead of his understanding, thus requiring a lot of 'catching up'. *(Srinivasa Ramanujan, 1887-1920, self-taught mathematician, said to be in the league of Euler, Gauss and Newton).

Many chess players have been shown in dreams how to play certain moves or a whole series of moves. The Marquis of Saint-Denys* reports that one of his friends had dreamt the solution to a problem that required reaching checkmate in six moves from a certain position. Inventions such as the sewing machine are based on dreams. Elias Howe ** had grappled for months with the problem of the right needle for his machine. Only after a dream in which cannibals had pursued

9

and threatened him with spears with holes in the spearhead, did he realise that the hole had to be drilled in the point of the needle and not at its end. *(Marquis d'Hervey de Saint-Denys, 1822-1892. He was a Sinologist and also made an intensive study of dreams, recording them from the age of 13. He was a lucid dreamer who wrote a book on the matter: "Les reves et les moyens de les diriger". Recently interest in his dream studies has overtaken his work on things Chinese.) ** (Elias Howe, 1819-1867.)

Thomas Edison ***, one of the most prolific inventors of all times, knew the value of dreams as problem solvers. He used to take afternoon naps, as did Kekulé on that famous occasion. In order to make sure that he would catch his dream, he placed a dollar coin on his head and a metal bucket between his legs. Once he nodded off he entered the hypnagogic dream state which often showed him the solution to a particular problem. Since he was falling asleep at the same time, his head would drop forwards and the clanging coin in the bucket would arouse him to catch the definitive vision. He found that a mere second or two were enough to perceive the answers he was looking for. *** (Thomas Alva Edison, 1847-1931, inventor of an endless stream of new devices among which are the phonograph, motion pictures, the light bulb and also mass production).

The dream as dress rehearsal. With such evidence, together with what Jouvet had said about the function of dreaming, it isn't such a big step to claim, as I do, that our dreams are the dress rehearsal for the stage of waking. By this I mean that we will never wake to a day unprepared for what it has in store for us. It also means that we, as the waking ego, have no say in what we will or will not encounter. Apart from the evidence already adduced in support of the claim that the dream is a dress rehearsal, there is also the fact that we never dream about well-practised activities like daily routines. If we do happen to dream about our usual chores for instance, it will be because something is going to happen in course of them that is unexpected, that is new and away from the well-practised routine.

Jung's belief that the dream is a 'reconnaissance flight into the future' in order to scout out new possibilities is yet another strut to the dress-rehearsal theory. Yet another thing that is underpinning this hypothesis strongly is the fact that premature babies dream up to 80% more in the period before the expected time of birth than babies that remain the full term in the womb.* This not only shows that premature babies are getting advance dress rehearsals to compensate for the loss of womb time, but that the time of their birth is known to the system and therefore predetermined. Another structural reinforcement is added from experiments requiring a subject to wear glasses that turn the world upside down. The effects in such cases were the same as with premature babies: a kind of accelerated dreaming called dream rebound. * (Full term babies spend about 66% in REM or the dream stage; by the time they are one year old this is reduced to 35%. Adults, on average, spend about 15-20% of their time in dreaming.)

The dream memory is our 'subconscious'. The dream memory also explains how we can know something 'subconsciously' about the future, how we can know it psychically, intuitively or instinctively. All such unwitting perceiving of things to come, all our presentiments, premonitions and foreknowledge of every description such as déjà vu, 'speak of the devil' and 'precognitive fantasies', come from our dreams. As we go through the day, we are constantly and unwittingly in touch with our dream memory. This is so whether we have remembered our dreams or not. Our dream memory will prompt our actions like a prompter at the footlights of the theatre but with one difference: we very seldom will 'hear' the prompter. In order to understand its cryptomnesic or incognisant workings we need to look at an important part of our brain.

The corpus callosum: The corpus callosum is the connecting 'nerve cable' between the left and the right side of the brain. It transmits information from one hemisphere to the other. If the image of a 'house' arises in the right hemisphere, for instance, we don't become aware of it until it has been sent over to the temporal lobe or the speech centre in the left side of the brain. There it is decoded and translated into the word 'house'. It is only then that we actually know that the notion of a 'house' had entered our mind earlier on. If the corpus callosum were severed for one reason or other, we would only be 'subconsciously' aware of the idea that came into our right brain. Here is the kind of experiment that will explain the situation: Present a flashcard with the word house on it to a patient who had his corpus callosum severed. Make sure that this information goes only into his right brain. This is done by sending the information through his left eye only. Ask him what the word says to which he will say: 'There is nothing written'. Then put a pencil into his left hand and ask him to draw what he sees and he will draw a house.* This shows that we can be aware of something without being able to say what it is until the information goes to our speech centre. This is erroneously called 'subconscious knowing' by psychology. This kind of awareness is very much there and not 'sub' to anything. All that is missing here is the ability to verbalise it. For this reason I have called this kind of knowing 'mute or incognisant awareness'. This situation explains to some degree how pictorial dream memories might prompt some of our waking actions throughout the day. * (Michael Gazzaniga, "the Social Brain", 'Psychology Today', November 1985.)

The dream as posthypnotic suggestion. What is a posthypnotic suggestion? It is a command given to us in a state of hypnosis. (Since this state produces Theta waves, as does the dreaming brain, the hypnotist's suggestions are perceived by the subject in much the same way as are dreams. In a way this process is the inverse of sleep walking) Once the command has been issued, we are then told to forget it the moment we 'wake up' from our hypnosis. This is exactly parallel to the forgetting of our dreams as we wake up. There is no way of escaping the posthypnotic command, nor is there a way of remembering consciously what it was. Yet the memory of the command is indelibly embedded in our dream memory and will force us to act in exactly the way it was suggested to us. It is as if there was something like a one-way-window between us and our dream memory. The memory can 'see' us, but we can't see the memory. As a consequence, the dream memory can direct our actions and feelings, but we can't reciprocate. All we can do is follow its commands like a sleepwalker. For this reason I see the dream memory as our hidden persuader. In a sense we are in a situation something like a split brain subject, as described earlier.

There is something extremely fascinating about a posthypnotic suggestion. Let's assume that a subject is told under hypnosis to grab the vase of flowers on the table and tip it over the hypnotist's head exactly five minutes after 'waking up'. What do you think this subject will do? Will he know when five minutes are up even though he is not cognisant of what he was told under hypnosis? The answer to that question is a decisive 'yes'. But 'knowing' here is not a state of full cognisance of what is happening, but rather a state of incognisance or mute awareness, which, as I see it, is perfectly parallel to our ordinary waking state as it is being directed by the dream memory without us having any recall of any dreams whatsoever.

This being so, it goes without saying that the subject will also 'know' when and what to do with the vase. And he will do exactly what was asked of him, even though he has only a hidden or cryptomnesic memory of the task.

Rationalisation of the posthypnotic command. And now for the most fascinating part: If the subject is asked why he did such an absurd thing, he will find a perfectly 'good reason' to explain it. He might say that the hypnotist needed cooling because he looked dangerously feverish. In short, he will justify his actions and be convinced that his reasons are completely rational. But will he ever find out the real reason for his actions? There is no chance of that, unless the hypnotist tells him so. And what if he did tell him? Would he believe him?

Rationalisation of the dream command. This is how it is with our dreams and their commanding power. Since there is only a one-way-window between us and our dream memory, can we ever hope to know who is in charge?

Somnambulism or sleepwalking: This specific aberration of regular sleep is one way to make some inroads into this question. One of the causes of sleepwalking is an insufficiency of the neurotransmitters that are designed to suppress the motor-sensory system. Unlike the case with new-born babies, physical movement of an adult during sleeping and dreaming is very restricted thus preventing the dreamer from acting out his dreams. This is excellent evidence that the dream does direct our body and mind. That this is so can in fact be demonstrated by wiring up the sleeper to an EEG (Electro-Encephalograph machine) which measures the electrical impulses in the various parts of the body. If a sleeping subject will, for instance, dream that he or she is playing tennis, the electrical impulses in the racket hand will be more powerful than in the other, free hand. This not only demonstrates clearly that the body is not entirely disconnected from the dreaming mind, but more importantly it also shows indubitably that the dream directs the body's motor sensory system, and with it the mind.

An extreme example of somnambulism is the case of an American woman who got up in the middle of the night, packed her dogs into the car and drove for 20 miles before she woke up at the steering wheel. I have had the opportunity to observe sleepwalking at close quarters. I saw a young boy of primary school age get up in the night, join the adults in the lounge and sit in a chair in order to grab a nearby coaster and put it on the sole of his foot from where it naturally dropped on the floor. He repeated this several times until I asked him what he was doing. His reply was: "I am putting on my sandals so I can go to school!" On another occasion, when this family was on holidays, he got up to go to the toilet. His mother needed to go as well, and went with him. By the time she came out of her cubicle her young son was already on his way towards the busy highway. The frantic mother only just caught up with him the moment before he stepped out onto the dangerous road. It was only when she grabbed him that he woke up from his sleep.

Sleep paralysis. This aberration is the exact opposite to somnambulism. In such a situation the sleeper partially wakes from his REM dream. Because of this the dream imagery changes to 'waking' hallucinations that are quite terrifying since the body is still anesthetised with those motor inhibitors that keep the dreamer trapped in his twilight world of terror. There is a famous painting by the Swiss artist Henry Fuseli that illustrates this predicament. It is called "The Nightmare". It shows a woman lying on her bed on her back with a dwarf-like creature on her chest. While this represents the choking pressure on the chest known as 'alpdruck', it was thought for a long time that the dwarf, or incubus, was a male demon that raped the female sleepers.

While this is obviously a mythologised view of sleep paralysis, there is a good reason for this symbolical representation of that late stage of REM, for it is then, just before the end of the night's dreaming cycle that the entire nocturnal drama is brought to a climax in much the same way as is customary with theatrical performances in the final scene of the last act. When in addition to this we realise that during this summary climactic event the sexual content of the night's dreaming invariably dominates the drama, the mythology of the incubus becomes perfectly plausible. More of that in Part II, the Freudian Interpretation.

Lucid dreaming: It is perhaps characteristic of the present era that interest in the work of Marquis d'Hervey de Saint-Denys has shifted from his Sinological studies to his records and work in the sphere of dreaming. As mentioned in the footnote above, he was particularly enchanted by what we now know as lucid dreaming. Just as the

Marquis in his time, so the young dreamers of today find this special kind of dreaming particularly enchanting. The reason for this is that in that state we suddenly realise in the middle of our dream that we are dreaming. But what makes this state of self-awareness truly exciting is that we also soon discover that we can actually direct our dream. In short, we are suddenly under the distinct impression that we are totally in charge of what is happening. And like the Marquis, our current young dreamers are convinced that this apparent control over the dream scenario will enable them to change unwelcome dreams and thus prevent them from carrying over into waking life. If that were really so, it would contradict my personal observations of a lifetime; it would clearly show that we could change our destiny; it would furnish proof that dreams are not the blueprint of waking life, but merely reconnaissance flights into the future as Jung had maintained.

In response to this, the first question we need to ask is this: If such apparent dream control over the current dream plot as well as over the scenario the dream had initiated could effect corresponding changes in waking life, would not all lucid dreamers end up as billionaires? Furthermore, should they not also become immortal, since changing a death dream would have to prolong their life indefinitely? As well as that, would they not also ensure that they would never suffer any pain or sickness and be permanently happy?

Without going any further we can see that lucid dreaming is not a means to control waking life at all. Indeed, the very fact that it is a dream that initiates the whole process shows that it is also a dream that prefigures the lucid state with all its apparent trappings of control.

There is one more question we need to ask about lucid dreaming. What is it then that gives us the sense of self-awareness while we are in the lucid state? It is the frontal lobe of the brain. This is the same part of the brain that in waking gives us our sense of self-awareness; in short, the notion that we are in control. Once we have been able to see behind the proscenium of dreaming and thus understand that the dream foreshadows all that we experience in waking life, we will understand that 'control' is nothing more than the feeling of control, a most subtle deception.

4. Who is the dreamer?

This is a recondite question and controversial. With the advance of investigations into NDE's (Near Death Experiences), and the experiments in OBE's (Out of Body Experiences) made by Monroe*, it emerges with increasing certainty that the dreamer is the etheric body, as it is called by some, the soul by others and the subtle body by the Hindus. As Pam Reynolds** testified, awareness is more acute when the contact with the body of flesh is severed since the subtle body can exist independently of the gross body. * (Refer to J. H. Brennan's book "Discover Astral Projection".) ** (See Light & Death by Michael Sabom, M.D., Zondervan Publishing House 1998; and posts on the Web under NDE of Pam Reynolds and others.)

But not only that. While unconscious on the operating table with all her blood drained from her body and chilled and no signals from the heart and brain, Pam was able to communicate with the spirit world, as some would call it, or, as I see it, with the fourth dimension. There the barriers of time broke down for her. The future, as well as the past, opened up for her into an inexplicable Grand Present which has been experienced and reported by mystics over the ages. Jung, who had this experience himself, describes it in his book, "Memories, Dreams, Reflections" (Page 327). For him, this moment beyond time was the mysterium coniunctionis which he says was an ecstatic experience where past, present and the future were all one.

As I see it, in the dream state, something akin to this is taking place. With the awareness of the body severely thwarted, as in a kind of NDE, we are able to slip into the fourth dimension which offers a view of things that still lie in the future for us when in the waking state.

Ultimately, everything we dream is first and foremost about ourselves. It's not about the people we meet and interact with, it's not about the animals we encounter or own, it's not about the landscape we traverse, but it is about us. After all, where are the other people, animals and landscapes without our mind perceiving them? The dream itself offers a wonderful parallel to this view. When we are dreaming, there is just one head on the pillow, just one consciousness at work; yet we see great numbers of other people, animals, trees, lakes and mountains. They are not independent manifestations; they all emanate from our mind and are contained in our single, solitary head.

The dream as playwright. The dream is the playwright of our nocturnal theatre. A playwright expresses his thoughts, his views, his convictions, passions and feelings quite generally by means of people and objects on stage. The stage itself is not a real place. The crucial thing about it is that it forms an environment that is most conducive to the mood of a particular scene and plot about to unfold. The same applies to the actors. The important thing is that they will convey the emotions that have motivated the playwright to take up his pen. So if he wants to air his feelings of oppression, for instance, he will naturally choose for that purpose a character who makes a convincing dictator. The dream does exactly the same. If it wants to say that we will shortly be in the grip of oppression, it will not cast a weakling in the role of the oppressor. It will choose a dictatorial father or the despot of a nation.

Dreams as plays on stage. So when we review our dreams, we always need to look at them as if they were plays on the stage of our personal theatre. We must regard the characters, actions and situations as an expression of ourselves, of ourselves today, tomorrow and beyond. And we need to do this even when a dream has become literally true, for the waking manifestation of a dream is in essence not different from the dream itself. It is simply another form of the same situation the dream had portrayed. In short it is an 'outward' expression of a previously 'inward' event and with it the dream's most accurate interpretation of itself!

The dream's workshop: Perhaps the best analogy of the dream's workshop is to think of it as a film studio where the producer and his crew, together with all the actors and the various prosceniums create a film later to be projected onto the more solid waking stage. The script for the drama has, of course, been provided by the author of all creation. It will have drawn subject matter from the day before which we now, thanks to Freud, know as the 'residue'. But it will also have reached back further, at times to the moment of birth or even before, if it was found to be an apt situation that will portray what is to be shown in the light of day. But there is also matter included in the script and its nocturnal enactment that has never before been screened. Some of this material may reach into the future by many years. In the case, for instance, of the aeronautics engineer Sikorsky*, the manifestation span of his famous boyhood dream of the air-clipper or S-wing, was thirty years. At the end of this time Sikorsky was flying in the very machine he had designed and built without ever recalling his dream. Only during the virgin flight of his plane, in which he was a passenger, did he suddenly remember his dream and realise at that moment that this was the materialisation of what he had seen such a long time ago. This gives us an idea of how complex and precise these nocturnal scripts must be for them to materialise at the predestined moment. * (Cf. Brian Inglis, "The Power of Dreams", Grafton Books, 1987.)

Kaleidoscope of the day: When I was in Grade Two of primary school, a fellow pupil lent me the kaleidoscope he had brought to school. I was stunned and fascinated by this magic tube which created a new pattern of crystalline beauty with each turn of the tube. I could not get enough of this intriguing chain of glittering designs. Each click of the tube had new surprises, yet all had a common grid of construction. I never forgot that first look through this tubular wonder. All my life I felt that I had witnessed something deeply essential, something wherein lie the secrets of everyday experience.

Today I understand what at first I only sensed 'through a glass darkly'. As I see it now, each turn of the kaleidoscope represents the outcome of a new night's dreaming, which is to be the blueprint of the day ahead. Each of these blueprints and their subsequent manifestations is different, yet in essence the same. The structure of the tube's crystalline pattern tells me that everything in our lives is ordered and intelligently integrated without a gap, without a flaw. But not only that: the pattern of this day reaches back to yesterday and beyond and also to tomorrow and beyond. Our whole life is as firmly integrated and beautifully constructed as the coloured designs of the kaleidoscope. It shows me that what I had discovered to be a serial manifestation of a dream with its thematic variations is very much like the crystalline design of the kaleidoscopic imagery where a particular configuration recurs in a number of variations. But it also demonstrates that if we look at life from the wrong end of the tube, it will look a disappointing mess. It will look like the confetti-like pieces that tumble in between the back end of the kaleidoscope and its prismatic glass.

5. Some more dreams and their later manifestations:

Dream H

'I went to a party with my girlfriend in separate cars. She had another guy with her. I wondered about him. Once we got to the parking area we again went separate ways to the party. She and her companion went up the stairs; I walked along a straight path.'

On the dream day this dreamer was feeling rather depressed. He was sure that his girlfriend would leave him in the lurch; that she would not go out with him. As is easy to see, these feelings were portrayed by means of having the dreaming self going separately to the party. But as it turned out in reality, all that was no more than his lack of confidence, a portrayal of his fears. These anxieties were allayed when his girlfriend did turn up and join him not only to go to the party, but also to make love at home afterwards. Thus the mystery companion of his girlfriend which the dreamer saw in his dream, and wondered about, was none other than he himself, his alter ego, his sexual self in fact, as the walking upstairs with his girlfriend showed. At times such scenarios of walking separately may also signify being of two minds.

Dream I

'I was looking over to the departure clocks at the Central Station. Where the clock faces used to be in reality, there were now computer screens. I watched the digits flickering but I could not read them properly. Suddenly a huge grizzly bear appeared from the dark. I panicked and ran to the ticket box.'

Obviously the dream put the stock market in the place where the station used to be. Clocks having changed to computer screens indicate this clearly. In light of this it is no great feat to see why the dreamer panicked and ran to the ticket box which in reality became the bank where he had invested his money. The words 'departure clocks' or indeed departure times, are ominous. They point to departure of money invested. The dream had obviously used the language of the stock market for times when values were beginning to slide. Examples of such jargon are phrases like: "The bear is about to emerge from its cave, the bear is digging in its grizzly claws, the market is desperately trying to free itself from the bear hug." This dream is an excellent example of how the metaphors of the waking life and the dream world can totally overlap. The only difference is in the presentation of the metaphors. The dream produces an actual bear while the stock market language only speaks of it. This sums up the chief difference between dream allegories and those that are spoken.

Dream J

'I dreamt that a swarm of bees descended on my left arm and stung me.'

The next day this dreamer went into the operating theatre where he got an anaesthetic injection into his right arm. Obviously the sting of the bees suggested an injection for medical purposes. This dreamer happened to know that bee stings relieved arthritic pain and were also reputed to cure multiple sclerosis; in other words they had medicinal properties. What should be noted here is the inversion of right to left. This is very typical of dreams as they become waking reality. Such matters must be regarded as part of the grammar and syntax of the dream language. It may be connected with the right to left wiring of the brain where the right brain operates the left arm for instance. As well as that the replication process of DNA to RNA may have a part in such inversions since it is antiparallel and complementary.

Dream K

> 'I dreamt that my canary became restless in its cage. He hopped from perch to perch and fluttered about crashing into the bars of the cage. Feeling sorry for him I opened the little cage door and out he flew.'

The dream described the dreamer's own longing to be free and his resolve to break free. Birds of prey, like hawks, will tell of the hunter and the hunted. If a hawk plunges onto a dove and carries it off, it will be the end of a relationship. Hawks may also be descriptive of sharp perception; after all we say 'he's got eyes like a hawk'. Or, 'I know a hawk from a hand-saw'. Crows are traditionally messengers from the underworld. Today that mythological place has been renamed the 'subconscious'.

Dream L

> 'I dreamt that my son came rushing out of the bathroom shouting that he couldn't see because something had splashed into his eyes.'

On that same day the dreamer got a phone call from her son asking her to pick him up in her car because he was too drunk to drive. The liquid had certainly 'splashed into his eyes' as it were. In waking language we say of someone who is drunk to this degree that he is blind drunk. Of interest here is that the dream dramatised the 'blindness' while in reality we simply use the verbal metaphor 'blindness'.

Dream M

'I dreamt that Angie came to see me. She picked up my favourite book and tore a leaf out of it. I was quite puzzled why her vandalism actually pleased me.'

The dreamer was pleased no doubt because Angie paid the dreamer a compliment by 'taking a leaf out of his book'. This again shows how the dream dramatises, or as I tend to call it, dreamatises, our spoken metaphors. This is a good example that shows that dreams are a kind of pantomime or charade. It is because we tend to read our dreams literally that they are so easily misunderstood. In order to get into the spirit of dreams we ought to practise communication without words and speak in body language every now and then as cats and dogs and other animals must do. Indeed, there is no difference between a cat sitting in front of our fridge in waking time or in dream time. If we know what the cat wants as it sits in front of a real fridge, we ought to know at once what it means when it is sitting in front of a dream fridge. Perhaps there is one little difference. When it happens in the dream we must not neglect to ask if the dream cat was also a reference to us, the dreamers. We must watch and see if we might be in a catty mood or just want to treat everyone like servants, or if our sex-drive has gone into overdrive.

6. How can a dream foresee the future?

The illusion of time. All things exist, co-exist in the Now. This is an ancient wisdom of which the Aborigines of Australia were well aware. Their 'Dreaming' or 'Altjeringa' says that the creation of the world does not lie in the past but in the eternal present that can be accessed any time by ritual means. This view is confirmed by the mystical experience known as the mysterium coniunctionis. Quantum physics has broken down the concept of linear time. It will eventually lead us to a borderless 'circle' as it were, or a point of view that concurs in principle with Altjeringa and the mystics' oceanic experience of the divine marriage.

In ordinary waking consciousness we have a sense of time that divides the ever-present Now into three parts. This is like being in a room that is divided by two partitions, so forming three compartments.* Although we are really in one single room, we are under the impression that there are three rooms: one for the present, one for the past and one for the future. While in the waking state, we are stuck in the middle compartment with only some peepholes into the compartment of the past and no view into the compartment of the future. *(Analogy by Amma of Jillellamudi, recorded by Richard Schiffman in "Mother of All"; Blue Dove Press 2001).

Memory of the future. In the dream state, on the other hand, these partitions are broken down. As a consequence we experience parts of the Now that lie in the future for the waking mind. In short, we wake up with a memory of the future. This memory of the future is in large part what psychology has erroneously called the 'subconscious mind'.

Past memories as models for future events. As everyone knows, we also relive things of the past in our dreams. However we do not do this out of a desire to re-create the past, as Freud speculated. One of the things that shows this is the fact that we never experience events of the past exactly as they were then. In the dream they always appear modified to a degree. Another thing that speaks against Freud's speculation is that there are things we have encountered in the past that we do not wish to revisit. So the purpose of looking into the past while in the dream state is to be sought elsewhere. This will become clear as we realise that the dream always talks in the future tense. In short, when the dream shows us something of the past it says: 'Look out, a situation like this will recur again.'

With older dreamers who have retired or are no longer in the job of their earlier years, this can be quite confusing until they realise that the dream often will use their work situation as the model for something that is to occur soon. But the situation need not be work at all, and the colleagues of those times gone by need not come their way again, but instead someone like the person they have dreamt about.

A retired physiotherapist, for instance, who had been working in a hospital, may dream that she is back there and doing a massage. This does not mean that she will go to a hospital and massage a patient, but that a situation comparable to that will arise which is, however, away from the old workplace. Or, if she had a love affair with a doctor at her old hospital, it does not mean that she will come across that doctor shortly, but that she will have an encounter with a man like him, one who is modelled after that doctor of long ago. Of course, we cannot rule out altogether that she won't come across that very doctor, or read about him or hear of him. But that is not as likely as interacting with his stand-in, his 'double', his 'representative'. So if this retired physio wants to know what is ahead of her after she has dreamt of a member of staff at that hospital, she will have to ask: "What does that member of staff mean to me, and also, what was going on in my life at that time?" Such questions will always bring the right interpretative thoughts to mind. By this I mean that the memories that will present themselves to the dreamer will pave the way to the meaning of the dream.

But there is another way such past acquaintances will figure in our life after we have dreamt about them. They can simply be the voice of our conscience. This may happen particularly with the appearance in our dreams of our mother or some other person that has died long ago and had played a critical role in our life while they were alive. People from our old workplace too may have a similar function. One of them could well be the critical voice in our head on the dream day, reminding us that we have a habit of being slack, such as in our way of dressing, for instance. In such a case we are not likely to meet that person again, especially if we have retired. But what will happen is that we will think of him or her and then be reminded that we are wearing something that our old colleague would have disapproved of. This person in a sense then acts as our Jiminy Cricket, or a personification of our conscience, of our self-appraisal.

The Jupiterian Flash. For the ordinary waking mind it is not easy to imagine that everything co-exists in the Now. Mozart might be able to help us a little to grapple with this apparently absurd notion. Consider the way he conceived his Jupiter Symphony. He said that he had heard it in a flash, with all the instruments sounding together, so making a single sound with a harmony of indescribable beauty. In contrast to this unified sound, he added, the same symphony appeared utterly insipid when played out in the usual twenty-one minutes.

Condensed dreamtime telescopes out to 'extended' waking time. This Jupiterian Flash gives us a bit of an idea what the world would look like if we had the capacity to see it in the manner of Mozart's Jupiterian Flash. In the dream state we are able to taste tiny morsels of such condensed time, for dreams are mostly extremely 'pressurised' events that will slowly telescope out into waking time. In computer language the dream could be regarded as a kind of zip program, a highly condensed piece of information stored on a CD, for instance. From there it can then be 'unzipped' and displayed in extended form so we can read it on the monitor screen or desktop. Because the dream is such a high-density program, it often seems quite bewildering and totally bizarre. One way the dream unzips itself into waking time is by means of the serial manifestation discussed in Part I, Point 14: 'Motifs and serial manifestation'. Other times when the dream unzips itself is in the second day manifestation and the protracted manifestation, both of which are also explained in Part I, Point 14.

For the Enlightened One, or the Awakened One such as the Buddha, the waking world is permanently like Mozart's Jupiterian Flash. For the ordinary person, on the other hand, the same world is always like the Jupiter Symphony played out in 21 minutes. The mystics of all ages and from all parts of the world have reported glimpses of the Jupiterian Flash or a taste of the 'Eternal Now' experienced in the mysterium coniunctionis. For those not so blessed, the nearest thing to the Jupiterian Flash is to be immersed in a dream. Its condensed time provides a kind of foretaste of the Eternal Now, for seeing the compressed episode of a dream telescoping out into the slow time of waking is not unlike watching the transformation of the Jupiterian Flash into a 21-minute 'symphony'.

7. More Dreams and how they came true.

Dream N

'I was preparing for my flight to Europe when I remembered that last time my baggage was so awkward. I had too many parcels. So I went about looking for a suitable box. The first one I found fell apart, the second one was too small and the third one was more like a crate than a box. I woke up before I could find a suitable box.'

This dreamer was actually thinking of flying to Europe, but he wasn't sure if his companion would be coming with him or not. He had to wait for her decision. (Boxes often refer to women, especially when the dream wants to target the female reproductive organs) The unresolved box question showed him that he was forced to wait. And wait he did - for three whole weeks. (Three containers) On occasions a box will indicate that it holds a secret. It may be that our body/mind is hiding something inside that needs looking at. As indicated, often a box is more specifically a reference to the womb, which too, is a secret place, although today we can have that secret scanned to a surprising degree.

Dream O

'My ex-husband came to see me with his lover. We were about to have lunch together. I wanted to go down the street to buy a fresh loaf of bread, but then I saw that my ex and his girlfriend were happy to eat the dry bread they had brought over and so I followed suit. I didn't bother with fresh bread.'

In other words the dreamer could see that it was pointless to try and make a fresh start with her ex-husband. And so it turned out in reality. As much as she would have liked to have him back despite his affair with another woman, it was not to be. It is worth noting the word bread when it occurs in our dreams. It sounds no different to 'bred'.

Dream P

'I dreamt of a Buddhist monk wearing the typical hat of a Tibetan monk. But not so typical were the many different crystals pinned to the hat. The monk greeted me saying: "I wear these crystals like this to keep my head cool."'

A few days after this dream flashing lights in the dreamer's eyes told her that she would almost immediately get a migraine. All the other symptoms followed as she made her way to the bedroom. Without properly realising what she was doing she reached for an amethyst on the bookcase in her bedroom. Once on her back on her bed she placed the crystal on her third eye. To her amazement the crystal felt like an ice cube. After only a short while the lights stopped and the usual migraine symptoms disappeared. She soon was able to get up and go about her business as if nothing had happened.

Dream Q

'I had gone down to the basement of a large building. It was quite dark down there, yet I could still make out the way ahead of me to some degree. It was a seemingly endless passage lined with tall marble-like pylons. Suddenly a massive elephant stormed towards me. I froze on the spot. I thought this would be the end of me. But instead of trampling me to death, the beast came to a sudden halt in front of me and gently wound its trunk around me and lifted me on its back. I breathed a sigh of relief and a feeling of great joy flooded me.'

'Dark' and 'seemingly endless' characterise the past of this lady. She had suffered from a long mental illness. But life changed for her for the better as the kindly elephant that sat her on its back illustrates so well. The 'pylons', the 'trunk' and the 'feeling of joy' are all promises of a new sexual relationship. It did come about, but, as the 'long passage' also says: It took quite some time before her new love appeared.

Dream R

> 'I am driving along a road from which I can see many elephants. Eventually I come to a part where a mighty bull elephant is grazing close to the road. I have to negotiate my car past him with the greatest care for there is a distinct danger that he would sit on my car and squash me.'

When I asked the dreamer in my usual way: 'Elephants? Where and when have you come across elephants?' The dreamer answered, 'at the zoo with my children'. No sooner had she said this that she recalled a most terrible Christmas where her father let her know that he did not approve of her husband. Worse still, he showed his displeasure to her husband directly and quite blatantly. From here on her memories leapt back even further to a time when she stood up to her husband for the first time in their long marriage. Superficially, the confrontation was about the purchase of a tablecloth. She had intended to make the purchase, but her husband pre-empted it. Up to then she had taken a very servile position and was regularly squashed by this arrogant individual who constantly let his wife know that he was the superior partner. With those two associations and her own expression of having been squashed by her husband, it was no longer doubtful as to who that bull elephant by the roadside was. What clinched the case was another memory that came to her mind when I suggested, after some discussion, that her husband must be somewhat psychotic and consequently unable to distinguish between reality and fantasy. 'Yes', she explained, 'once he returned from an ashram in India telling me that he was the god Ganesha'. We both laughed, for Ganesha is, of course, the Indian deity in elephant form.

But this was not all. After the dream day came the second day manifestation. This turned out to be a most terrible confrontation with her parents. It was a kind of repeat of the awful Christmas day, only the father's displeasure was not directed at the dreamer's husband this time, but at the dreamer herself. Again the confrontation was about the purchase of something. The parents had given the dreamer some money with the expectation that she would buy a washing machine. But she spent the money in a different way. This caused uproar. It was now her father who did the squashing of the dreamer's independence. So he too was that bull elephant that had represented her husband. It isn't without basis that daughters marry their fathers and sons marry their mothers!

8. Recall of our dreams

Recording and coaxing recall. Reading and talking about dreams will encourage our recall. Also having a pen and writing pad next to our bed, together with a pencil light, will bring our dreams back much more readily. If we do wake in the middle of the night with a dream, it is best to make only brief notes, a few key words will do. When reading them in the morning, the dream will readily resurface. If we write out the whole dream during the night, it will disturb our sleep patterns. Writing out the whole dream is a day job.

Recall tricks. If we have particular trouble in recalling our dreams in the morning, it is best to stay put for a while. Lying in the position in which we have woken up helps. In that posture we need do no more than just watch what goes on in our head. This will often bring back our last dream, since all of the things that we think about upon waking up are direct emanations of our last dream. If our dream won't come back, it is safest to hold on to the most dominant words or ideas that float in our head. They are manifestations in thought form of the last dream, and if we follow the events of the day with keen attention, we will see that some of these words were predictive of occurrences of the day as it unfolds.

A woman at one of my dream workshops complained that she could never recall a dream in the morning. Since there was a second workshop on the following day, I asked her to watch the next morning for any words that might pop into her head immediately upon waking up. The next day she had again no dream recall but had heard the word 'gas' in her head as she woke up. At morning tea we were about to boil the electric kettle. There was a power failure. We had to resort to the gas camping oven to make the tea!

Waking up with a song in our head: The 'gas episode' shows that sparse fragments in our head at the point of waking up are sure to be remnants of the last dream we had. And, as this episode demonstrates, such fragments are no less predictive than whole dreams recalled. This is most certainly also the case with waking up with a song reverberating in our head. Here is a classic example of this phenomenon: My wife and I had driven to the highlands where we were to attend a wedding. After the wedding we stayed in a motel from where we departed the next morning to find our way home. It was a long way and on roads we seldom travelled. When we woke in the morning my wife said that she had woken with a song in her head. This was not at all unusual for her, since she has an incredible memory for popular songs. "I am not surprised!" I quipped and asked her to sing it. It turned out to be "Nowhere Man", a song of the Beatles. The crucial line that was so uncomfortably prophetic contained the words: "… knows not where he's going to…" And yes, it isn't hard to guess what happened on that fateful day. I was driving and missed the crucial turnoff that would have got us home the short and smart way. We finished up making a detour of over a hundred kilometres before I found my way back home.

More on improving our dream recall. The attendances at my dream workshops are invariably 95% to 100% women. On the whole, they seem to be better dream recallers than men and are accordingly more interested in their dreams. There can be little doubt that the ability to recall easily is partly conditioned by our brain structure and partly by our life style. Women's brains, in the main, operate quite differently from those of men. Men are mostly left-brained, meaning that their left hemisphere is generally the more dominant unit. When they grapple with a problem, for instance, that area of their brain lights up like a single searchlight in the dark. Women's brains on the other hand are sparking all over, like Las Vegas at night. Apart from this their corpus callosum, the nerve 'cable' linking the two hemispheres, is thicker than that of men, which allows for more information to pass from the right to the left. Since dream recall appears to be right-oriented, woman, in the main, recall them more easily than men. As everyone knows these days, the right brain operates the left side of the body and vice versa. It has also been found that when the left nostril is 'open' to breathing, the right side of the brain operates more efficiently. From this we must conclude that if we engaged the left side of the body and at the same time did left nostril breathing, we would stir the right hemisphere into maximum performance. In short, an exercise like standing on the left leg while closing the right nostril by pressing against that side of the nose with our thumb before going to sleep will in time stimulate our dream recall.

The other part of dream recall is conditioned by our life style. If we are always busy and immediately upon waking rush out of bed, the brain waves will instantly accelerate from the recall range of 8-12 Hertz into Beta waves of 13-30 Hertz. Such a sudden jump that forestalls a gradual increase from the calm to busy brain waves will naturally block the dream recall.

Spontaneous recall. When we recall a dream 'out of the blue' at any time of the day or night, we must make it a habit to stop and look about. We will soon recognise items the recalled dream had featured. Such spontaneous recalls occur because at that time, parts of our dream are manifesting as waking realities. An interesting study would be an investigation into the frequency of the brainwaves at such spontaneous recalls. I would imagine that they would be in Alpha mode, which has the 8 cycle frequency in common with Theta waves. Those Theta waves are most conducive to recalling dreams, or, put another way, most conducive to getting consciously in touch with our dream memory which psychology, as I have said before, erroneously calls the subconscious.

9. Our dream diary

The necessity of a dream diary. Once we have decided to take our dreams seriously, we will need to keep a dream diary. This will not only stimulate our dream memory, but it will also preserve our dreams for long-term study. This is of vital importance if we wish to see how dreams become waking facts, especially in view of the fact that some dreams may take months and indeed years before they materialise. Upon re-reading our dreams we will also discover that we have missed some of the things the dream had foretold.

Re-reading our dreams. Because we do often miss quite important dream manifestations at first readings, regular re-reading at the end of each day is absolutely crucial. Regular re-reading on a monthly basis is also important for the same reasons because it will reveal to us recurring themes and ongoing concerns. They will show us important facets in our life that we may have missed. They may be pointers towards unrecognised talents we have, or they may reveal solutions to certain problems that we have not considered as yet. They may also highlight characteristics of ours that have remained hidden from our awareness so far.

Keywords as memory joggers. We may not always feel like writing down our dreams in the morning. We may want a rest for a day or even days. Providing we have kept those keywords of the night in mind, we will be able to catch up on recording later on, for the keywords will prompt our memory sufficiently to recapture all of those dreams, or at least the most important parts of them.

Another important reason for regular rereading of our dreams is the fact that often one dream will help to throw light on another one.

The highlight of a dream. Every dream has a highlight. It is the climax of our dream; it is the moment that stands out like a red spot in a green field. It is a good idea to choose this highlight for the title of our dream. Once we have decided on the title, it is even a better idea to add a simple drawing of the highlight to it. This will not only help us find our dreams in our diary quickly and easily, but it may also furnish the best evidence in support of our psychic abilities in the dream state. Put another way: a drawing of a dream object that matches its corresponding waking manifestation on the ensuing day or later, is better evidence of the dream's psychic abilities than words. This is especially true when we have drawn something that we have never seen before.

But there is something else useful about the highlight of the dream. Because it is the dream's climax, its quintessence, it is capable of providing the key to the dream's essential meaning. In other words, it is not necessary to work with the entire dream in order to find its flavour and most basic message. It is quite impossible to miss the highlight of the dream. It is the most impressive part, the most memorable part, the bit that fades last when the dream evaporates. It is the scenario that is least forgotten. It is the 'orgasm' of the dream. I mean that both metaphorically and literally. I mean it literally because the dream foreshadows an orgasm of our waking experience through the climax of the dream. If in the highlight of a man's dream he was picked up by a lioness and tossed through the window that then breaks, it would foreshadow an orgasm induced through intercourse. Breaking an object in a dream invariably indicates an orgasm. But there are anticlimaxes too. They will still be recognised as the highlights of the dream. A woman may dream, for example, that her husband prevents a predatory fish from attacking an egg she possesses. This would then manifest in waking as the withdrawal of her partner's penis (the fish) in order to prevent fertilisation of her ovum.

All this goes a long way towards explaining why we remember this or that dream, this or that part of a dream, and not some other dream or another part of it. In short, it is the emotional highlights that fade least and last, and these emotional highlights are anchored in our sexuality.

Recording the waking manifestations. It is a good idea to leave sufficient space after every dream description for observations made on the dream day. The most important part of these will be the waking manifestations we will discover. In order to save time and space, it is a useful practice to simply highlight in red all the passages of our dream record that are literal manifestations, and in green those that have materialised metaphorically.

Noting the associations. Another important thing to do when recording our dreams is to note all the associations we have with certain dream images as we go over our dream. These spontaneous associations are an invaluable key to the meaning of our dream. We should always note them immediately after the word or situation that brought them to mind. A good idea is to put them in brackets marked something like this: (@, reminds me of my cat), (@, remembered a childhood playmate), (@, recalled the time my father spanked me).

Memories of the past. When we reflect on such associations they will take us back into the past. By past I mean anything that happened before we had our dream. Often we will be astonished just how far a dream may reach back. In the dream state we will be able to recall things that would never resurface in our waking state. I have said earlier on that the dream uses these memories to show us that something like it is in store for us. We ought to bear in mind that the dream most often talks about the future in terms of our past. So when an item in our dream puzzles us, we should ask ourselves: "When and where did I encounter such a thing, animal, person or incident?" When we have recalled that 'when' and 'where', it is then time to ask ourselves: "What were the circumstances under which I encountered that item, animal, person or incident?" Once we have remembered that, we must then read the plot of the dream in light of such circumstances, and then we will know what exactly the dream has foreshadowed.

The previous day's residue. Freud, who coined this term, observed, like most dreamers would, that the dream always features something we had experienced yesterday. Since he could not believe that the dream was able to look into the future, he incorporated these parts of the dream into his wish fulfilment theory. But dreams are not wish fulfilments.

They are pregrams for tomorrow and beyond. So yesterday is not a special kind of past as Freud suspected. It is a past experience like any other. And the dream always talks in the future tense even when it refers to the past. See Part I, Points 3-4 and 12. Also refer to Part II, Point 5, 'Past referencing'.

10. The five steps of interpretation

Step 1: Focus on the title given to the dream and/or the highlight and its drawing. Find a word or phrase for the general mood of the dream such as: sad, terrifying, delightful, reassuring, made me uneasy, nervous, fearful, frustrating, strenuous, relaxing and so on. Such key words will take the interpretation in the appropriate direction. Dwell on all of these points: title, highlight, drawing and mood for a while before going further. Note down the ideas and feelings that come to mind.

Step 2: Read the dream like a story written by someone else. Dreams are indeed stories authored by someone or something else! While reading, keep the results of Step 1 in mind. The dream will acquire a new meaning. Much that was obscure will be understood.

Step 3: Retell the dream with the meaning gleaned in Step 2 in mind.

Step 4: Deal with the associations. There are usually two sorts of associations: The first of these are the spontaneous associations. They are the ones we have noted in brackets.

The second of these are the 'requested' associations, which I usually mark with (@). As the word 'requested' suggests, they are the kind of associations that do not come to mind of their own accord. They are hauled up from our memory bank by focusing on a part of the dream that remained unclear. If there are no such parts in our dream, there is no point in looking for requested associations. On the other hand, if there are gaps in our understanding of the dream under analysis, such associations will throw light on the obscurities. For example, it may puzzle us why we dreamt of our old girlfriend Laura. In order to find the meaning of this, we had best ask ourselves: 'Where does Laura take me?' In response to this we may remember a particularly good time we had with her at Luna Park. Once that is done, we can substitute 'Laura' for' a good time' and reread the dream in that light. We will find that it will suddenly make sense.

This is also the way we can use our spontaneous associations. First we have to ask ourselves where the association in question will take us. Whatever comes to mind first and freely will be the meaning of that association. After that we are ready to re-read our dream in light of what came to mind when we reflected upon our spontaneous association. The use of both types of associations is the same. The only difference between them is that one will arise spontaneously, while the other is triggered off by means of deliberate focusing on one or the other obscure part of the dream.

Step 5: The final step requires us to interpret our dream in light of Steps 1 to 4. On the basis of this we can now make a forecast of what is to be expected. If it does manifest in the way we predicted it will of course be a verification of our interpretation. As I have said, a dream only very seldom comes true literally. Once we learn to recognise the waking correspondences of our dreams and their interpretation, we will discover a great deal about the peculiarities of the dream's language. We will see what parts appeared directly as seen in the dream and what parts came true associatively. The manifestations of our dreams are, in fact, the only true interpretations of our dreams; anything else remains chiefly speculation! Only in this way can we be sure that we will truly learn the language of our dreams. And it is as well to remember that some dreams will let us wait for months, or even years, before they fully materialise, verifying our interpretation.

11. Aids to interpretation

Unlocking our dreams. It is a good idea to tell our dreams to someone we can trust. Discussing them helps enormously. Our listeners will act as a sounding board that will bounce things back in a new light and also bring to mind things we have overlooked. When we come across a part of a dream that we consider unimportant or not worthy of our attention, we must make a point of 'digging deep' right there. Something that we are trying to hide from ourselves is sure to surface through such digging. I have in fact often found that such points provide the very key to the mystery of the whole dream.

Dramatising our dreams. Another way of getting to the meaning of our dreams, or at least parts of them, is to relive them by dramatising them; acting them out in other words. In view of the fact that dreams are in essence dramatisations of our state of mind to be, acting them out is the most natural way of dealing with them. In this way we are dreaming them again as it were, but with the added advantage of being not only the actor, but also the spectator. In short, we will no longer be tied to just one point of view as in the dream state, but we will be able to see the same drama from two points of view. It is this which brings to light so many answers about our dream actions and situations that might elude us otherwise.

12. Some fears about the future-factor

Fear of bad dreams. The worst thing about knowing that dreams foretell the future is that we fear that bad dreams might come true literally. The greatest anxieties are caused, of course, when we dream for instance that someone near and dear had died. In my experience things seldom come true precisely as we dream them. More often than not dreams of death and dying mean a change in a relationship or the transformation, for good or for ill, of the person that died in our dream. Another point to be remembered in this respect is the dream's characteristic of associative identification, or, in regard to persons, ego-transference. This means that we may have a dream that we died in some way or another, but then it will turn out that it was someone else who had died in reality. It may be no more than a death reported on TV or in the paper. But of course this will not be a matter of total indifference to us. There is at least something of symbolical significance in such a death for us.

Death dreams among pubescent children. Dreams of death and dying are particularly frequent among pubescent children. They will often dream that they have died, or that the world has blown up in an atomic holocaust, or the like. They do so because such events are a dramatisation of the change that is taking place in them. They are dreaming of dying because they are indeed dying: to their childhood. Their childish world is annihilated to become the world of adults.

Dreams that forebode physical death. Such dreams are usually quite allegorical. One such allegory is that the dreamer sees himself departing through the wall of his room. Another allegory is that our grandfather might be seen off at the railway station by all his kith and kin. If he has no baggage with him, then it could well mean that he won't return. Another example is that we might see someone close to us gathering sticks in order to build a raft to cross a river. Crossing a river is an ancient allegory for crossing over to the place of our ancestors. That such a crossing is implied in this particular example is revealed by the words 'sticks'. Those who are familiar with Greek mythology know that the river Styx is the border between the living and the dead.

Here is a death dream that confused and scared the woman who had it:

Dream S

'I dreamt that it was night. As I was walking along the street I spotted a lady cloaked in a long black robe. She looked terribly skinny. I could not see her face because she was walking well ahead of me and in the same direction as me. I woke with a start.'

Before I recount what happened on the dream day, I must report another, similar dream. It came to the girlfriend of this dreamer on the very same night.

Dream T

'I was hugging a tall, skinny man. Just as we were about to kiss, a gaunt lady in a long black dress and long blond hair leapt between us. I could not see her face because she hugged the man now and took him away from me.'

Both of these dreamers were quite clear about who the lady in their dream was. They both called her Lady Death. They were right, for on the dream day both of these dreamers heard the news that a common friend of theirs, a woman of forty, had passed away.

Of crucial interest here is that both dreamers did not see the face of Lady Death. This simply meant that death was not for them, but someone else. Neither of the dreamers could see that someone else.

What the second dreamer saw was the husband of the woman who had died. This is confusing because we would expect that Lady Death would have taken him away to the other world. Instead, she took him away from his wife.

So what is the dream doing here? It is playing its favourite game of associative identification (or ego-transference). This is tricky. But if this dreamer had asked, as I suggest in Step 4 of the 5 Steps of Interpretation, 'Where does this man of my dream take me?' she might have thought of her friend who had died. Well, it's precarious, but life must have its surprises and be free to preserve its mysteries!

13. More about the language of dreams

Allegories and metaphors. Fears of the future-factor recede as we begin to understand more and more that dreams speak mostly in allegories, that they are full of metaphors just like everyday language. At first we fail to see this because the dream speaks extensively in dramatic visual imagery. Since we are in the habit of thinking that anything presented visually must be a literal fact, we can't see the dream's real intent. In short, if we are attacked in a dream, for instance, by someone sticking a knife into our back, we may fear that someone will actually stab us in the back sometime in the future. The interesting thing here is that if I say in everyday language that someone had stabbed me in the back at work, no one will have any difficulties knowing exactly what was meant. We will not ask, as if our right brain had been removed: 'Did they have to call an ambulance?'

The main difficulty with the dream language. The fact that we can read figures of speech in waking language quite naturally shows that the real problem in understanding the language of dreams is not with their metaphors in themselves, but with the habit of reading visual imagery literally. When things come to us by means of everyday speech, the situation is different. Even though there too we have no obvious signs to indicate to us which way to interpret what has been said, we will know somehow what is really meant. We will quite automatically 'read between the lines'.

This used to be exactly the reverse. This becomes evident when we remember that we dream as babies in the womb long before we understand the spoken word. In short, the first language we comprehend and learn to master is the picture language of the dream.

Dream language is not only the first and most fundamental language we learn, but also the most universal one. It is in fact so universal that all dreaming creatures, no matter what they may otherwise be, actually understand it and indeed 'think' it. Then, after we leave the womb, we begin to superimpose the spoken code on the pictorial metaphors and scenarios of our dream imagery. As we become proficient in the spoken metaphor we gradually forget how to deal with the original, pictorial kind. We even forget and have to relearn body language which is an integral part of the dream language.

Reading between the lines. We all know, of course, that in everyday speech, reading between the lines is managed with the greatest of ease. In fact, we manage this so well that we are not even aware of it unless we take special notice. Since it would be a most useful preparation for the interpretation of dreams, it is a good exercise to set a day aside, on which we watch carefully just how many metaphors we use ourselves, and how automatically we understand them to be metaphors and not literal truths. This will convince us that we must be prepared to read many dreams and watch them come true before we will feel thoroughly competent in interpreting them. Although this will help us to be more awake to the metaphors of the dream, it will not get us out of the woods easily. For, as we have just seen with regard to the metaphors for death, they may foreshadow a physical death, while, on the other hand, the physical representation of death may look towards a metaphorical death.

Undifferentiated reality. This changing of the 'rules', inverting them as it were, is not the only trick the dream has up its sleeve. There is one that may delude us time and time again. This is the fact that the dream projects much of its plot on an undifferentiated level of reality. By this I mean that the sense of reality in the dream will be the same whether it intends to foreshadow something we will see in ordinary reality or on the level of virtual reality such as a show on television or the screening of video games. The dream will also present as a live experience an event that later will turn out to be something we will read in a paper or book. And, to make matters worse still, the dream will often have us as the hero, when in waking reality we will be no more than an onlooker, or the reader of the news or the story.

Ego-transference and inverse projection. I call the confusion of 'you' with 'me', and 'me' with 'you', ego-transference. Ego-transference is quite a common occurrence. It happens in waking as well as between dreaming and waking. A case of waking ego-transference is hero-worshipping. We identify with our hero. A typical situation is when we say, "we won the match", although our participation in the match was nothing more than watching it. Transference from our dreaming self to someone else's waking self will become apparent to us as we watch our dream manifestations carefully. We may discover for instance, that although we dreamt of getting an injection in our right arm, on the dream day it will be our daughter that gets an injection in the left arm. This is not only ego-transference, but also inverse projection. In some ways then, the dream is like the photographic negative for the waking experience that is to become the positive. (Also compare with Dream J)

From a technical point of view this may come about because of the left to right wiring of the brain where, the left side of the brain controls the right side of the body. But it goes deeper than that. It happens because there is a perfect complementarity between dreaming and waking. These two phases are really one process. One fits into the other like the pieces of a jigsaw puzzle. It further highlights the fact that the outer process of waking is a reflection of the inner process of dreaming. And, as happens in reflections on the surface of water, the original and its 'clone' are identified one with the other, yet inverted.

Associative identification. Ego-transference is a special case of associative identification. When the transference is from a dream object to a waking person, or from a dream object to an associated object in the waking state, I call it associative identification. We could also call it associative transference. This is a very common occurrence. We may dream of a scene where a cup of tea was the focal point. On the dream day we may then come across the same scene. It will seem to us like a kind of déjà vu. But in the waking state our centre of attention will not be the tea cup before us, but the person who is drinking from that tea cup.

Such associative imagery is based on the fact that the dream and its corresponding waking manifestation are an interdependent whole. We might say that the dream is the mould into which the liquid plaster of our waking experience is poured. This means that if we want to see what is to emerge in the light of day, we often will be compelled to look at the dream's language in the same way a sculptor looks at his moulds.

As we come across ego-transference time and time again, we will realise suddenly that when we look at our fellow humans we are really looking at ourselves. In the same way we will get to see that associative identification is a demonstration that dreaming and waking are two complementary halves of one process. The two will be as inextricably connected for us as an object and its shadow. The two worlds of dreaming and waking will be seen as one world. In time, we and the world will become an indivisible unit.

Composite imaging. Related to associative identification is the dream's curious characteristic of creating composite images such as a centaur. The dream resorts to this 'artistic' device partly because of its need to employ a kind of shorthand language discussed at length in Part II, Point 5. But it also makes use of it for the same reason an artist or sculptor would. It does so because a composite image acquires a meaning that the individual parts cannot express by themselves. Thus a lion with a serpent's tail is able to express a might that is beyond the strength and courage of the lion and also beyond the venomous lightning strike of the snake.

Dream compounds of this kind have a habit of 'disintegrating' as they become manifest in the waking hours. By this I mean that the two components of a centaur, for instance, who is part horse and part man, will separate in waking reality and manifest as a man riding a horse, or leading a horse along, or just walking beside it.

Another example of associative linkage is this: we may dream of a girl who has a cold sore on her lips. Then, on the dream day we will go out looking for a cold sore ointment. When we ask the shop assistant what there is on offer in that line, we will suddenly realise that she is the girl we dreamt about. But instead of having a cold sore, the girl of the waking world will only respond (with lips) to our request about cold sore ointments. Sometimes composite images are due to 'spatial contraction' occurring in the dream landscape. A dream image of a man with flames issuing from his shoulders may manifest in reality as a man seen in front of a distant flue spewing out fire. The distance in question could be several miles. Events of such 'disintegration' seen in isolation often appear too trivial to deserve further attention. But when we know that they are part of a series of manifestations, and at the same time indicators of crucial happenings, it will be difficult to ignore them.

Sorting out our dream images. Because dreams are like distorted 'reflections' of waking, sorting out our dream images can be rather bewildering at first. In order to find a footing in this jungle of imagery it is best to focus on one particular facet of dream manifestations for a start. The most fruitful one is that of distinguishing between literal 'reflections' and metaphorical ones.

Literality versus the metaphorical. Fortunately, learning to distinguish between the literal and metaphorical meaning is not quite as horrendous an ordeal as it may seem. This is because there are certain visual images and experiences in the dream that are simply impossible in the waking state, so they can only be read as metaphors, or allegories. One of these is sailing on a cloud. The linguistic equivalent of this is 'I am on cloud nine'.

Figures of speech not likely to be taken literally. Metaphors that will be fairly readily recognised, are figures of speech of the waking language that we would never consider taking literally. One of these is the situation where someone says to us that he was plastered. So, if we saw someone in a dream covered in plaster, we could be almost certain that we were face to face with a metaphor. In short, we would not expect to meet someone the next day, or later, who was covered in plaster.

Wishful thinking and intentions. Before I shall leave you to try your hand at interpreting such tricky dream language, I want to mention yet another uncertainty. It arises from the fact that dreams not only foreshadow hard and fast facts, but also wishful thinking and intentions. For example, we may dream that we have bought a boathouse by the sea. This may lead us to think that we will actually buy such a building. But some months later we may find that we will only toy with the idea of buying one. Or we may actually go to the real estate agent and enquire about such a building and even inspect one. But then, when it comes to the crunch, we may walk away from the deal.

The conditional tense. The grammar of the dream is difficult because all that is shown in a dream is happening in the present. It will picture past events as happening right now. But when we wake up we know that the dream was talking about the past because we can remember the event as it was. We will also notice that those past events, people, animals or experiences of the past were not in reality exactly as the dream presented them. This means that the dream is not just making us re-live the past, but wants to tell us something about the future as well. So the dream not only talks in the present tense about the past, but also in the future tense. Where it gets particularly tricky is when the dream also talks in the conditional tense. This is akin to the problem of wishful thinking and intentions just discussed. In other words, the dream might have us step over a snake with its mouth wide open, showing its fangs. A couple of days later we will see that snake, but we will stop short of stepping over it, and so it will not open its mouth, but just raise its head. Here the dream used the conditional tense. It was saying that if we had gone along the path without heeding the snake's presence, we would have looked into its wide-open mouth with its threatening fangs. It is, of course, this very picture of threatening fangs that is saying: "Don't come closer!" Naturally it is easy to say all this after the waking encounter with the snake. Before that it is nearly impossible to determine if the dream talked purely in the future tense or the conditional. So we must beware of making rash interpretations.

The feeling test. Although there is no sure way of predicting what the outcome of any dream will be, there are nevertheless certain indications in most of our dreams that will help us arrive at a fairly accurate prediction. Such indications are to be found in the feelings our dream leaves us with. The basic feelings or moods of the dream are positive or negative, interested or indifferent, happy or sad, ecstatic or terrible. They must be taken as our overall guide when making an interpretation. With regard to nightmares and other dreams of terror it must be remembered that the dream is a pressure pack, or, in computer language, a 'zip-program'. It must therefore be much more intense in every respect than its later manifestations. In other words, the terror will be watered down as the dream telescopes out into waking time. The lightning strike of the Jupiterian Flash will draw out into the sunshine of the Jupiter Symphony, as it were, and the compressed zip program will unravel slowly in the form of much scrolling on the desktop.

The dream game as Charades. So we can see that dreams are seldom what they seem. In fact, interpreting them is very much like the parlour game, Charades. However, the dream game needs a lot more patience, for we will often have to wait very much longer before we will be told by the waking manifestations whether or not we had guessed correctly.

Everyday metaphors. As a reminder of how often we use metaphors in everyday language, I add here a short list I compiled while listening to the evening news one day: under a cloud, wages system blown apart, high stakes involved, inflame the debate, target Asia, take the heat out of it, Sinclair is showing the flag, Howard caught in a vice, stops the build-up, undermining the status quo, cuts in migration, the numbers cruncher, political wings, raise the heat, a drop in the market, the shadow minister, the policy is dead and buried, it's all hot air, he put his foot in it, don't run away with that.

Dream metaphors and their translations

Heading towards barren country	A woman in danger of becoming barren
Floating on a cloud	Being on cloud nine
Missing the bus	Missing the bus as an opportunity
A rat gnawing the sole of a shoe	Something is gnawing at my soul
Another me sitting next to me	Being beside myself
He is pulling a sweater over my head	He is pulling the wool over my eyes
Being covered by bugs	Something is bugging me
Keeping your feelings in a bottle	Bottled up feelings
He is chasing a ball	Chasing a homosexual partner
Vomiting	Being fed up, unable to stomach something
Knees giving way	Weak-kneed
A run-away baby carriage	Miscarriage
Wearing a suit with unlikely fabric	Suits me to fabricate something

14. Manifestation span of our dreams

Motifs and serial manifestation. Dreams begin to manifest the moment we wake up. All dreams have a main theme or motif. A motif will manifest several times on the dream day, which is the waking period immediately after our last dream. I call this multiple recurrence of a dream motif on the dream day the serial manifestation of a dream. These manifestations are, of course, varied in the way the theme of a piece of literature or music is varied. Because they are often strikingly similar, they appear to be what Jung called synchronistic events. But since all waking experiences are manifestations of one dream or another, they are more properly seen as serial manifestations of a dream, and not synchronicities.

Here is the serial manifestation of the highlight of a dream about huskies pulling a sleigh. The motif of the highlight was a 'V' shape, the formation of the huskies as they pulled the sleigh. Its mood was 'going out amidst great excitement'.

• 6:50 a.m. Wake up very happy. Sitting up in bed, stretching my arms. Recall the dream I just had. Before I can relate it to my wife, who was already awake, she asks: "Are we going to go out anywhere this weekend?" While considering her question, my attention is somehow drawn towards the corner of the room where the architraves meet, forming a 'V' that fans out towards me. We decide to take the children on a picnic.

• 11:18 a.m. On the way to the picnic the girls spot a flock of swans overhead. Flying in typical V-formation. General excitement and jubilation in the car.

• 1:47 p.m. Picnic at Love's Creek. Fluked this spot so expressive of today's happy vibes. After meal, girls clean up the papers on the grounds. Cut stakes for each of them and sharpen points. They spear the papers and burn them on the stakes in the fires. The spearheads glow and they stick them in the nearby creek to hear the sizzle. They shriek with delight. They get the idea of holding the burning points of the stakes together to keep the flames alive. They walk to the creek holding them in V- form.

• 8:10 p.m. Out in the garden with baby son in arms. Point to moon. He too points with great excitement. Our fingers meet in V-shape.

• 8:15 p.m. Go back into lounge. As I walk in Elizabeth R is on TV. Mary Queen of Scots is to be executed. Lunging forward to lay head on block she spreads her arms backwards like the wings of a bird. V-form and weird excitement runs through me.

• 9:56 p.m. Girls clamour for bedtime story. It is to be Odysseus's adventures. They catch a glimpse of the illustration where the Cyclops is being blinded with a glowing pole. The figures form a V-shape.

• 11:45 p.m. Exuberant lovemaking. Legs and arms form two V's around the 'polar' region during climax.

A series does not end with the dream day. There is always a second day manifestation that often features one element or another quite literally. The series may echo on over days, weeks and months, even years.

Second day manifestation. A dream motif will not only manifest on the dream day, but also the next day. I call this the second day manifestation. I have found these to be often very literal. In short, if we dreamt of a scene with a lion in it, on the second day the image of our dream lion might well appear quite photographically.

Protracted manifestation. A dream will often take days, weeks, months or even years to become manifest. Such manifestations are really part of the serial manifestation of the dream that begins on the dream day. But because they echo on for such a long time I call them protracted manifestations. Because some dreams will take years to manifest, dreamers who do not keep a dream diary and regularly re-read their records will miss their manifestations. The fact that dreams take such a long time to manifest also demonstrates how complex the co-ordination of our dreams with their waking manifestations and other following dreams must be. For a dream of today (which is going to manifest, say, three years from now) must mesh perfectly with the dreams we will be having three years from now. I have observed a case where three dreams pointed to one and the same waking event thirteen months after the first dream. The second dream, which had to be spliced into the first one, took place nine months after the first dream. And then the dream of the night before the waking event anticipated thirteen months ago also had to be meshed in with the previous two dreams. Each of those three dreams, which I had recorded, described different facets of one and the same waking event. What amazing co-ordination, what imponderable foresight!

The nocturnal theatre. But that is not all. We have several dreams in one night. They must all be in perfect harmony with one another; indeed they must be no less integrated than a stage play in four or five acts with several scenes each. They also must be completely co-ordinated with all the other dreams, especially those that describe the various facets of one and the same waking event anticipated. This being so, how much room is there for us to make decisions independently of our dreams? For 'The manifestation span of the sexual plot' see Part II, Point 9.

15. Tips and reminders

Never dismiss dreams as silly or absurd. After all, we don't think that it is either silly or absurd if our mate claims that he is 'on cloud nine today'!

All dreams are the dress rehearsal for our waking stage. This means that our dreams only know one tense: the future tense. In other words, they speak of the future even when they show us things of the past.

This dress rehearsal is a total dress rehearsal. By this I mean that it covers absolutely all facets of life. Put simply: the same dream story that describes our work and play, our hopes and fears, our worldly and spiritual aspirations, also describes our sex-life. Just how the dream does that is explained in Part II, 'The Freudian Interpretation'.

Because the dream is a total dress rehearsal, both the Freudian and Jungian interpretations are valid, providing they are read in the future tense.

Since our dreams are a memory of the future, they are also the basis of our intuition, premonitions, psychic and prophetic abilities, déjà vu, instincts, telepathic communication, and so-called 'subconscious' knowledge. The latter ought more accurately to be called dream memory! And let's not forget that which Jung called 'Synchronicity" is really a serial manifestation of a dream or part of it.

Colour in a dream is crucial, for the more intense the colour is in the dream, the greater will be the emotional highs. Also the manifestation span is usually longer with regard to highly coloured dreams.

Recalling a dream 'out of the blue' means that its waking manifestation is upon us. A typical exclamation at spontaneous recall is: 'You've just broken my dream!'

Recording of a dream is not complete until we have also noted its waking manifestations. They are the only true and complete interpretations of our dreams. They are in fact the basis of our personalised dream dictionary.

Listen to the language we use when we retell our dreams or record them. Often a word throws light on the meaning of the whole dream. …'more on'… may read 'moron' and vice versa. The dream is full of puns. Often we don't get the real meaning of our dream until we recognise the pun. A 'faucet' may mean 'force it', while 'tulips on the organ' will really read as 'two lips on the organ'.

Take heed of all associations. It is a good idea to place them in brackets and mark them with (@) when reflecting upon a dream and attempting to decode it. Remember the dream's favourite language is associative talk. Part of associative talk is ego-transference and integration that becomes disintegration as the dream manifests.

Highlights of our dreams are our guiding stars. Focus on them, meditate on them, and consider them as titles of our dreams.

We must remember always that all we dream is about ourselves.

We need to verify dreams forever in the days, weeks and months and even years after we've had them. See Part II, Point 10.

16. Some more examples of how dreams may manifest

Dream 16A

> I am standing by a spring that is a mere trickle. There are lots of boxes next to it with kitchen utensils in them. Suddenly the phone rings. To answer it I have to go into the house close by. My ex-sister-in-law is calling. I carry the phone to the spring. As I arrive there, the spring starts to gush like a geyser; eventually the gushing stops. We were talking a lot about spiritual matters.

Manifestation: (The dreamer's report) "On the dream day, that is in the evening after the dream, I am watching a video. There is a scene where two little girls walk along a creek. Eventually they cross it below some cascades. The phone rings. In order to answer it I have to go into the study. My brother is calling. He tells me that he has bought a ticket to fly to New Zealand. He will visit his Maori friends who consider him to be their spiritual brother. While talking to my brother, my foot rests on a box of books. Before I could continue my conversation with him, I have to go to the kitchen to see to something. I have to do this because my brother talks endlessly."

Comments: It is interesting to note that the dream makes no distinction between what is to be seen in a film and what is going to be 'real'. (See Part I, Point 13, Paragraph 5, 'undifferentiated reality') It is also easy to see why the dream had changed the creek of the film into a spring and made it gush like a geyser: because only that way could the dream say in one image that the brother, who is the associated manifestation of the ex-sister-in-law, would be gushing like a geyser, and include in that way that he would also go to New Zealand, the land of geysers. It is also evident that the spiritual conversation in the dream indicated the purpose of the brother's trip. Similarly the box of kitchen utensils by the gushing spring was giving notice that there would not only be a box at the dreamer's feet when the brother phoned, but that there would also be a need to go into the kitchen at the time of the phone call.

Dream 16B

I am walking with a man (@ who reminded me of my first lover whom I never married) in the inner city. We come to this unit in the middle of the shopping centre. As we are going up in the lift, he says: "Thank you for choosing me! I'll even sell one of my racehorses." But I don't want him to do that. We come to his apartment which is very modern. The furniture is grey-green. (@ The same colour furniture I and my first husband had). As he is buzzing around full of excitement, I think: "No, I have to withdraw the offer. I have to stop saying 'yes' to satisfy others!"

Manifestation: (The dreamer's report) "During the morning following this dream (i.e. on the dream day), I got a phone call from an acquaintance of mine who lives in precisely the sort of apartment the dream had featured. He is well-off like my first husband, and of the same ethnic extraction. He said: 'I have something to tell you! I love you! What do you say to that?' 'Well thank you very much, but that's where it has to end, I am so sorry!'"

Comments: Although the dream could have shown this man as he was in real life, it preferred to portray an associative figure. In this way the dream made it clear at once that the man was in love, but would not get his wish to marry the dreamer. The next association, the furniture, revealed the suitor's ultimate intention: 'Not to be just her lover, but her husband'. That this was just a pipe dream of his is made all too clear by the plot of the dream which explicitly states: "I have to stop saying 'yes' to satisfy others!"

Dream 16C

I went up to Helen (@ an acquaintance of mine who is an artist and member of the Women's Society of Artists) and swallowed nervously. Then I found myself saying that I had a lot to offer, and was not too bad to look at, and that I also had a talent for painting. Helen and her friends then covered themselves with carpet which made them appear like soft sculptures. I could not understand their advice. All I could see when looking at the carpet was facial shapes, mouths moving, and I could hear only blurred speech.

Manifestation: (The dreamer's report) "One month after this dream I had to submit examples of my work, both paintings and sculptures, to the Women's Society of Artists. They would be evaluated and if found adequate, I would be made a member of the Society.

Under these circumstances it is quite clear why 'I swallowed nervously'. No less clear is why Helen featured in the dream, although in reality I was not at the judging of her work.

No less obvious is why I said in the dream that 'I also have a talent for painting'. Yet this needs some qualification. As I was leaving the premises of the Society, one of the members who was just arriving walked towards me, and touching my face said: 'I bet you are today's model!' I had to correct her and say that I was not the model, but the new applicant'.

This incident explains why the dream had me say 'I also have a talent for painting', and it makes it clear why it made me say: 'I am not bad to look at'.

Because I was told to wait for the result of the judging, I left the Society and spent the waiting time at an art gallery. There my friend, who came with me on this day, pointed out a landscape he found particularly pleasant. I looked at it and said: 'That green there is exactly the green of the new carpet I have chosen.'

Being excluded from the meeting of the judges I naturally could not hear what they were saying, I could only guess at it, and that's why the dream let me hear only blurred speech. It was all hush, hush, as if 'swept under the carpet'.

I thought that 'Helen and her friends' appearing in the dream like soft sculptures was a good sign. I knew that the Society was particularly keen to get a member who was not only a painter, but also a sculptor. And I took their appearance, which reminded me of soft sculptures, to mean that they would be a 'soft touch.' This seemed true even in the literal sense since one of the members had physically touched my face. But it also turned out to be true in the metaphorical sense, for the judges welcomed me with open arms."

Comments: The manifestations of this dream began before midday and ended about two-thirty in the afternoon. This shows palpably, how a dream will package an event into a short space of time that will later spread itself out over several hours of waking time. It also serves as a reminder that dreams may take weeks or months before they become reality. This highlights the necessity of keeping a dream diary, without which protracted manifestations would almost certainly escape our attention.

Dream 16D

'I was travelling up a mountain in a bus with several of my colleagues. About half way up the road became rocky, very narrow and steep so that we all had to get out of the bus and change into a smaller, open vehicle'.

Manifestation: (The dreamer's report) "On the day of the dream I attended a workshop with several colleagues of mine. At first the lecture was easy and quite general. About half-way through things got tough. It became necessary to be totally open about one's innermost thoughts and feelings."

Comments: Travelling in a bus, in public transport, is always an indication of social interaction on a broader scale. If we are driving the bus it means we are in a leading role in a public matter. As is clear from the manifestation of this particular dream, changing from the general, spacious transport to a smaller, open vehicle as the road became rocky, narrow and steep, meant that the going was getting tougher. But, as well as that, it also indicated that it was now necessary for everyone to be much more open with each other on quite intimate matters, if any progress was to be made. A smaller vehicle requires us to move closer to our fellow travellers, getting physically in touch with each other; in short to become intimate.

Dream 16E

> 'I dreamt that my son and his friend were sleeping under a bus in the neighbouring town'.

Manifestation: (The dreamer's report) "My son and his friend had gone to visit a mutual friend in the neighbouring town that has no regular public transport to where we live. I myself was staying with a friend when my son rang me late in the evening to get him. My car had broken down and so I could not fetch him. I worried all night about what could happen to the boys. The next day, when I got home, I found that they both had managed to catch a bus home that had been put on for a special occasion."

Comments: This dream is a splendid example of the economy of the language of dreams. For further explanation see Part II, Point 5,

'Condensation'. While the dream was clear enough regarding the fact that the boys would get their sleep, it is rather misleading with respect to their whereabouts. This is because the dream contracted the trip home and the boy's safety and rest into one image.

Dream 16F

'I am travelling on a bus through a barren landscape. Everyone disembarks to take part in a 50 km horse race. There are two types of horses, a different race for each. Mexican cowhands run the first race on wild stallions. We bus people run the second race on ordinary horses. A girl, a shadowy figure that I can't quite identify, yet seems familiar, is in this race. Suddenly she comes back to the start, claiming that she had completed the race and won it. She was told that she had taken the wrong course. So I plead with the judges to be permitted to take her place. I am given the OK and before I mount the horse I am given the Ten of Hearts from a pack of cards. Then I enter the race and fly through it to win'.

Comments: Clearly a success story. But there are two parts to it. The first one is a failure. Who ran that first race? 'A shadowy figure that seems familiar'. That figure seems familiar because it is the dreamer herself. It was she who failed in the first attempt. The one that will win is the dreamer in her present state.

The Ten of Hearts is of great interest here. 10 equals 5+5. One hundred equals 50+50. The first race was 50 km, half of a 100 km. So it seems that we are dealing here with two races of the same distance, which translates to two activities of the same kind.

It was fascinating how the dreamer and I, together, solved the riddle of this dream. I said to her, holding out my arms in a gesture of 'help me': "You have been given the Ten of Hearts, 5 and 5 are Ten...' And then the dreamer, staring at my arms and hands with their outspread fingers, shouted: 'The fallopian tubes!'

It was then that the young lady told me that she had to have one side of these arms of the womb scraped because she had been in danger of becoming barren. 'Aha,' I exclaimed, 'you got the Ten of Hearts because it talks about love and children. The first operation was unsuccessful, but the second one will be a success. The Ten of Hearts will vouch for that, because it is the traditional card of success in love, and in your case, it is the full 100 km race." And so it was.

Dream 16G

'I dreamt I was with friends and one of them waved a $1000 note under my nose. I saw the colouring and the number very clearly. I said to him, "Don't be funny, we don't have $1000 notes in this country!"'

Manifestation: (The dreamer's report) "The next day I sat in a waiting room that had a magazine from Italy there. As I opened it, there was a 1000 Lira note just as I had seen it in the dream. It was as if it wanted to prove the point that dreams foretell the future!

Comments: The dreamer had a discussion with me the day before about dreams being able to foretell the future. He thought this was utter nonsense and we parted, each with his own opinion intact. The next day I got a phone call from the dreamer telling me of his dream and his own interpretation. The line of the dream that says: "Don't be funny, we don't have $1000 notes in this country!" was of course a stand-in for the dreamer's view that dreams don't come true!

Part II
The Freudian Interpretation

1. Freud

A household word. FREUD has been a household word for a long time. It is synonymous with sex. The reason for this is the fact that Freud discovered that many psychological problems arose from sexual conflicts. He believed that repression of sexual impulses made us not only dysfunctional in the realm of Eros, but also caused serious neuroses and abusive sexual behaviour including rape, incest and child abuse. When Freud first suggested that the rapist was more likely to be a family member than a stranger, in other words the father, brother or uncle, the Victorian world was in uproar. Today this attitude has vanished. Instead we have help lines and other means of guarding against such abuse within the family. In short, Freud's view in this regard has been vindicated a hundred years later!

So how did Freud detect this social problem when seemingly everyone else remained ignorant of it? It was dream analysis that uncovered this sinister state of being. Freud discovered that some of his patients occasionally volunteered a dream quite spontaneously during consultation. He soon found that such dreams would throw light on the illness diagnosed and often helped to trace its origin. Because these origins seemed to be mostly of a sexual nature, he mentioned this in his famous book 'The Interpretation of Dreams'. This caused yet another storm of indignation in the sexually furtive society of his day. He defended himself against the ensuing public outcry by reminding his critics that he didn't say that all dreams required a sexual interpretation.

Strikingly erotic wishes: And of course, he did not. However he maintained that apparently 'innocent' dreams clearly embodied erotic wishes, which could be demonstrated by numerous examples. And this he most definitely could, and he did so in abundance. For someone who understands dream symbolism it is not difficult to uncover rape and other sexual abuse. A typical dream of sexual violence, for instance, is one where the female dreamer is being chased through her house by a dark, shadowy, figure with a knife in hand. The knife is, of course, easily identified as the pursuer's penis. This same meaning is also often attributed to the knife in waking time, as well. It becomes apparent in the wedding ceremony, for example, where the bride and the groom are cutting the cake together, each holding the same knife at the same time.

Freud's social mould. Freud grew up in a social milieu where sex was generally taboo. The exception was, of course, sex for begetting of children. Even that was kept as much in the dark as was humanly possible. Or should I say 'is still kept in the dark'? Considering what a country doctor said to me recently, it should indeed be stated in the present tense. He reported a case where a teenage girl came to him utterly distressed. She thought she was bleeding to death. Her mother had been unable to bring herself to pass on that age-old feminine wisdom of menstruation.

Conflict as basis of Freud's dream theory. In light of this it is not surprising that Freud based his dream theory on the conflict between our natural sexual impulses and the social taboos imposed on them. This found him on a path that ended up in a world of further conflict and contradictions. Instead of being able to help us in this sphere, which was his undoubted intention, he added to the confusion that already reigned in the domain of sexuality.

2. Freud's first mistake

Disguising our sexual desires. Freud believed that our so-called 'unconscious mind' was hiding our sexual desires by means of innocent dream language in order to save us from the truth of our base nature. More often than not, he said, our dreams described our sexual activities in a furtive way by portraying them in the 'guise' of indifferent objects and innocent acts, thus shielding us from the raw truth about our natural passions. Let me exemplify this by a common, indeed even stereotypical dream of a husband:

Dream F1

> 'When I came home I found the front door locked. I searched in my pocket for the key to the lock. When I finally found it, I inserted it and opened the door.'

Freud believed that this sort of dream story was a covert description of a man wanting sex with his wife. He maintained that the house stood for his wife, (the house-wife), the lock for her vagina, and the key for his penis. He added that dreams of opening doors were a very common euphemistic plot for sexual intercourse. Incidentally one of our vulgarisms for penis is 'Peter' because St. Peter, the Keeper of the Pearly Gate is the man with the 'key' to heavenly bliss. While the meaning of such symbolism has not found too much resistance from critics of Freud, the reason he gave for such symbolism was often attacked. Jung was perhaps his severest critic in this regard. He said that the dream was simply a parable with no intention to hide anything, but rather to teach.

3. Freud's second mistake

Dreams as wish fulfilments. Because Freud also believed that our sexual inhibitions often frustrated our passions, such dreams were there to compensate for our unfulfilled cravings. He thought, for instance, that opening doors in a man's dream would fulfil his wish to have sex. This led him to the ill-conceived theory that all dreams had a wish fulfilling function. He doggedly adhered to this view even in the face of the critique that surely no one would wish to have nightmares of suffering in hell.

What evidence did Freud have for his wish fulfilment theory? The simple answer to this is "none". It was all conjecture. We might well ask why Freud never asked his patients outright if his interpretations were correct. Had he done so, he would have had direct evidence that his sexual interpretations were mostly right even though his wish fulfilment theory might well have been completely wrong. But there was a problem with such direct verification of his analyses. If an astronomer wants to verify his calculations of stellar behaviour, for instance, say the return of Halley's Comet, he has to make a prediction. If the comet then arrives as foretold, his calculations are vindicated. So why did Freud not follow this age-old, tried and tested and indeed utterly simple procedure to prove the veracity of his interpretations? The answer to this too is simple: He did not believe that dreams were anticipations of things to come. This despite the age-old saying of "a dream come true", and despite the fact that the ancients firmly believed that dreams were messages from God of things to come. What is even more surprising is the fact that he had learnt the method of interpretation from an ancient dream diviner named Artemidorus, who believed that a certain class of dreams came true. Freud rejected this idea point blank without ever testing it. Had he done so, he would have had a weapon in his hand with which he could have won that heated argument between himself and Jung. This argument concerned the sexual content of the dream. While Freud saw no conflict in interpreting the sexual aspects of a dream physically and the non-sexual ones symbolically, Jung regarded this as untenable.

In my own extensive dealings with the dream I have come to the conclusion that Freud was perfectly right in interpreting the sexual meaning of the dream physically. On the other hand he was mistaken when he saw the dream as mere wish fulfilment. Anyone who doubts the flesh and blood interpretation of the sexual aspect of the dream, but is capable of interpreting its symbolism, can test this for himself. The procedure is simple, since in most cases the sexual meaning will become physically manifest on the dream day. This is the period of waking that follows the dream. This contrasts with Freud's dream day since for him it was the waking period before the dream.

At this point it might be helpful if we looked at one of the dreams listed in Part I which definitely came true in the way reported there. From what I said on that occasion, it is clear that its manifestation was anything but sexual. But when we look at this dream again and read its symbolism in the Freudian manner, things change radically. Let us then re-examine Dream G in a sexual context:

Dream F2

'I hurried to the liquor shop to buy a bottle of gin. Just as I stepped towards the door, Lucy the attendant closed it in my face saying: "Sorry sir, I am closed!"

The first question we should ask here is what sex the dreamer might be. In the first posting of this dream I did not indicate this. Not to know the sex of the dreamer, is of course, highly unusual. But not to know this also offers an excellent exercise in interpretation since it makes us look at the text more carefully. In this case the dialogue is the give-away. It would be highly unlikely to address a woman as 'sir'. So the dreamer is male and the fact that he addresses a female attendant, the desired object in this plot is not really gin, but the one who serves it. This is associative language, which is extremely common in dreams, and certainly not unknown in everyday talk, especially when it comes to sexual matters. We will refer to our genitals in all sorts of ways in order to avoid directness. 'Down below', the 'family jewels' and so on.

So the question here is: did this dreamer have sex on the dream day? There is little doubt that the craving was there. There is even less doubt that it was not satisfied since the attendant quite clearly said: "Sorry sir, I am closed"! She said 'I am closed', not 'the shop is closed'. Could it possibly be clearer that she was unavailable? Incidentally, this total identification of her with the shop is yet another associative characteristic, not just of dream language, but also of everyday speech. Yet another associative factor is that the attendant was a representative of the dreamer's wife. The dreamer did not actually want the attendant, but the one she stood for. So we can see that this dream not only foresaw that the dreamer would lack in spirit, but also in sexual interaction.

4. The real reasons for 'coding' the sexual plot.

If the dream is not using 'code' to hide, is it using 'code' to reveal? My observations have shown me that the dream is a dress rehearsal for all of our waking experiences. Put another way, the dream is a total program or pregram of things to come. This means that it will not only foreshadow our general everyday concerns, but also the specifically sexual episodes, and more generally, the sexual state of the day. This includes the whole gamut of sexual feelings from indifference to ecstatic passion, from repression to wild arousal.

Understandably this requires a massive amount of programming. Because we dream for only a restricted amount of time during the night, the dream's programs have to be severely compressed. In other words the dream is compelled to resort to a kind of shorthand or computer zip program in order to cover all of our behaviour of the next day and beyond. Part of this zip program is the ingenious device of telling the sexual story by means of non-sexual everyday happenings. It means that the sexual plot of the day is not prefigured in a separate plot, but will ride, as it were, on the non-sexual plot of the day. So when a man, for instance, dreams of a problem with the lock of the front door, he will subsequently come face-to-face with an actual lock problem and also find it problematic to have sex with his partner. Clearly, since the dream's nature is susceptible to a predictive interpretation, it makes nonsense of the view that the purpose of its code is to hide rather than to reveal. Because of this 'code', we can determine not only whether or not sex will take place, but also what kind it will be and where and when it will materialise. This double-headed plot of the dream is the strongest evidence yet, that Eros shadows us wherever we may go and in whatever we may do.

5. Dream shorthand

What else is there to this shorthand or zip program the dream is able to employ? Basically it consists of two different methods.

The first method.

Condensation. Part of the first method is condensation. By this I mean that all dream actions and situations are 'pressure packed' by means of temporal and spatial contraction. As indicated, it may be seen to work like a computer zip program.

The serial manifestation. Another form of condensation the dream uses is this: Instead of featuring every variation of a motif or theme in the dream itself, it simply shows a single, basic motif, but then projects its many variations into waking time at different intervals in the form of serial manifestations. (For a short example of how this works, see dream F23 at the end of Part II)

The static series. Yet another form of condensation or of 'time saving' the dream resorts to is showing long, repetitive actions by means of the static series. Thus a picket fence or a staircase will indicate repetitive manipulation in an instant, for the many pickets or the many steps simply stand for doing things over and over. Rows of items, boxes or poles, vases or jars, are used for the same purpose. Lines of pillars, palings, pickets, bunches of keys, packets of matches, assortments of knives and stacks of cigarettes are all typical items to suggest manipulation of the penis. Its female equivalents, on the other hand, are representations of rows of boxes, cases of tomatoes, oranges, a series of picture frames and rows of windows. Here is a man's dream to illustrate this concept:

Dream F3

> 'I found a packing case in a dark corner of my daughter's house. The boards were widely spaced like on a pellet. With a bit of chalk I wrote on it H A P P Y X M A S, each letter on an individual board.'

Sexual play followed on the dream day. The daughter's house was an associative representation of the dreamer's wife. The dark corner won't leave us guessing. The writing on the individual boards prefigured the kind of foreplay that took place. The fact that the boards were part of a packing case shows where that foreplay was to lead.

It might be helpful in this context to point out that not all straight items are references to the penis. While a hose with a nozzle, for instance, is definitely penile, a hose without a nozzle refers to the clitoris. In the same way not all trees are representations of the penis. A tree growing in a volcano is decidedly clitoral.

Past referencing. But to save even more time, there is also past referencing. By this I mean that the dream refers to past experiences; it tells us that something like it is going to come up again. In this way the dream does not have to present a lengthy explanation of what is in the pipeline, for all we need to do is recall the relevant past events for us to understand what lies ahead. But of course, that understanding won't come unless we uncover these past experiences by means of noting our associations and reflecting on them. When we actually do reflect on these associations we will see how a single moment of the dream will telescope out into minutes or even hours of waking time. This again is akin to the computer zip program.

The second method.

Recycling. The second method of saving time and space employed by the dream is recycling. By this I mean that one and the same plot, like opening locks and going through doors, is a pregram for both the non-sexual and the sexual events of the day.

Lock and door dream as a model for sexual intercourse. Let me expand on this a little by means of the lock and door dream recorded earlier. (Part II, Point 2 & 4) This dreamer would actually find himself in course of the dream day in front of a locked door. After some time he would gain entry just as the dream had said. If this door happened to be the door to his own house, finding it locked would have to be something unusual, otherwise the dream would not bother portraying such a situation. An example might be that his wife had gone out, which she never does at that time of the day. Indeed, if we observe our dreams carefully, we will find that we dream only of things that are not strictly routine. After all, we don't need to be prepared for things and situations that have become automatic.

Two messages in the same plot. As already outlined, the same plot not only prefigures the hurdle of a locked door, but also the hurdle of gaining entry in sexual terms. In other words, in this case the dreamer would find himself on the dream day before a reluctant wife, but since the dream plot allowed him to find his key and then permitted him to open the door, his wife too, would relent and eventually welcome his advances. In such a case the dream would clearly be a sexual allegory as well as a literal message.

All dreams feature sexual concerns. While Freud said that most dreams contain sexual concerns, I found that all do in some way or another. And why not? After all, once puberty has set in, our whole body is constantly flooded with sexual hormones. There is no way to filter them out. Also, the central position of our sexual organs on our body is quite symbolical of the centrality of our sexual concerns. Indeed some psychologists maintain that some men will think of sex every three minutes. In view of this it would seem to be no exaggeration to maintain that everybody, no matter how under-sexed they may appear to be, would at least entertain several sexual thoughts within an hour. But what is even more convincing than these considerations, is the fact that the dream's sexual plot rides on non-sexual everyday concerns. It transpires that our life force, our libido, is a firmly twisted twine made of sexual and non-sexual strands.

Covert sexuality in our thoughts and feelings. When we realise just how much of our thinking and feeling is covert, or if you like, 'subconscious' sexuality, the frequency chart of sexual thoughts looks more like a three-minute curve. But even if it were only a ten or twenty minute curve, it would still be unavoidable that every dream, (and with it its many manifestations) was shadowed by a sexual undercurrent; providing of course, that my contention is right, that our dreams are a total pregram of our waking life. Whether or not that is so, only consistent and extensive dream watching will determine.

Are thoughts and fantasies pregrammed too? In view of what I have just said about sexual thoughts, both overt and covert, we should wonder if not only our actions were pregrammed, but also our thoughts? In my experience they are, and this brings us to another realisation. It is the recognition that the sexual content of a dream is not just about active sex and orgasms, but also about fantasies and sexual feelings away from intercourse and masturbation. This includes sexual frustrations, inhibitions and wishful thinking! In short, in a total dress rehearsal nothing is left out.

Sexual overtones in all we do, feel and think. Earlier on I have suggested that much of what goes on in our head is charged with sexual overtones. We might well ask if this is really so. At first sight it seems far-fetched, but when we become aware of how intricately sex and pleasure are intertwined, it begins to look more and more likely. Let's take the innocent word of 'joy' for instance. It is everyone's experience that there are a variety of joys. There is the joy of the toddler who watches his cat performing its antics with a ball of string. Then there is the joy of winning a contest. There is also the nasty kind of joy we may feel when our enemy gets hurts. And then there is the book entitled "The Joy of Sex". 'Joy' comes in a variety of packages.

When we reflect on this we soon come to the conclusion that there is a bit of sex in every kind of joy; even in the apparently most innocent one. I'll never forget the little two-year old boy who was surprised by a massive flock of seagulls on the lawn in front of the town hall. Utterly astonished by this extraordinary sight he advanced towards the birds that fled before him slowly enough to allow him to be surrounded by hundreds of fluttering wings. Overwhelmed by this he threw his arms up in the air, but then immediately dropped them again in order to firmly clasp the fly on his shorts and stomp among the 'whooshing' feathers in broad and giant steps. Freud would have been overjoyed had he been able to witness this scene, for it vindicated his conviction that pre-pubescent children too, had sexual feelings. He often pointed out that the cries of excitement by tiny tots when an uncle or bigger brother tossed them in the air was testimonial to this.

It would seem then that even the purest of joys and the most innocent of pleasures will always bear traces of sexual joys and pleasures. Indeed, if joy may pervade sex, why should sex not pervade joy?

What about anxieties? There are many feelings that seem far removed from sexual sensations, yet they are nevertheless coloured with definite sexual hues and tints. Anxiety is one of those. We can see this in cases of acute anxieties. They can actually induce erections and orgasmic episodes. Indeed sexual excitement is in principle not different from anxiety. When we look at an orgasmic build-up more closely, we realise that it is really a form of anxiety. It may be more pleasurable than other forms of angst, yet we seek release from it as promptly as from the more unpleasant variety.

What about spiritual emotions? But, we may ask, what about spiritual emotions such as the love of God? Are they too, tinged with sexual overtones? Our first reaction to this question may well be a decisive 'no'. But is this the right answer? Are not such emotions, no matter how 'spiritual' they may be, also filled with pleasure? If they are, then we have no choice but to come to the same conclusion we had come to before; that anything bound up with pleasure is never free of sexual tinges. It is certainly of intense interest here to note that the saints speak of their devotion to God in terms of love. Moreover when they are separated from their object of devotion, they seem to suffer the same kind of anguish any lover does who has been separated from his or her beloved. As well as that, we need to remember that in India there is a spiritual practice called Tantra that encourages a special kind of sexual interaction which leads to other-worldly ecstasies.

Kundalini rising. It is often forgotten that sexual urges are part and parcel of the life force. The two are an integrated whole like the light and warmth of sunshine. Studies made of the Kundalini experiences such as those of Dr. Lee Sannella show that the awakening Kundalini which ultimately leads to enlightenment and a sexless state often goes hand in hand with sexual sensations. (Dr. Lee Sannella, "The Kundalini Experience", Integral Publishing, 1987)

Freud's preoccupation with sex. Jung once described Freud's preoccupation with sex as numinous. The dictionary defines 'numinous' as relating to the divine, as something that arouses spiritual or religious emotions, something mysterious and awe-inspiring. It makes us wonder then why Jung fought Freud's sexual interpretation of the dream tooth and claw? Why indeed, for Jung himself loved to emphasise the mysterious, the awe-inspiring, the metaphysical and the mythological interpretation of the dream.

Many levels of interpretation. This brings us to the question of whether or not the sexual interpretation has to stop at the sexual level? It does not, much in the same way as the non-sexual reading can be pegged to various levels. To sum this up: Every dream, like any waking situation, has many levels of meaning. Whether or not we explore these depends on the interpreter and not on the dream itself.

The paradox of explicit sex in dreams. It seems curious at first to realise that when the dream features overt sexual intercourse it is rarely foreshadowing sexual intercourse; instead it will picture symbolical sex. By this I mean that intercourse will become nothing more than 'getting on' with someone in an amicable manner. The hidden sexuality in this situation both reveals itself in the phrases of 'getting on' and the word 'amicable'. The latter means being friendly, as we would be with someone we like or pretend to like. And liking is a form of loving, and loving is never devoid of sexual implications. But as is usual with dreams, they may just surprise us and make an exception and manifest literally! In general, the overtly sexual dream will manifest more often as symbolical sex than as physical lovemaking.

Inverse projections. That a sexual dream plot may manifest in waking as innocent 'getting on' is an inversion of the case where the non-sexual plot will manifest in sexual activity. Such inversions reveal a kind of complementarity between dreaming and waking, between metaphor and literality. In other words, when the dream speaks in anatomical terms of sex, waking manifests this in metaphorical sex, and when the dream speaks in metaphorical terms, waking acts it out anatomically. There seems to be the same sort of complementarity in this as in a game of charades, which is a game of associative thinking.

6. Freud's third mistake

Freud's teachers. Although Freud had learnt his technique of interpretation from the ancients such as Artemidorus, he could not accept their belief regarding the dream's prophetic nature. This is not so difficult to understand, for having been reared in the west he was moulded into believing that the future was in no way accessible. Neither in dreams nor any other way.

His rejection of the future factor without testing. What is not so easily understood, on the other hand, is the fact that he was not at all prepared to test this crucial belief of the ancients, even though he prided himself to be the first scientific investigator into dreams. Because of this reluctance he came to assert that the dream looked forward only from yesterday's waking period to the dreams of the ensuing night. In other words, he thought that our desires/wishes from the day before were taken up by the dream and then 'gratified' in that state. In order to illustrate Freud's view of the dream's function, let's go back to the lock and key dream once more, and see how Freud would have explained it:

Freud's view of the lock and key dream. First the dream again.

Dream F4

> "When I came home I found the front door locked. I searched in my pocket for the key to the lock. When I finally found it, I inserted it and opened the door".

Freud correctly assumed that the lock and key stood for the vagina and the penis respectively. Equally correct was his reading of the initial part of the plot. The man coming face-to-face with a locked door is coming face-to-face with a reluctant wife. Where he goes off the track is in his conclusion. He believed that this dream compensated for the man's inability to have sex by allowing him, in his dream, to open the door and enter the house. In this way, according to Freud, his wish to have sex, which was frustrated in his waking hours, was fulfilled in his dream of the night.

It is in conclusions of this sort that Freud committed the greatest of scientific sins. And he continued stubbornly in this manner. Instead of having his speculations verified, he went on with such speculative interpretations to the end of his career. It is difficult to comprehend that Freud never once asked his patients after such a dream: "Well then, did you get your way, or were you refused entry despite the fact that the dream let you open the lock?" Was he too shy or too arrogant? If he was too shy, he could have asked himself this question after a similar dream; after all we know from his personal life that his wife was not always so obliging. And then there was always masturbation as a test piece. Ultimately there is only one explanation for Freud's refusal to consider that question of verification: destiny, which determines all of our thoughts and actions.

Dreams are definitely not wish fulfilments. We can decide this question without looking further into Freud's bedroom. But even before moving onto our own dreams to see them becoming reality, we can safely infer that dreams are not wishes we seek to have fulfilled; after all, not all dreams are pleasant or indifferent encounters. What about a nightmare of being burnt at the stake?

7. Summing up so far

Freud's reasons for the covert language. Freud was mistaken when he believed that the dream spoke in a clandestine way in order to shelter us from our true and passionate self. His belief that the dream was a wish fulfilment was equally wrong. And his view that the dream could not look ahead to the next day or beyond was misconceived as well.

Freud's sexual interpretations were essentially right. Freud was perfectly right in as much as his translations of the dream's euphemistic language was concerned. He was right to assume that the house stood for the dreamer's wife, and he was right in saying that the lock was his wife's vagina and the key the dreamer's penis. Incidentally it was from Artemidorus, who believed that our dreams could foresee the future that Freud had learnt the meaning of such 'euphemisms'. And Artemidorus in turn had learnt it from the Greeks, the Greeks from the Arabs, and the Arabs from the Babylonians.

So what is the real reason for the dream's euphemistic sexual language? The real reason is the dream's need for saving time and space which it achieves by means of the two methods shown earlier.

8. The marker phenomenon

The dream's intentions are not to hide, but to reveal. Just how wrong Freud's reason for the dream's euphemistic language was, will only be fully appreciated when we learn of the true function of the enigmatic 'symbols' the dream uses to describe our sexual encounters. As we shall see, it is in complete opposition to camouflage. In short, the dream's intentions are not to hide anything, but rather to reveal.

Time and place of sex encoded in the dream's covert language. What is it then that the dream reveals by means of its 'covert' language? It indicates not only what our sexual state will be, but it also shows with amazing precision just where and when any sexual activity will take place, providing there is any activity to eventuate. In short, the very imagery the dream uses to describe our sexual interaction will also mark the time and place of the occurrence.

A point of special attention. We have already seen in the context of the lock and key dream that the purpose of representing the sexual act by means of opening the door of the house was to show what kind of sexual act would follow in its train. We have also seen that the dream used this scenario because there was something unusual about the real door of the dreamer's house on the day of the sexual realisation of his dream. In other words, it was something that would catch the dreamer's special attention on the day he would have sex.

The marker phenomenon. This phenomenon tells us loud and clear that the dream chooses so-called 'symbols' for its sexual scenarios. These will become material fact in the course of the dream's manifestation, a material fact that will come to the dreamer's direct attention one way or another. In the case of the dream of the lock and key, that material fact is the unusual (locked) state of the door to the house. Thus this circumstance will serve as the marker of the place and time of sex. To repeat this in another way, sex will occur in the house with the troublesome door on the day the door in question gives that particular kind of trouble.

Two birds with one stone. If it had not been for the fact that the door of the dream in question had been troublesome on the dream day, the marker would have been too ordinary and nondescript to be noticed; it would have been wholly unsuited as a marker. Fortunately, such situations can never arise because our dreams only program those situations that are not strictly routine. In this way, the dream 'kills two birds with one stone'. The first one achieves economy of language while the second one guarantees the provision of a distinctive and unmistakable marker.

The marker as a new item. Unlike its occurrence in this example of the lock and key dream, the marker will often appear as an entirely new item on the day and in the place of sex. The marker object may come to rest right next to our bed, or even in our bed, or somewhere near the location of our sexual activity. Often it will be an item we have never encountered before, like a new book beside our bed, a magazine with a certain picture, a report in the newspaper, a scene on television, an unusual visitor or something on the outside of the house.

Here is an example:

Dream F5

> 'I dreamt that I climbed up on the kitchen cupboard, opened its door and found a packet of liquorice. The packet was torn in one corner; someone had obviously opened it and had tasted some of the sweets. I helped myself to one of the lollies. As I did so, I spotted the brand name of the sweets written in large letters over the celluloid packet. It was CLINTON.'

Manifestation of the dream. In the afternoon following this dream the dreamer's wife brought home the local paper, an unusual thing for her to do. She put it on the kitchen bench opposite the kitchen cupboard where some days ago she had placed a packet of sweets given to her by someone. As the dreamer casually opened the paper, his glance fell on Clinton, who was in danger of being impeached for his love affair with Monica Lewinsky. This moment became the marker of the day and place of sex. It was consummated in the evening, however not in the kitchen, but in the bedroom. This shows that the marker need not be right next to the bed of the lovers, and need not appear at the exact moment of the sexual embrace.

Perfect simultaneity of sex and marker. But perfect simultaneity can actually occur, especially if the television or the radio is on while sex is taking place. By this I mean that the very object the dream had used in the night will later appear on TV or will feature on the radio at the very time of sex. A variation of this is when the lovers will discuss a particular object that was the highlight of a dream just before, during or immediately after sex. These are often very tenuous markers that will easily escape our attention. So, if we want to catch all our markers, we can't lose ourselves entirely in our passion. Another difficult marker to catch is one that appears vicariously or by mere association. Here is an example of a marker close to the bed of the lovers:

Dream F6

'As I walk into my studio, my attention is drawn to a workbench on which is a square wooden frame. Stepping closer, I have a good look at its contents. It is filled with terracotta clay. At the very moment I realise this, a shower of rain begins to pour into the mould, leaving pockmarked impressions in the soft clay.'

The marker of the sexual manifestation of this dream was extraordinarily interesting. This dreamer's little boy had brought a book from school the afternoon of the dream day. In other words, the dream foresaw that this book would come to the attention of the dreamer after he had dreamt about it. He and his son had a good look at it together. After they had their fill, the dreamer placed it on the bedside table on his side of the marital bed. So it happened that in the evening of the dream day he was making love to his wife right next to this book. It clearly served as a marker of the place and the time of lovemaking. There were pictures of fossils in the book and instructions on how to make artificial fossils by means of a square wooden mould and plaster. One of the pictures showed fossilised rain. The obvious sexual codes of this dream were of course the 'workbench' which is a well-known vulgarism for the bed of lovers; the 'square wooden frame' which in dream language is feminine because it is a 'container'; and the rain which is an unmistakable representation of an 'ejaculation'. What on the other hand is not so obvious is the phrase "my attention is drawn". The word drawn gives a clue: there is a definite attraction implied. But attention too, signals concentration on urgent matters, on passion, on sex.

Literary pheromones. I have dubbed the expressions that forewarn of sexual encounters literary pheromones because they are unmistakeable indicators of our libidinous state. It's worth paying attention to these terms when they occur in our dream report since they are strong signals of a sexual plot hidden in an apparently innocent story. Some further expressions and situations of this ilk are: attractive, delightful, arousal, spellbound, alluring, bewitching, enchanting, surprise, interest, close-up views of images, curious, shock, shocked, shocking, terrified, terrified of heights, vertigo, awesome, astonished, amazement, unexpected, jerk, perfect, focus, exquisite, intense, fantastic, fame and fortune, fun, joy, excitement, fire, explosion, fascinating etc. Whatever else these expressions may signal, they are all descriptive of sexual highs, which, when they occur in our dream diary, forewarn us more often than not, of sexual scenarios. The last one of these literary pheromones, 'fascinating', is derived from Latin with the following meanings: 1. 'To attract and delight by arousing interest or curiosity'. 2. 'To render motionless, as with a fixed stare or by arousing terror or awe'. 3. 'Archaic, to put under a spell'. All symptoms, of course, observed among lovers.

The marker as part of the serial manifestation. In Point 5, 'Dream Shorthand', I have said that the theme of a dream will manifest several times in different variations. Because of this, it is certainly to be expected that the marker items will appear more than once during the day. They will occur scattered throughout the day. It is because of this phenomenon that the marker will not always make its appearance at the exact time of sex, but before or after it. In other words, the time of a marker's appearance will depend on which particular serial manifestation will come to our notice. In dream F18, recorded towards the end of Part II, more than one manifestation of the dream came to the dreamer's notice, so there was more than one marker. One of these was the potting of the bonsais that occurred long before the sexual manifestation. Another marker was the spider story told by the wife while the lovers were in embrace. That became the simultaneous marker. Both of these markers were anticipated by the dream and portrayed by it in one short, condensed scene. In waking reality they were wide apart due to the phenomenon of the serial manifestation. But the main point to be remembered here is that in a regular relationship the time of the sexual manifestation is generally on the dream day.

9. The manifestation span of the sexual plot.

In normal relationships and masturbation. In the case of masturbation the dream nearly always becomes sexual reality on the dream day. (The dream day being the waking phase immediately after the dream) With regard to plots indicating sexual intercourse it will be on the dream day if the dreamer is in a reasonably balanced relationship. If sexual relations are strained the manifestation may take longer, perhaps two or three days. When in a precarious sexual web, a frustrated partner may dream of intercourse several days ahead. The dream will build into its plot an indication of the delay of intercourse, but that's not always easy to detect. A seemingly endless road or a vast landscape often represents a longer waiting time. Sometimes an object changing into another object, or several others, will indicate it. At other times we may be in the foyer waiting to go upstairs or be trapped in some other waiting area.

In the case of single persons. When we are not in a relationship the sexual manifestation span is especially difficult to determine. This is because a dream with an intercourse plot may look far ahead. But every dream always manifests at least in some respect on the dream day. For instance, a woman without a partner may have a typical intercourse dream that on the dream day may result in an orgasm, but not induced through intercourse. Instead it might be triggered off quite spontaneously through a sexual fantasy. Remember I have said that thoughts too are pre-figured by the dream. Since the dream does not distinguish between thoughts and things (between 'thinks' and things) it can be a devilish item to handle. So be warned: when we deal with other people's dreams we must first ascertain their personal circumstances, particularly partnerships, before we stomp on a wasps' nest. But it is precisely in such uncertain circumstances and especially in extended manifestation spans where the marker will play a decisive role. If it does appear on the day of the sexual consummation in the location or circumstances the dream had indicated, then we are face-to-face with the materialisation of the dream that had featured it.

10. Verification of the sexual meaning of the dream.

Freud was too sure of his interpretative skills to ask the dreamers if his sexual interpretations were right or wrong. To my knowledge there is no evidence in his writings that he asked any of them. Yet he knew that the Arabian dream interpreters always made sure of their clients' sexual relationships before they ventured a reading. In contrast to this, Freud was more likely to say that popular symbolism enabled him to interpret the dream without help.

Jung, as is well-known, evaded the sexual issues whenever he could. This is perhaps the clearest distinguishing mark between the two dream giants. Although Jung did verify his interpretations in some way, he never developed strict guidelines that tested the verity of his interpretations. He was satisfied if his readings helped the patients in their return to mental health. He was the dream doctor and not the dream diviner. In fact, he thought it was difficult to imagine a controlled way of obtaining reliable results from formal testing.

Verification by means of the marker. I have found that it is not quite as hopeless as Jung suspected. The sexual facet of the dream does give us access to a controlled way of verifying our interpretations, for we can hardly miss noticing an orgasm or a frustrated attempt at having sex in the waking state. If we predict intercourse to follow a dream and then it does, we have proof that our interpretation was right. And, as I have indicated before, we will have an even better substantiation of the accuracy of our forecast when there is a marker to identify the sexual episode. It is clear from this that the marker provides that very 'controlled method' which Jung had said was difficult to imagine.

The incubus revisited. I wish to return to the lesson that sleep paralysis has afforded us in order to expand on the importance of the last dream phase before waking up. Contrary to popular opinion, this phase can last between 20 to 40 minutes before we become fully awake. During this time, sleep gradually becomes lighter. By the time we are about to wake up, some of the motor inhibitors will have weakened to an appreciable degree so that some of the dream content will evidence noticeable repercussions in the body. As I have said earlier, if we dream of playing tennis, the electrical charge in the racket hand will be stronger than in the free hand. Now if it is as I suggested, the sexual content of the last dream will assert itself over the 'neutral' content of the dream. This means that although the dream's imagery will consist of ordinary everyday objects, its plot will be charged with sexual energy. In other words, if the dream of the lock and key was to foreshadow impending intercourse, the body would release at that time a sufficient dose of sexual hormones to trigger off sexual arousal.

Such a situation is quite palpably exemplified in the case of wet dreams. They occur most markedly in young males who are supercharged with sexual hormones by the time they are about to wake up. The most distinctive physical symptom of such a state is of course, the proverbial morning erection which will accord with the plot of the dream. If now the blocking of the motor sensory system has been weakened, as will happen towards the point of waking, the sort of acting out of a dream as occurs in sleepwalking will quite readily take place, resulting in an orgasmic ejaculation. For this to take place it would, however, be a precondition that the plot of the dream foreshadowed masturbation. This is still more evidence of predestination.

11. Some examples of how dreams will manifest sexually

Dream F7

'I am chiselling a mortise hole. I know I am doing this although I am not using my hands and I am not holding a hammer. I can see the rectangular mortise hole very clearly. Suddenly I break through the back of the hole and a portion of timber breaks away. I am a bit concerned that I might have caused some damage. Luckily the mortise wasn't wrecked, yet I was somewhat disappointed'.

Manifestation: On the dream day this dreamer had sexual intercourse with his wife.

Comments: It isn't difficult to see that this was a man's dream, nor is its meaning much of a puzzle; after all, everyday language refers to a man's potency as his tool. What is of particular interest here is that the dreamer knew he was chiselling although his hands were nowhere to be seen. There are two reasons why the dream does this sort of thing. The first one is to determine the kind of sexual manifestation, the second one to pinpoint the marker. If the dream had shown the dreamer using his hands, he would most likely have masturbated. Since his hands were absent in the dream, intercourse followed on the dream day. The chiselling action without hands shows that clearly. The breaking through the hole and the breaking away of timber represent the orgasm with the breaking away of timber picturing the ejaculation.

The Marker: As I have said, the second reason for the absence of the dreamer's hands was to be sought in the marker phenomenon. This particular marker had its roots in the waking phase before the dream. (Freud's 'residue', see Part I, Point 9). On that day the dreamer had given the joiner some final instructions regarding the small bookshelf to be installed in his lounge. On the dream day the joiner came to set it up. It was then discovered that the shelf did not fit exactly into the area it was designed to go. The joiner expressed his disappointment before he went to work to make the necessary alterations. In short, it was the joiner's hands that did the chiselling of the timber while it was the dreamer who did the sexual joining. The reason for the dream's identification of the carpenter with the dreamer is rooted in the dream's need for this shorthand style of communication. (See Part II, Point 5; also see Part III dreams 6 & 92).

Dream F8

> 'My mother-in-law had taken all my dolls away. I was determined to get at least some of them back. So I went to her place and retrieved an armful of them.'

Manifestation: This dreamer lived at a different address to that of her lover. For safety reasons her mail was posted to his address. On the dream day she went to visit her lover. At first it seemed the two would not make love. Eventually they did.

Comments: Again, the dreamer's gender is perfectly clear. The same plot also tells us who determined to have sex. Dolls, being 'pretend babies' and a pet name for 'toy-girls', are a common allusion to sexual intercourse. In this case, the dreamer could actually recall a time when she wanted a particular doll as a little girl. The doll's name was Kitty. At the time she had cried until her mother had given in to her plea. The name Kitty is also linked to 'kitten' and so is a euphemistic reference to 'pussy'.

The Marker: Almost immediately after the two had made love the postman arrived. He brought a card for the dreamer. The two lovers looked at it together while sitting up in bed. On the card were two figures. One was a woman and the other a little girl. The woman was putting something into the basket the little girl was holding up to her. Although there were no actual dolls to be seen in the picture, the figures themselves were stiff and stilted as if they had been painted from dolls set up for that purpose. The card was from the mother-in-law of the dreamer's niece. She lived in the very town in which the dreamer had lived as a little girl and had seen Kitty in a shop window there. This shows how childhood wishes are used by the dream to pre-figure adult sexual desires. (Cf. dream 75) This in turn exposes the essential sexuality of apparently innocent desires. Incidentally, the story told by the dreamer of her 'Kitty episode' was a sufficiently strong marker of the dream's sexual manifestation. It is often the case that markers will be no more substantial than that. On such occasions they are easily missed. It means keeping our eyes peeled and ears open.

Dream F9

> 'I am holding a ladder made of treated pine in my hand. Several large nails are sticking out at all angles from the timber. Some of them are clearly bent from extensive banging and bashing. Suddenly I toss the ladder up high. It gets caught between the two top rungs on a piece of timber sticking out from the wall. It was a perfect shot.'

Manifestation: This dream resulted in sexual intercourse after some extensive foreplay that is indicated by the involvement of the hands. Another indicator of this is the word 'treated pine'. Pine trees are often representative of the penis, (pines/penis), while treating not only suggests an orgasmic treat or working at something, but also genital manipulation. (See dream F19 of Part II)

Comments: Perhaps it isn't so easy to say from the dream alone whether this was a woman's dream or a man's. Because ladders look so very masculine we might suspect that we are face-to-face with a man's dream. But then, when we look at the ending of the dream where the ladder gets tossed up in the air and is caught between the two top rungs on a piece of timber sticking from the wall, we might rightly suspect it was a woman's dream. The problem in this case is that the ladder represents as much the male's sexual anatomy as that of the female. There is no doubt of this because of the sharing of the sexual anatomy during intercourse. In the beginning of the dream the ladder introduces the erect penis in the dreamer's hand. At the end the dream changes it into the woman who hooks up the man's protrusion from his body, the dream wall on which she comes to 'hang'. Also the nails sticking out from the ladder see it as the woman's body. This becomes clear when we understand that the nails, which suffered much banging, are a representation of her clitoris. Many nails mean many blows. So it was a man's dream. He started off by stimulating his partner and himself. Then, as they reached the top rung, he got 'hooked' up on her and it all ended in a 'perfect shot'.

The Marker: On the dream day the dreamer's wife asked him to dismantle the damaged ladder to the children's bunks so it could be replaced by a different one. It was the wife who tossed the old one out on the wood heap.

Dream F10

'A lady who was doing a survey regarding a new, red wine came up to me. She asked me what it should be priced at. I very meanly said five dollars knowing very well that this wine was worth more. When she protested I added two more dollars. She then gave me the curiously shaped bottle that was also a glass at the same time. I took the cork off and dipped my finger into the wine. It was totally exquisite.'

Manifestation: This dreamer, a woman, had sex with her partner on the dream day. The partner was a man, not a woman, as it might seem at first sight.

Comments: Because the dreamer dipped her finger into the wine it might look like a masturbation dream. But it wasn't; the curious bottle that is also a glass shows that. This strange bottle/glass is a clever picture of the male (bottle) and female (glass) partners in sexual embrace. Dipping the finger into the wine in this context meant grasping the penis (with her fingers) and dipping it into herself.

The Marker: On this day the dreamer shared a bottle of wine with her partner. If the two had been regular drinkers this would have to be disregarded as a valid marker. But they seldom drank. The dream actually makes this quite clear. Once we understand that the lady doing the survey is the dreamer herself, we see her debating with herself as to whether or not she should have some wine. Her mean underpricing of the wine reveals her reluctance. The low value she puts on it reflects the low value she gives to wine. But then, as she increases the value of it by two dollars, we see her warming to the idea of having a drink. There was something else in the dream that showed the dreamer's resistance to having a drink of wine. But we can't know this until we learn that she did not like red wine at all. The wine the two partners shared was actually white wine. So it seems that the dream featured red wine in order to stress the dreamer's reluctance to have a drink. Nevertheless, wine became the marker of the sexual episode even though it was of a different colour.

Dream F11

> 'A young, blonde woman, the life of the party, came up to me holding out a long, green bottle of wine. It was unusually elongated. I said to her: 'I don't want this', but almost immediately after I had said it I changed my mind and I cried out, 'Where is my glass, my glass please!'

Manifestation: On the dream day this man had sexual intercourse with a blonde woman. She was actually the lady who had the dream that was just discussed. (Dream F10)

Comments: Here we have a rather unique case where we know the dreams and their manifestations of both sexual partners. It is evident at once that this dreamer too was reluctant to have a drink of wine at first. This supports the claim I have made on behalf of the two lovers that they were not regular drinkers. But unlike his partner, this dreamer did not agonise over the question whether or not to have a drink for too long, and almost immediately cried out for his drink. But was it really the drink that made him so impatient? This becomes doubtful as we look at that unusually elongated bottle the lady had held out to him. It doesn't need much reflection to see that it was 'the life of the party' that actually had caused the dreamer's 'bottle' to stretch itself so that it became a matter of urgency for him to find a glass to pour his wine into.

The Marker: I have said in connection with the marker of dream F10 that the two had white wine together. It was actually in a green bottle just as the man's dream had said; so in his case both the colour of the wine and that of the bottle stood for markers of the most literal kind.

Dream F12

'My wife and I are walking towards a flat area of high ground, a sort of platform. At the end of it is a picnic type of fireplace. While walking there my wife asks me: 'What are we going to do?' I answer: 'We are going to have some fun!' 'That's what I like' is my wife's response. Then I go up to the fireplace where I get hold of a long log of firewood that's jutting out from it. I then press it downwards. Somehow this lifts the cooking pot up. The branch must have acted like a lever on a fulcrum. I didn't actually see this; I made this assumption in the dream. To my astonishment this large, bone-shaped lever catches fire at the end, which lies in the middle of the fireplace where it also seems to touch the cooking pot. In contrast to the burning log which I can see very clearly, I only feel that the hearth and cooking pot are there.'

Manifestation: Both the dreamer and his wife went to bed in a particularly amorous mood. As they cuddled up to each other the husband lifted up his wife's thigh and pressed his erection against it. After some caressing he inserted from underneath, so lifting her buttocks at the same time. On that night they had sex in the dark because they had visitors. Normally they leave a light or two on or have at least a candle burning.

Comments: In the Upanishads, sacred books of Hinduism, there is a description of sexual intercourse with the woman being the sacred fire and the man being the owner of the fire stick. Pubescent children relate to this allegory quite readily. They tell a joke where a nun and a man have to share the only bed available in the inn. The man touches the nun's feet asking: 'What is that?' The answer is: 'My sacred feet'. Then his hands go higher and higher, each time waiting for the nun's answer. Her last one is: 'My sacred fire' and he responds with: 'May I light my cigar please?' In short, all the sexual euphemisms of our daily language are those that the dream gives us. We merely copy what the dream dictates. All our euphemisms and metaphors come from our dreams.

It is worth noting that the dreamer called the level ground a 'platform'. This is the 'work-bench' in an outdoor form. The particularly sexy mood of the lovers' was foreshadowed by the dream with 'going to have some fun'. Here we have proof that no matter how innocent our fun may seem to be, it is manifestly sexual. We can also see quite easily how descriptive the levering of the cooking pot was of the particular position the lovers assumed on this occasion. Even the detail of the penis pressing against the woman's thigh was prefigured. We will also have noted the passage: 'To my astonishment this large, bone-shaped lever catches fire'. This is solid testimonial that astonishment is decidedly rooted in sexuality. Literary pheromones like it, such as amazement, surprise, shock, intense focus and so on, characterise a dream story at once as a sexual plot.

The Marker escaped the dreamer himself in this case. But it is there in his manifestation report. It was the unusual thing of making love in the dark. As well as that, the dream only let him assume that his fire-stick touched the cooking pot and only gave him the feeling that there was a hearth and cooking pot present. Of great interest here is that the husband's inner feelings of the dream translated in waking reality to feelings caused by touch. This is yet another example of the complementarity between dreaming and waking, and ultimately between the inner and the outer world.

Dream F13

'Because I couldn't find my husband waiting for me in our car, I just hopped into the nearest one available. The driver promptly took off. After some time I opened the door and placed my foot on the ground which was grassy. This eventually stopped the car and I hopped out. Soon I found myself in a huge house by a narrow waterfront. I was quite fascinated by it and surprised that I never knew it existed. I walked around with amazement. Apart from the living quarters there was a large working area. It was a hive of industry with people busily practising their particular crafts. Although they seemed poor, they were confident that their craft would bring them fame and fortune one day. Walking around this house which was built half on land and half over the water, I became concerned that the floor would be dropping down exactly where the pylons were supporting the part of the house that was over the water.'

Manifestation: There was sexual intercourse on the dream day.

Comments: The lady was actually quite in a hurry to make love. This is evident from the fact that she wouldn't wait till the driver took her where she wanted to go. Instead she took over control by putting her foot down, not to stop sex, but to have it sooner. First there is the grassy ground (pubic area) and then the arrival at a narrow waterfront, which vouches for that. The house is the dreamer herself as is usual with a wife. Being half built over water emphasises the focus on the 'watered ground'. In the fact that she 'never knew it existed' is hidden the carnal knowing which for most people is a clandestine affair. What guarantees her sexual interaction with her husband is the 'concern over the floor sinking where the pylons stood'. Her concern about the floor is yet another form of that much sought after orgasmic anxiety. On the face of it we might think that it is a worry, but the contrary is the case. True, it is a kind of tension, but the sort that is the prerequisite to an orgasm. So the dreamer is secretly looking forward to the floor sinking over the pylons standing in the water since it is the essential action that will bring about her arousal and raise her orgasmic tension. That there was plenty of pre-orgasmic activity is evident from the fact that the house was a 'hive of industry' with people striving towards fame and fortune. It should be remembered here that 'clitoris' is a Greek word that actually means divine, Goddess-like and famous! 'Fortune' is no less of an indication of a sexual high since it suggests happiness and being well-satisfied. And finally, if there is one single word in the whole of the dream text that practically guarantees the dream to lead to sexual intercourse, or at least to an orgasmic event, it is the word 'amazement,' a favourite literary pheromone of the dream. What makes this even more convincing is the circumstance that this voucher for sexual joy is supported by two more such words with the same drive towards orgasmic thrills. These are 'surprise' and 'fascinated'.

Fascinating is usually said to mean enchanting, bewitching. But the Latin dictionary gives two meanings for 'fascinus'. 1. 'an enchanting' and 2. 'membrum virile'.

The Marker: The marker for this sexual episode was a newspaper article that came into the house on the dream day. It was called 'Beauty in Craft Exhibits' and featured an artisan couple who worked from their home! While they lived in modest circumstances, making everything from clothes to furniture, the quality of their product promised a great future. Here, with the artisan couple working from home, the notion of the workbench as the lovers' bed is not only reinforced, but also expanded, thus showing how in the final analysis creativity is inextricably entwined with procreativity.

Postscript: This dreamer met a new man two years after this dream. The two moved to a different state where they started an art & craft business from home. Now, twenty-two years later, they are still the happy proprietors of a thriving souvenir factory.

Dream F14

'I am looking at a large hall-like building from the front. It is wide open and looks a bit like a huge garage with its door up. The inside of this building is filled with a faint haze that is of a beautiful light green colour.'

Manifestation: There was sexual intercourse on the dream day.

Comments: Although there is only a fragment of a dream before us, it is still possible to determine what its sexual implications are. In short it was 'open house'. It was obviously a husband's dream since the house is almost certain to represent a wife, or at least her equivalent. True, there is no interaction indicated apart from looking at the building that was like a garage with the door up. The garage is a useful association because it houses cars, which are vehicles, especially fast ones that are strongly suggestive of sexual intercourse. The previous dream, No. 7, began with a car ride and manifested as intercourse. This dream only alludes to it. Yet there is one element that is almost as reliable an indicator of sexual excitement as the 'amazement' of the previous dream. It is the word beautiful. To make it even more 'sexy', its beauty is grounded in a colour. Beautiful colours are predominantly a sign of beautiful sexual encounters. This is even more certain when the colours fill an open house, as in this dream.

The Markers: Because all dreams are susceptible to serial manifestation there will always be more than one marker to every sexual episode. It was certainly the case with the sexual event that resulted from this dream. Provided we are able to spot the various manifestations, we will also recognise the various markers. Naturally, some of these markers will be closer to the time of sex than others. In this case, I shall only mention two markers that tagged the sexual episode of the dream day. One of them occurred well before lovemaking and the other during lovemaking. The earlier one was a newsflash that was reported on television in the house where the sex took place. It was about a large building in New York that had collapsed and consequently split wide open. When the shot of this collapse was taken, there was a man seen inside the building doing some welding. He was wearing a green helmet that was shining with an almost phosphorescent glow. The second marker was a group of words the wife said to her husband, together with what she pointed out to him as she inserted his penis.

Comments on Marker 1: It is at once apparent that the first marker contains words that are clearly descriptive of sexual intercourse and so compensate for the lack of dream recall or dream text. The first one is that the building was wide open because it had collapsed. If we take the building to be the wife of the dreamer we will know that the collapse was that of sexual tension, in short an orgasm. The other indication of sexual activity is that there was a man inside (!) the building doing some welding. Welding joins separate pieces of metal together by means of heat, thus it is an activity that bespeaks a heated kind of union.

Comments on Marker 2: I have said that the second marker was something the dreamer's wife had said as she pointed something out to her husband as they began their lovemaking. Her words were: 'Look at the moon out there; everything is so lovely and bright outside'. This, together with the fact that the moon had a beautiful misty aura around it, formed an unmistakable marker. The colour of the haze that graced it was not actually light green, but it was at least faint, as the dream text said.

Dream F 15

'My wife and I arrive at our holiday home in the bush. Before I go inside I walk around the house. While doing so I notice that there is a blazing fire on the horizon. It is travelling fast towards us. It is quite a spectacle. I call out to my wife: 'Come and have a look at this! Quick, let's get the hoses ready.' As my wife comes out she says: 'It doesn't look too bad.' Then, while I am looking at all the grass around the house, I decide to go to the place where the hoses are. When I finally get there, I see that they had burst into a thousand pieces.'

Manifestation: Yes, there was lovemaking on the dream day.

Comments: A classic dream. Its manifestation verifies everything Freud said about the house, the bush, grass, fire and hoses. The whole dream seems made up just for that purpose. It certainly needs no explaining in that regard. What does need a bit of clarification is the word holiday house. This couple didn't own one, nor did they go to one on the dream day. But the husband had a day off. When he woke up he had his usual morning erection. That was, of course, the fire on the horizon. But because his wife got up to attend to the kids, the fire, although quite spectacular at first and threatening to envelope the 'holiday house', died down for a time. This was anticipated by the words of the dreamer's wife when she said: 'It doesn't look too bad.' But then, after she had attended to the children and had sent them off to school she returned to bed. This was the time of the second arousal with the dreamer going to the place where the hoses were. And when he finally got there the hoses burst. The use of the plural is of interest here. It means to say that there was just a single hose that, however, was in repetitive motion.

The Markers: There were several markers, but I shall mention only two. The first one was the unusual situation of having a holiday during the week. The second one was something his wife had said as they became engaged in acting out the scene of the fire around the holiday house in the bush. Just before the husband went inside, he put his arms right around his wife and lifted her up from her pillows. To this she said: 'What are you trying to do? Is this a hold-up or an ambush?

Dream F16

'Because there was something wrong with my Kundalini, I went to see the family doctor. When I got to the clinic it wasn't my usual doctor that attended to me. It was a friend of mine. His wife was with him and when he examined me she left the surgery. I sat on a stool and my friend inserted all of his ten fingers into my vagina. It felt ecstatic. Then he gave me a little bottle with some bittersweet syrup for me to take. It looked a bit like sperm. He assured me it would cure my Kundalini problem. Then his wife came in and asked if we had finished. When I said 'yes', she stepped towards me and turning in a distinctive way slightly to her side, she held her hand out.'

Manifestation: As it happens so often with explicitly sexual dreams, there followed no sexual activity. Instead there was 'orgasmic ecstasy' of a different kind.

Comments: This dreamer, because she was an ardent spiritual seeker, had been a member of an ashram for ten years. But when her husband left her for another woman, things started to go wrong at the ashram, as well. The dream points this out by means of the Kundalini problem, which begins to make sense when we know that the central practices at the ashram were Kundalini-oriented. The ashram too, would have been her usual family doctor in the sense that it was, up to the time of the dream, the regular carer for her spiritual health.

The dream anticipated a turning point in the dreamer's life. It eventuated during the dream day when she visited her friend and his wife before she made one of her usual ashram visits. While the three were conversing with one another, her friend's wife left the room to fetch something. When the wife came back, she turned to the dreamer in precisely the way the dream had pictured it and handed her a sheet of paper. Because the dreamer didn't have her reading glasses on, she could only make out the shape of the typescript which formed a stylised female figure whose lower end was in the shape of a vulva. The dreamer was so shocked that she hurriedly put the sheet in her bag. Later on she departed to visit the ashram. The session there so disgusted her that she went home at once and took out the sheet of paper she had been given earlier on. With her glasses in place, it became clear to her that it was a poem about the Mother of the Universe in the shape of the Willendorf Venus. The bottom end of the vulva of the poem ended in the sacred syllable OM. When she realised that, there was an internal explosion of spiritual ecstasy. She understood at once that the dream had anticipated this by means of the 10 fingers of the poet-doctor in her vagina of the dream. She read the poem over and over for three hours. It changed her spiritual course radically. At one stage she wondered if the poet-doctor had used ten fingers on his keyboard while composing the poem. Later she asked him about it and his answer was 'yes'. It isn't difficult to see that the bittersweet medicine the poet-doctor gave her induced on the one hand a pleasurable experience with new hope in sight, while on the other hand it also required facing up to the bitter reality of the loss of her husband and the fallout with the ashram. The medicine in the bottle, reminiscent of sperm, suggested spiritual impregnation with the expectations of a new baby, meaning a new way of looking at life and her spiritual aspirations.

The Markers: There were several, which is apparent enough from the manifestations described in the comments. These manifestations took place at the poet-doctor's place as the dream suggested. His wife was in attendance, but she left the room for a moment to bring back the paper that she handed to the dreamer in exactly the same way she had done in the dream. Because there was no sexual interaction, these markers could not tag any sexual event. Instead they tagged the innocent events the dream had anticipated in sexual imagery. This dream example of explicit sex with its non-sexual manifestation shows too, that contrary to Freud's presumption, the dream is not afraid of sexual imagery. It also shows quite splendidly how the ten fingers touching the vagina in the dream became in waking ten fingers touching the heart of the dreamer via the keyboard. And above all: how non-sexual matters, indeed spiritual matters, are portrayed by the dream unashamedly in terms of sexual interaction. This again supports my contention that all our waking experiences, no matter how innocent they may appear, are shadowed by Eros at every step of the way.

Dream F17

'I was in bed with my spiritual advisor. He was very caring. There was an atmosphere of great love. We were going to kiss but he left it to me whether we did or not. Then we were going to have sex together, but again he left it to me whether we did or not. I thought it wasn't what I really wanted. My thirst was of a different kind. So instead of having intercourse with him I lay my head on his erection.'

Manifestation: There was no sex of any kind but a visit to her spiritual counsellor to get advice on very crucial matters.

Comments: What is interesting in this case is that all the explicit sex, which could have happened, did not, or was toned down as in the last act of the dreamer. So does this mean that the dreamer and her counsellor didn't get on as well as they might have? It does not. What it means is that the dreamer actually restrained herself from getting physical in the counselling session. According to the American model of psychiatric help to patients, allegedly 60% of counsellors will have sex with some of their patients. This dream shows that in this tête-à-tête there were not going to be such liberties. The emphasis was on a love that was able to function without physical or indeed overtly sexual contact. Yet it was best expressed by means of sexual symbolism. As in the dream before, where the ingestion of semen-like medicine suggested healing love, the dreamer's head on her counsellor's erection meant that she was getting emotional succour, since an erection shows sexual excitement and the possibility of inducing pleasure and providing the fertilising power for a baby, which in this case would mean a new start, a new way of looking at things. Since the head instead of the vagina made contact with the erection, it showed clearly that the sexual excitation was not meant to give sexual pleasure but intellectual, or indeed, spiritual satisfaction. In other words, the dreamer was craving understanding and the quenching of her emotional thirst. But just as the dream did not hesitate to employ sexual imagery, so the soothing of her emotions would not have been utterly free of sexual undercurrents. Nothing is, and this dream demonstrates it brilliantly. It says: 'they could have easily made love, but they didn't'. And this possibility was not the least factor in passing on emotional balm to the counselled. It is in such dreams that we see the penis very much in the sense of the phallus Jung had experienced in his boyhood dream.* There it was unmistakeably the divine link between heaven and earth, a link that in today's Hinduism is still worshipped as the Shiva Lingam. In short, the emphasis on the penis is here more on en-light-enment than on dowsing the fire of burning passions. Phallus is etymologically rooted in the Greek word 'phos', light. * (Cf. "Memories, Dreams, Reflections", pp. 26/27)

The Markers: One marker was the counsellor since the dreamer went to see him on the dream day. The other was the dream itself as it came under discussion with the counsellor. This might seem trivial. But the dreamer might have been prevented from seeing her counsellor either because of circumstances at her end or at his.

Dream F18

> 'I am to select two or three stilettos from a whole row of them for a mock fight. Before I can get my hands on any of them, three of them suddenly and surprisingly appear on the belly of an elephant I am to ride. While I am pondering whether I should take two or three of them, they change colour from black to bright red. I select two and then wonder if I should take a third. As I focus on one of them, I notice that it has an 'eyelet' to pull a belt through.'

Manifestation: One hour after this dream intercourse took place. Not long after that there was the 'come again' which the second stiletto promised. Approximately twelve hours later there was mutual petting that soon died away and ended in sleep. The doubtful stiletto.

Comments: The way the dream begins we might think it was a woman's dream. But it wasn't. Yet there is an element in it that indicates that the woman would take a leading role in every case. This is the word stiletto that refers both to a dagger and stiletto heels. But there is no doubt about what these stilettos are in anatomical terms. The change of colour from black to red unequivocally points to a rise in temperature and a passionate response to a woman's overtures. The stilettos being daggers points to another feature of the sexual manifestation. Because daggers are hand-held weapons, this prefigured extensive handwork at the beginning of loveplay. Forty minutes in one case. By then the dreamer's excitement became so maddening that he rose to one knee. At that moment he matched the dream picture of stiletto(s) protruding from the elephant's belly. A little later he changed from the aroused elephant to the rider the dream had said he would be. This sort of double role (subject-object) of a dream item is typical of the dream's complementary tendencies. Another feature that foreshadowed a lot of handwork was the eyelet through which a belt could be pulled. This image bespeaks both petting and the intercourse that was the end result. It is already clear that the hesitation regarding the selection of a third stiletto turned out to be petting only. Sleep overtook the couple before anything else could happen. They had a long outing on that day quite apart from the sexual saturation in the morning. Another quaint revelation is that the dream showed their sex-play and intercourse as a mock fight, which is what copulations looks to a child.

The Markers: For the first two manifestations the markers were a steel ruler that the dreamer had used and left on the bedside table. The marker for the last episode became apparent to the dreamer while his wife was already in bed. She was bothered by a slight headache and so had left the TV show they had been watching together. After she had withdrawn, there was a scene on TV that featured an actual elephant. That, together with the steel ruler that was still on the bedside table when the husband joined his wife in bed, aligned the marker even more to the dream image. It was the sexual actions that, however, animated the markers to bring them close to the dream scenario. Such animation is typical of the dream. While in reality we will find that the marker objects are generally inanimate and lying quietly in the vicinity of the sexual action, the dream will fuse the two situations together into a unified whole, into one animated scene where the marker performs the sexual action. In this case, that was the sudden appearance of the stilettos on the elephant's belly.

Dream F19

'At a river flat. I am preparing for work. My wife has much advice to give. The work will be potting bonsai trees. As I am fetching one of the little trees, I snap one of its branches. Two tiny spiders fall out of it and get caught in my hair. Feeling with my hand I find them and squeeze them until they pop. After that I hop on my bike and ride along a narrow track to work.'

Manifestation: The plot clearly shows two stages. First the preparation and then the actual work. The preparation was the dreamer giving his partner an orgasm by means of oral sex; the subsequent ride to work was their sexual intercourse.

Comments: As I have said before, the dream often sees the bed or place of intercourse as the workbench. The same notion recurs here where preparation for sexual intercourse is portrayed as preparation for work. In the context of the oral sex given to his wife, it isn't difficult to see what her advice proffered in the dream turned out to be in waking reality. Interesting is that the clitoral stimulation was portrayed by miniature trees. Trees and branches too could be either the penis or the clitoris, depending on the context. The latter is made quite plain in this case. Spiders are mainly a reference to the vagina. Just as it is risky for certain male spiders to approach the much bigger female, so is the male's sexual approach to his female partner often an uncertain affair. That the two spiders came to drop into the husband's hair reveals that his head was in touch with the vagina. At the same time one of his hands assisted the oral stimulation, which the dream saw as him feeling for the two little spiders caught in his hair and then popping them. This together with the breaking bonsai branch foreshadowed the woman's orgasm. His own followed as he 'rode to work along the narrow track' which is a classical dream scenario for sexual intercourse.

The Markers: On this dream day the dreamer actually potted some of the bonsais he and his wife got the day before from a river flat. While they were engaged in sexual play, the wife suddenly remembered that earlier on she had encountered a big spider as she got the mail from the letterbox. So she promptly told her husband about her experience. In view of what Freud had said about boxes in general and posting a letter, this marker is itself a 'dream plot' indicating sexual intercourse. There are, of course, several markers in the day because the dream will manifest serially with each member of the series referring to one or the other aspect of the day's sexual manifestation. Whether we spot them or not will depend on our alertness.

Dreams F20 & F21

We dream many dreams in one night. They all are thematically interrelated like a good play on stage. Every act has its scenes that are perfectly integrated into a meaningful whole. The various acts or dream phases of the night too are a perfectly integrated work of art developing two or more themes in course of the night and interrelating them, leaving absolutely no loose ends. That being so, every dream we recall must contain some element or other that will serve as a marker for the sexual event or other events of the day if any were predicted. Here are two dreams of the same night, each supplying a particular marker to tag the sexual event of the day. Naturally the two dreams also predict, each in their own way, the same sexual episode.

Dream F20

'Coming off the football field where we have just played a match. I go into the crowded cafeteria. It's a huge hall. At the end of it is a whiteboard with the football-ladder listing the performance of the various teams. I notice with great satisfaction that our team has only lost one game and so is on top of the ladder.'

Dream F21

'From a distance I am watching a play on stage while leaning against a huge pole. The stage is crowded with lots of colourful actors. The scene is set at a royal court. The king is sitting on his throne with his retinue and other courtiers surrounding him. It looks festive with banners over the centre of the scene. Suddenly I realise that I am here because I am waiting to come on stage. So I move closer to where the action is. Going towards the entrance, I notice that it is more like a dark tunnel than a door. I try to remember my lines. I can't think of a single word. I panic. I notice two boys who also seem to be in the play. I wonder if they might know my lines. It's too late, I am on. My panic intensifies to such a degree that I lose my awareness of my surroundings. All I know is that I am bravely stepping onto the stage just hoping for a miracle.'

Before looking at the usual parts of manifestations and markers, I want to draw attention to the thematically related parts of the two dreams. Both dreams are about playing. One is playing sport; the other is a playing on stage. Because of this the central attention is the respective performances. In both cases we meet crowds of people and teams that must act together. It is worth noting here that crowds and crowded situations in general hint at closeness in sexual interaction. There is yet another correspondence between the two dreams, which may not be so obvious because one of the items is an abstraction, while the other is a concrete object. I am referring to the ladder of success, which the dreamer notes with satisfaction, and the pole on which he leans while waiting to 'come on'.

Then there is the motif of 'being on top of the ladder' of dream 13 that corresponds to a number of situations in dream 14. These numerous circumstances are in fact a clear development towards 'being on top of the ladder'. The beginning of this development is to be seen in the fact that the dreamer is waiting to come on. Although this is not spelled out in the first dream, it is implied, for crowds at a football match too are waiting, however not to get on stage, but for excitement, and they will encourage it by calls of 'come on the Blues' and so on. The same crowd that barracks for a particular team will be anxious regarding the performance of their team. The dreamer, while waiting in the wings, feels the same sort of anxiety, or even more so since he is to be on show. Hence the panic that increases as his cue approaches. Clearly there is a steady rise of anxiety along the 'ladder of emotions' until it reaches the sort of intensity that blanks out all outside awareness. There is only one thought left: the miracle of remembering the forgotten lines.

Manifestation: It's not difficult to know what the sexual outcome was of these two dreams, for all the thematic correspondences I have singled out between the two dreams are not just an apt description of what goes on at the football field and the theatre, but also in bed with two lovers. Yes, there was sexual intercourse.

Comments: Here, as in so many other cases before, we see again with consummate clarity that the so called innocent actions or situations are in irreproachable accord with those of sexual interaction. Although this may be hidden to the spectators' eyes as they follow a match, it is precisely the sexual energy fuelling any excitement that draws the crowds to the football fields and to the theatre. (That is why in Roman times the brothels were right next to the Colosseum). Freud was quite right when he insisted that once we examined a dream thoroughly enough, it would nearly always yield some sexual concerns. Since dreams are the pregrams of all waking events, it follows that all of the waking happenings, no matter how innocent they may appear on the surface, are invariably pervaded by sexual concerns. In such a framework sexual interaction will, with adults at any rate, become the climactic events as it were, of all the apparently innocent, yet nevertheless sexually charged episodes. It is as if then the sexual interaction between two lovers summed up all their other daily concerns. And indeed, we can see this blatantly when two people are hopelessly in love: everything else is rosy no matter what the real circumstances might be. On the other hand, when love has faded and bedtime is no longer 'fun, but fight', then everything else that has to be shared between the ex-lovers, will be nothing but emotional warfare.

The present dreamer's sexual relationship was still intact even though lovemaking with his wife was foreshadowed by means of anxiety and panic. We have seen before that anxiety in dreams is an expression of pre-orgasmic tension. In this particular example it is a growing tension as the increase in panic shows. There is an interesting point to be observed with regard to the word panic. Not only is it a sign of anxiety with certain sexual symptoms, certainly bladder symptoms, but the word itself is actually derived from the ancient fertility god Pan. When he used to appear unexpectedly to a group of picnicking ladies, for instance, panic would arise. In view of this, the dreamer's relationship must have had certain undertones of disquiet.

Also pointing to that is the fact that the dreamer forgot his lines as he was about to step on stage, which latter means becoming engaged in 'performing' intercourse. A perfectly confident man would not have his sexual highs prefigured both by panic and having his memory wiped out at the same time. Yet sex did go ahead, as I have said, and was in fact initiated by the woman. It was also orgasmically successful, as the words 'coming off' that opened up the first dream, indicate. Also the football match seemed to suggest that the two were still a suitable match despite certain apprehensions that obviously must have been there for the man. The ladder and the pole were, of course, a reference to the dreamer's erection while the two boys, who also seemed to be part of the show, were indicating that his penis would be engaged in the festively decked-out centre and the dark tunnel.

The Markers. When the dreamer got up, he found his two boys watching television. At the exact moment of walking into the TV room, a show was on which featured a king's court in the open air. The king wore a wreath of laurel leaves as a crown. A great gathering of people was around him, some carrying spears. Above their heads were flags flapping in the wind. When the dreamer asked his boys who the king was, they said it was Kronos. Then one of the boys asked his father if he could rejoin the football team that he had left because he recently had an operation. These two events were then not only the markers of the sexual episode that took place an hour later, but also showed a fusion of the markers, and with that a fusion of the themes of the two dreams.

Dream F22

'I am in charge of a children's camp. It is lunchtime and I have to make an announcement. Because there aren't any loudspeakers, it takes quite a while to get all the kids together. Just as I think I've got them all assembled, a little boy runs up to the entrance of the main building. Its doors are flung open outwards and so the little boy rushes behind one of them, opens his fly and does his 'little' hard against the entrance.'

Manifestation: Extended and playful intercourse between two heterosexual lovers.

Comments: I have included this dream and its manifestation for two reasons. The first one was to warn against rushing into an interpretation of 'camp' sexuality just because the word 'camp' appears in a dream text. This was, in fact, an undoubtedly heterosexual man's dream presaging intercourse with his equally heterosexual female lover. The second reason was to draw attention to the peculiar behaviour of the 'little boy'. The fact that he was little is enough to alert us to who he really was. Yet the dream emphasised his function by letting him actually do little as well. But it wasn't just for emphasis that the dream showed him in that mode. The really clever thing was that he was doing what he had to hard against the entrance and not into it. This would have been difficult to decipher had it not been for the waking manifestation of this act. It turned out that the dreamer's lover had her period at the time. While any other time they practised withdrawal at the point of orgasm, which would have meant ejaculation next to the 'entrance', they considered it safe at this stage for the dreamer to stay inside for ejaculation. So the little dream boy doing 'little' behind the door instead of into the entrance, prefigured a form of ejaculation that was equivalent to withdrawal and thus safe from a contraceptive point of view.

The Marker: It is here where the word 'camp' came into play. The two lovers, while still in each other's arms, had a conversation about a certain famous personality who was rumoured to be homosexual and was allegedly abusing the little boys who were attending his camps.

The next dream example demonstrates how a serial manifestation works. It shows how the dream compresses or, as Freud would say, condenses the various waking events into a short, composite event. There are three manifestations recorded.

Dream F23

> 'I dreamt that I was swimming in a pool with my clothes on. Suddenly I thought of my watch that isn't waterproof, but only water-resistant. I quickly lifted my arm out of the water and wiped the watch with my other sleeve.'

Manifestation 1: Shortly after, the dreamer, a young man, got up and dressed and went into the kitchen to run some water for his kettle. Because the full stream of water hit the concave side of a spoon in the sink, it bounced upwards and splashed his wristwatch. He wiped it dry on his other sleeve with some urgency.

Manifestation 2: In the evening of the dream day he went to his girlfriend's place where he watched a show on TV with her. There was a scene in which a large dog was told to jump into a stream. Because the animal had to leap from a very high embankment, he made an almighty splash. Shortly after that his girlfriend looked at his watch saying that it was time for a cuddle.

Manifestation 3: The two lovers went to bed. The clothes and the watch of the dreamer lay beside it. Their lovemaking was more passionate than usual. Because they practised the withdrawal method, the ejaculation wet both the lovers and the bed.

Comments: If at the end of this day we look back from the three manifestations to the morning's dream, we see its incredible artistry. By this I mean that the dream does something akin to what an artist would do who was told to make a collage of the three events, combining them into one brief event. We will object, of course, and say that the dream contained no such creature as a dog, and that the pool was in reality a stream. We will also point out that there was no sign of a bed in the dream, or sexual intercourse, or swimming in clothes. The only thing which we will accept as a more or less straightforward manifestation is the watch getting literally wet and then wiped dry at once.

But dreams do not manifest literally holus bolus. As we know by now, much of what the dream says is allegorical and is therefore going to become reality in an associative manner. Thus, in the second manifestation we have a dog making a big splash instead of a man, as he jumps into the river. Once we know that a dog represents a man's libido, such apparent manifestational licence makes perfect sense. We will also see that although the dog was not wearing a watch, there is nevertheless the notion of 'watch' associated with that sort of animal. So, forgive me if you will, for saying that this watch-dog too, like the dreamer in his dream, was given no time to get undressed before he had to jump into the wet!

Linked with that same scene is the girlfriend's glance at her lover's watch which then prompted them to go to bed. Freud pointed out over a hundred years ago that watery places correspond with the vagina. So when the dreamer 'took the plunge' in bed, he was figuratively swimming in a pool. True, in the dream he had clothes on, but isn't passionate loving like jumping in clothes and all?

If we now go back to the first realisation of the dream, the pointer manifestation as I call it, we see a tap squirting the dreamer's watch. This is of intense interest because this manifestation is just as symbolic of an ejaculation as is a facet of the dream scene itself. That facet is the wetting of the watch that the dreamer had to wipe with some urgency. It was like saying to him: "Watch it, she is not 'sperm proof', you must keep her works dry, or else!" Put in this way we are able to see why the dream had the dreamer 'quickly lift his arm out of the water'.

The closer we look at the serial manifestation, the more we realise just how fantastic the dream's artistry is, how intricately everything is interwoven, how devoid of loose ends the whole artefact is, and how it all dovetails with the series of manifestations. Dream and waking experience merge into one brilliantly interwoven tapestry where no part is more real than the other, where no piece is less meaningful than the next.

The Markers: Yes, there were two: the dog scene on TV and the watch next to the bed of the lovers. While we have less ammunition in arguing against the dog incident as a legitimate marker of the day and place of sex, we will protest even more strongly against the watch next to the bed of the lovers being one. This, we will say, is because it was unlikely that the watch being close to the dreamer while immersed in lovemaking was anything new or unusual. That is quite so. But there was a renewed interest in the watch on that day, a special focus on it. This was so because of the fact that it got splashed earlier in the day, which is not something that happens every day. It is also not something we dream about every day, and so it rightfully becomes a legitimate marker.

Part III

101 more Dreams

Freud was right when he maintained that absolutely every conceivable object and situation could be used as a stand-in for our sexual organs and their encounters. This fact alone is massive evidence in favour of the all-pervasiveness of sex. However this general observation is also supported in a more specific way. It is the fact that every dream is not only a pregram of our ordinary everyday concerns, but also the blueprint of our sexual disposition of the dream day and beyond. Although I have dealt with this question extensively in the second part of this book, I have learnt that nothing will open up our eyes as widely to this fact as the study of a good number of dreams. For this reason I have appended to this book one-hundred-and-one more dreams and their interpretations.

You may be aware that it was the sexual interpretation of the dream that rent the association and friendship between Jung and Freud apart. Freud insisted that the deeper one delved into the dream the clearer it became that its bedrock was pure sexuality. Jung on the other hand objected to this, saying that it was not justifiable to take the sexual language of dreams absolutely concretely. Indeed, Jung believed Freud was obsessed with sex, regarding it as something numinous. If Jung meant this to be a reproach it failed miserably. It failed because numinous really relates to something divine, to something mysterious, arousing religious or spiritual emotions. And that is precisely the way our ancient forebears saw sex.

For them it was not something that should be hidden, something to be ashamed of and denied, but something to be venerated (this word comes from Venus and is related to venereal) for after all it forms the basis of our earthly existence. Indeed, if it were not for the fact that our parents and their parents back to Adam and Eve had sexual congress, we would not be here to discuss this.

Survival on this planet depends first and foremost on the s-twins: sustenance and sex. The formula is simply s + s = S: sustenance plus sex equals Survival. The two S's are as inseparable as Siamese twins. Indeed if one of them should die, the other would follow on its heels. This, of course, has to be understood in the larger context of life where sex is also fertilisation of the plant world.

If dreams are about life, about survival, then an interpretation without the sexual facet is nothing short of castrating the dream. While saying this, I am, of course, quite aware that there are exceptions to every rule. After all there are freaks of nature, castratos and Buddhas whose dreams may be devoid of sexual consequences in the ordinary sense.

However, for us ordinary beings, only the dual interpretation of the dream will yield a true precursor of our everyday existence. Our ancient forebears were only too conscious of this simple fact of earthly life. They realised that the earth by itself was like a woman without a husband. If the earth was to be Mother Earth, and thus capable of bearing and nurturing mankind and other life, impregnation was paramount. This boon would come from the sky which was also heaven where Father God was at home. In their eyes he rode at times in the storm clouds, struck the earth with orgasmic lightning bolts and impregnated it with gigantic ejaculative downpours.

In Sumeria, the cradle of human civilisation, rain was not just water, but it was also strong water* which meant semen. We need go no further to see what our forebears did when they spoke in such terms. It is all too obvious that they projected the human condition into their surroundings. When they saw in the thunderstorm the same phenomenon as in sexual intercourse, they did exactly what the dream does every night. Indeed, if we observe the dream attentively, we will see that it constantly identifies the human body with the body of the earth. For example it will feature twin hills when it wants to draw attention to a woman's breasts. A minaret or the steeple of the church will be an unmistakable reference to the penis. On the other hand, a terrestrial cleft, a hole in the ground, a pit or a cracked rock will just as surely point to the female genitals. And so does a door. After all, with the exception of those that have been lifted from the womb by Caesarean means, the vagina is our door into this world. * (See Allegro, the sacred Mushroom and the Cross, Hodder and Stroughton, 1970).

For the ancients there was no distinction between the sacred and the secular, between the physical body and spiritual realities. Indeed the body was the icon for things spiritual just as the sky was the icon for heaven beyond the sky. For our forebears, the bodies of their women were no less sacred than the temples they had built. Indeed, in the Near East, all temples were modelled on a woman's reproductive system. The lower end of the vagina up to the hymen was the template for the porch of the temple. The hall was fashioned after the vagina proper, and the uterus provided the pattern for the holy of holies, the inner sanctum. * (ibid page 25)

When we reflect on this we suddenly realise that as a foetus we developed in the inner sanctum of a living temple. At the same time we realise that modelling the temple on the vagina does not vulgarise this sacred structure, but instead ennobles its fleshly counterpart.

It is only through the separation of the sexual from the sacred that sexual interaction becomes something other than a divine union, something other than the two aspects of one and the same divinity finding reunion in the heavens of ecstasy.

Here then are one-hundred-and-one examples of dreams and their manifestations. The majority of dream interpreters tend to treat the sexual interpretation of the dream like Cinderella. For this reason I have sided with Freud ensuring that his manner of interpretation is not forgotten. I am hoping that this will restore some kind of balance between the Jungian and Freudian interpretations.

1. Challenging destiny

'I dreamt on three successive nights that I lost my striped handbag and that in the end it would be returned to me.'

Here is the dreamer's story: "I was very concerned about this dream. After all I was travelling across Europe carrying my passport and other valuables in my striped bag. To prevent losing it I emptied the bag and stowed it away in my suitcase. I distributed all my valuables among other, smaller bags. Another reason why I did this was to defy destiny which is said to be recorded in our dreams. Everything went well until the last port of call. At my home-airport I went to the baggage department waiting for my three items to appear on the carrousel. Two of them soon rolled towards me. The third, however, let me wait and wait. It was my suitcase with my striped bag in it. In the end I had to report the loss to the baggage department. I was assured that they would do everything to retrieve it. There was nothing for me to do but to return home without my lost bag. It was midnight when there was a knock on the front door. It was a special courier with the third case holding my lost striped bag." A 'lost bag returned' promised joyous sex.

2. Acrobatics

'I dreamt that junior wanted to go upstairs while I was examining a plumbing problem. He climbed as far as the steps would reach and then stretched out his arms to grab hold of the upper floor above him. He pulled himself up to the next level like an acrobatic mountain climber. Finally he somersaulted onto the top floor.'

The thrust of this dream scene is teeming with expressions that reveal the urge to get a high through sexual interaction. They are upstairs, climbs, steps, stretches, upper floor, pulls himself up, acrobatic, mountain climber, somersaults, top floor. In such a context junior easily translates to the dreamer's penis. Mountains in dreams mostly suggest mounting. They also evoke the highs attained through sexual climbing. Floors and grounds in general refer mostly to the female partner or to her pelvic floor. The top floor indicates that the height of an orgasmic build-up has been reached. Floors put sex in a fundamental position. They are the basis of life's regeneration. At times tables or even walls will take the place of floors. But the floor is indeed the ground of propagation. It is a favourite representation of the female partner - of mother earth.

3. Alligators

'I dreamt that an alligator climbed my tree in the back yard and wrapped itself tightly around its green crown.'

At the time of this dream this woman was drawing crocodiles. While she was busy pencilling these relatives of the alligators a friend came to see her. They talked about jobs. The dreamer had heard that a position at the local library was vacant. She told her friend of her intention to apply for the job. After the friend had left she was suddenly compelled to consult an old dream book she owned. She had looked it up on other occasions but had never been impressed. Under 'alligator' it said: "A creature we can't trust. A sign of betrayal." And so it turned out to be. The friend of the dreamer went straight to the library and applied for the job. The tree in the dreamer's backyard was the tree of life and of sustenance. It stood for her livelihood that was now 'strangled' by the alligator.

Of special interest is to learn that the dreamer's husband came from a clan with a heraldic shield that featured a lizard wrapped around a tree. In the sexual scenario that followed this dream the dreamer became that very tree.

4. Elephants and guru Ganesha

'I dreamt that my guru gave me a little elephant. When I looked at it closely I realised that its face was that of my guru's right hand man. Suddenly my dog rushed towards me. I was afraid she might harm my elephant. I held it up high into the air. I turned away from my dog keeping the elephant up high.'

The two animals of this dream represent opposite tendencies in the dreamer. The dreamer followed a Hindu guru. In Hinduism the elephant stands for the god Ganesha that removes all obstacles. It also points to the dreamer's spiritual aspirations and practices. These had been endangered by her libidinous urges characterised by her dog rushing at the guru's gift. Her gesture of holding the elephant up high speaks for itself. So does the fact that she was keeping it up and out of reach of the assailing dog. Obviously sex was ruled out for the time being.

5. Antiques as dead relationship

'I went into the lounge and found that all the furniture had an antique look. I wondered what had happened. As my eyes scanned the room, my glance settled on a photo of my husband among a lot of nick-knacks I had gathered up to give away to charity.'

This dream speaks for itself. The relationship is dead. The lady is ready to give it up and feel good about it. Love has turned to pity. The lounge is mostly a reference to the dreamer's womb. Its antique furniture signals that it is well into menopause. Photos are memories. The husband's photo is among the nick-knacks. He is remembered in much the same way as nick-knacks are.

6. Strong residue and serial manifestation

'I dreamt that someone asked me to do a job. I obliged without hesitation. It was a matter of removing a sheet of rusty steel that was wrapped around an old oven. Magically an axe appeared in my hands. With it I hacked at the rusty steel cover. Although I could not see my hands, the axe did its job. Soon I could fold the rusty sheet over and away from the oven. I stopped hacking before the cover came off altogether. The oven looked in good condition. Its shape was tubular. As I looked at its fresh green colour the idea that this was really a fuel tank entered my head.'

Freud coined the term 'residue'. It is material the dream incorporates from the day before. Because the residue is based on a waking experience, we clearly know what its various ingredients signify. For this reason it is an excellent guide to the meaning of the dream. Here is the residue: The dreamer watched a documentary entitled "Rome wasn't built in a Day". The series was about the construction of a Roman villa. The men doing the job were all volunteers. All the work had to be done with the tools and methods of the ancient Romans. The TV instalment of the day was about building a kiln in order to fire the tubes for the floor heating of the Roman villa. They supported the floor while simultaneously supplying the heat to warm the floor. The brick kiln was covered with a rusty, funnel-shaped metal flue and green lawn sods. The timber for building the wooden structure of the villa had to be prepared with axes and adzes. The wood for firing the kiln was also cut with axes.

We see at once that the dream built its plot with a surprising amount of residual elements. Some of these were slightly modified. The kiln became the tubular oven of the dream. The green of the lawn cover lent its colour to the oven which at the end of the dream became a fuel tank of tubular shape.

Even without the plot of the dream it becomes evident that the residues alone promise a steamy sexual encounter: the kiln, the floor, the heat, the tubes are sufficient to hint at this.

The action of the dream also followed residual elements. The dreamer happily volunteered to do a job for someone like the volunteering builders. But there was also the axing which the dream had in common with residual actions. After that the plot of the dream went its own way. The steel flue of the kiln transformed itself into a rusty steel cover around the dream oven. The reason for this was the couple's lengthy abstinence from sex. Striking at the rusty steel cover in order to remove it meant bringing the 'oven' into renewed usage. The fact that the dreamer did not cut away the steel cover totally signalled absence of an ejaculation. The dreamer practised Tantric sex. All this happened in the morning shortly after waking up.

The reason for the curious change from an oven to a fuel tank came to light in the afternoon. The dreamer went under the house to get the mower out. His house was built on stumps emulating the tubular pipes that support the floor of the Roman villa. Next to one of these stumps was kept the container for the mower fuel. It was a petrol-can of cylindrical shape. Almost touching it was a green cardboard box of the same shape as the Roman floor-heating tubes. But there was also an axe with a green handle not far from the petrol can. This associative network of articles clearly served as the markers, since the need to go under the house was not something that happened every day.

The axe motif recurred once more later in the evening of the dream day. The dreamer watched a documentary on the Amazon. There was a lengthy scene showing loggers at work in the jungle. There was much axing. But there was also a scene with a chain saw. The latter is another item the dreamer kept under the house not far from the fuel can.

7. Rape as betrayal

> 'I dreamt that someone grabbed my wrist and held me tight like in a vice.'

On the surface this dream doesn't look much worse than the proverbial 'twisting of your arm'. Questioning the dreamer revealed a more serious side to it: "Was there a time in your life when you were actually raped?" "Yes, when I was a little girl." We might ask if this will be repeated now that the dreamer is a grown woman. Alternatively it is possible it may turn out to be just a broken trust. A later report confirmed that the new boyfriend betrayed the dreamer.

8. Walking upstairs with baby on hip

> 'I was walking along the central corridor of the building and saw my eldest son off. When I started to walk up the stairs at the end of the corridor, I was holding a baby girl that had perched itself on my hips.'

Just as house and home in dreams most often represent women, so do buildings in general represent the human body. In view of this, the central corridor of this dream points to a passage in the centre of the dreamer's body. Seeing her son off looks back to the loss of what an eldest son represents in dreams. The dreamer was a widow. Walking upstairs at the end of the corridor with a baby girl on her hips manifested as an orgasm. Walking in dreams often suggests sexual motions. This is mainly because walking is movement of feet and legs. Both legs and feet issue ultimately from the genital area. But as always, the context should have the last word. (There are women, such as this dreamer, who have spontaneous orgasms).

9. Grooming the body as honing speech

> 'A mediocre actress whom I saw last night on TV came
> to my place for a bath. I scrubbed her clean and groomed
> her hair to make her look like someone successful.'

This dreamer went to a public speaking competition as one of the judges. While judging a mediocre competitor, she "cleaned up" the many faults of her presentation. She groomed her for future public appearances. Hair often refers to thought, so grooming it became in this case honing it before speaking. Scrubbing hair and grooming it easily translates to sexual activity. Since this dreamer was without a partner, the actress represented the dreamer's sexual self. Scrubbing is often intercourse. Here it became self-indulgence.

10. Owl crashing against window

> 'I dreamt I was lying on my bed in the middle of the
> night. Suddenly there was a whoosh and a bang. An owl
> had crashed against my bedroom window.'

It's not difficult to see that this dreamer was a bit of a night owl at the time. What kept her up was her attempt to write a book for which she needed all the wisdom the owl of her dream could bring her. It is interesting to note that it is an old tradition that wisdom and inspiration occur in the night. Clearly this is indirect evidence that it is our dreams that bring us wisdom, knowledge, inspiration, intuition and so on. It suggests that dreams themselves are like birds that fly to the other world to return to this world with messages of new ideas. But windows are always also a reference to the vagina and so the crashing of the owl against the bedroom window points decidedly to a sexual event. 'A whoosh and a bang!'

11. Breaking communication

'My sculpture of Mother and Child was standing near the phone. It had two breaks; one was in the head of the mother and the other was between the child and the nursing mother.'

Because these breaks are near the phone, it shows clearly that communication will break down. The crack between mother and child points to splitting up and the break in the head of the mother is a reflection of the pain this is to cause her. Under such conditions the break is not expressive of a sexual high, but indicative of the breaking of an emotional tie. Of course the break in communication also implies a break in sexual interaction. If in a dream we can't reach our partner by phone, it signals that there won't be any sex on the dream day.

12. Nurturing breasts

'I was drifting down-river on my back. I pulled one of my breasts towards my mouth and then sucked on it.'

This woman had neglected herself for some time. As someone had said: "Only dead fish drift downstream." The dream announced a change. She would soon make up for her disregard of her own needs and nurture herself. This nurture is, of course, also erotic self-indulgence on this occasion.

13. Put it where it belongs

'I heard a sharp, regular banging. I wondered where it might come from. As I looked in the lounge, there was my son pulling my partly extended tape measure along. The casing was bumping against the floor with every step he took. As he went outside I followed him and called out: "Put that thing back where it belongs!" At that he dropped it into the green grass and disappeared.'

The dreamer awoke from this dream in the early morning. He went to the toilet and while he was there he heard a sharp clatter. When he returned to the bedroom his wife explained that she had fumbled for the watch in the dark to see what time it was. While doing so the tape-measure the dreamer had left on the dressing table got knocked off its perch. It dropped into the half open drawer below making that noise. (The marker) Clearly the dream had anticipated this. After returning to bed he and his wife cuddled up to each other and soon began to pet each other. After the husband had taken the plunge his wife said: "This is where he belongs!"

Here the lounge points again to the room that represents the womb while the floor of the lounge looks to the pelvic floor. Tape-measures that can be readily extended are a classic representation of a man's penis. The dreamer following his son who disappeared in the green grass is the dream's way of saying that he followed his penis that disappeared in the pubic hair.

14. Back to the snow

'I dreamt that I went back to my country of my birth. The town was covered in snow. I walked from one end of it to the other, but I could not recognise any parts of it. It looked more like an Australian town, yet there was snow everywhere.'

This dreamer came from a country with severe winters. Two days after this dream he moved to a new place that looked just like the dream town. However there was no snow. Later he found out that this town had a fall of snow a few years back. As well as that he heard that a lot of its inhabitants came from the same snow-ridden country as he did. Four months later there was an actual day of snow. It iced up the roads and the snow lasted till the next day. 'I could not recognise' also turned out to be a signal for no sex. The dreamer's libido was under a blanket of snow.

15. Bullying bull

'I was walking along the footpath with my husband when a great big bull came galloping towards me. Luckily there was a house nearby with a picket fence around it. I managed to slip through the gate to safety.'

On the dream day this lady did actually walk on a footpath with her husband. An argument broke out and her husband started to bully her. He was wearing a T-shirt with the head of a bull on it. Like in the dream, she took refuge in a house they were passing at the time. So did they have sex on that day? Not with a picket fence between them.

16. Hotfoot

'I dreamt that my son's feet were burning in the open fire. His grandfather stood by and shouted: "Good on you boy, see what the boy is doing!?"'

The dreamer was totally puzzled about this dream. "We have no open fires", she mused. "So what could burn my son's feet?" The answer to this came a few days later. As a young P-driver her son had travelled at excessive speed through a township. He was intercepted by the police and fined. The young hotfoot got his fingers burnt as well. It is not difficult to see that this dream had a speedy sexual episode in its train. Of interest here is that the sexual manifestation occurred on the dream day while the non-sexual episode became a protracted manifestation.

17. Repressed urge

'I was in a large, official building. Suddenly I was overcome by the urge to urinate. I looked for a toilet. I was unable to find one that was not occupied. Every time I thought I found an opportunity to relieve myself, someone would appear from nowhere and make me move on to look for another place.'

On the dream day this man's wife had gone out. The two had an excellent relationship and both were always ready to make love. But on this dream day the dreamer's wife arrived from a gruelling outing. Because she was so very tired the husband refrained from all attempts at sex. This shows that toilet inhibitions need not be a sign of psychological inhibitions. They may arise out of a need to repress the sexual urges.

18. Lizard awaking

> 'I saw a lizard breaking through the mud. It raised its head looking at me with knowing eyes. I was fascinated by it and touched its head and then the whole of its body. I stroked it lovingly.'

After waking, this dreamer felt her husband's morning erection against her thigh. She reached for it and began to stroke it lovingly.

19. Sorry, no screws

> 'I went to the spare parts shop to find a screw which was missing from some part of the car engine. When I got to the store the guy who served me went off to find the item. After a short time he came back saying: "Sorry, no screws of that kind.'

This dreamer missed out on the other kind of screws on that dream day. Car parts frequently stand in for body parts. The clutch easily becomes the vagina, the dipstick or the feeler gauge the penis. On the non-sexual level it is not hard to see that the dream also spoke of a frustrating day.

20. Convents and tractors

'I ran to catch a bus to the convent. I missed it. Not far from the bus stop there were several tractors ploughing the fields. They were all named after the various sisters of the convent. I approached the one called Sister Stella and asked the driver if he could give me a lift to the convent. He agreed and I hopped on. We hadn't gone far when we hit a giant tree lying across the road. I catapulted high into the air but landed safely on my feet.'

Having missed the bus the dreamer caught a lift with a tractor driver. It suggests that initially the dreamer had in mind to go into the public domain. Bus is short for omnibus where 'omnis' means 'all'. But before she could do so she was 'dragged' into making love to her partner. The word 'tractor' is derived from the Latin 'tractus'/'trahere'. It means 'to drag'. At first sight we could easily be misled into thinking that this dreamer was on her way to become a nun. We would soon be enlightened after checking the etymology of 'convent'. This word is derived from Latin and means 'coming together'. 'Coitus' too is of the same origin. On the dream day the tractor driver became the dreamer's lover. The dream portrayed the lovemaking as getting a lift (a high) on a tractor. The tractors being named after the sisters of the convent suggests the fusion between the male and female partners. The tree that lay across the street causing that massive collision was, of course, her lover's penis. The street was a reference to the dreamer's vulva. Ploughing the fields is a metaphor that can't easily be misunderstood. The field is here what in other dreams is often the ground or the earth, the floor or the pelvic floor.

The marker of the dream's manifestation was a tractor working the grounds of the catholic college not far from the house of the lovers. The name of the college was Stella Maris.

21. Sex kitten

'I come to a large, hall-like room in the middle of which stands a science table with lots of people congregating around it. I join them. Suddenly a black and white kitten runs across the table. I reach out to stroke it. It slips through my hand.'

Science means knowledge. In dreams it stands for the proverbial 'biblical knowing'. The hall-like room signals an augmentation of the feelings that are engendered in the bedroom of the lovers. The 'science table' represents the woman and with it the 'bed of carnal knowledge'. The table in the middle of the room points directly at the middle of the female partner. It also hints at the centrality of sex. The kitten is, of course, referring to the pubic hair. Stroking the kitten suggests foreplay. The kitten slipping through the hand of the dreamer indicates an abrupt end to the sexual prelude.

22. Walking on water

'I dreamt I was at the shore of the sea where there was a plethora of fish swimming near the surface of the water. A flock of crows was pecking at them and a number of people were filleting them. Everybody could walk on water. An old guru was filleting some of the fish and putting the pieces in precise order.'

This dreamer was in the middle of writing a book on yoga. She was new to such a task. The sea is, of course, the source of inspiration. It represents what psychology calls the 'subconscious mind'. It should, however, be recognised as the dream memory. Its water also shows how much of what kind of emotion will be involved in the writer's project. The fact that everybody could walk on water alludes to the spiritual aspect of the book. But the dreamer also confessed that it would require a miracle to pull it off since she was not a confident writer. The crows point to critics who would pick her work to pieces.

People filleting fish are those who would be giving good advice to the prospective writer. An interesting feature of the dream is the plethora of fish. They stand for the latent ideas surfacing from the dreamer's 'subconscious mind'. This outpouring of ideas is shown to be regulated and ordered by the guru. He is the guiding spirit of the project. Fish in dreams are always also a reference to female sexuality. Filleting fish becomes therefore sexual stimulation. The interpretation of the fish motif is not straight forward because it can refer to the vagina as well as to the penis. For this reason it is essential to know the personal circumstances of the dreamer before attempting a sexual interpretation.

23. Wrong focus

'I was watching black and white TV. But there was something wrong with the focus. The picture was all wishy-washy. As I squinted my eyes to see a little better, I realised that I wasn't wearing my glasses. So I lent forward as much as I could. It was all in vain since I still couldn't make out the picture clearly.'

Not an easy dream to decipher if we don't know the circumstances of the dreamer. This is precisely why Artemidorus always said that one and the same dream meant different things to different dreamers. Here is what happened: The dreamer was about to sit for an exam on the dream day. It was a psychology test. One of the books he had to study was so big and dreary that he refused to read it all. After waking up he pondered the dream. It suddenly hit him that this must have to do with vision. He opened the neglected book at once and hurriedly read the chapter on vision. One of the exam questions was on that very chapter. The dreamer passed with flying colours. But in the sexual realm things followed closely the dream scenario which showed that "there was something wrong with the focus". It is reinforced in the last sentence with the phrase: "I still couldn't make out."

24. Driving without licence

> 'I was at the wheel of a semi-trailer without a licence to
> drive such heavy vehicles. Careering down the main
> street I was kept busy dodging the oncoming traffic. I
> had several near-misses. I got away without a collision!'

This dreamer woke up from this anxiety dream on the day she opened
her new shop. She was totally new to the business and wondered
how she would get through the day. Driving a heavy vehicle without
a licence simply meant being in charge without previous experience.
Despite this the day ran its course without mishap. 'Dodging the
oncoming traffic' and getting away 'without a collision' meant that
there would also be no bumping into each other in bed at night.

25. Screwing as approval

> 'I went for an interview with the manager of "Kwikest
> Union P/L". Instead of asking me a whole lot of questions
> he simply said: "I want to screw you!"'

This female dreamer became the successful applicant for an office
job. The interview was on the dream day. On that day the dreamer
also had sex. Not with her future boss, however, but with her partner.
The application for the new job was still on the kitchen table as they
enacted the dream boss's desire. It clearly served as the marker. Their
hurry was aptly prefigured by the name of the new firm.

26. The eyes have it.

> 'I am travelling with my family in a train. My wife has sat
> our youngest daughter on the edge of the open window. I
> am wondering how safe this might be and so I stick my head
> out of the window next to hers. Suddenly a bit of the baby's
> faeces flies off her nappy and hits me in my eye.'

My prediction was that the dreamer's wife would fall pregnant and have another daughter. Nine months later this was confirmed. From this it is clear once again that there is a direct connection between the eye and the vulva. This is not just because there are certain similarities of form, but also because the eye plays a major role in sexual attraction. Interesting is that in popular language the penis too is associated with an eye. On the one hand it is known as the 'one-eyed trouser snake' and on the other it is said that the divine phallus has an 'eye' that receives the light from the transcendental world.

What seems to be somewhat surprising is that faeces will represent semen. But this is explained when we remember the dream's associative language. Note the concern the dreamer had about the safety of the child sitting on the window ledge. This reflects, of course, the dreamer's concern about a possible pregnancy. Equally noteworthy is the fact that the little girl was sitting in the open window. This too is pointing to conception, for the window is also a reference to the vagina, and so is the little girl in that position.

27. Fed-up

> 'I dreamt I was changing my grandchild's nappy when suddenly a bit of excrement flicked into my mouth.'

This dream contrasts with the previous one. Instead of predicting a pregnancy it expresses being utterly fed-up. Fed-up both in non-sexual and sexual terms. The latter is hinted at by the fact that the nappy to be changed was that of a grandchild.

28. Tiger as flesh-eating bacillus

> 'I dreamt of a man who had a tattoo on his leg. As I looked at it the man turned into a tiger saying: "I won't eat you this time!"'

Upon waking this dreamer noticed a large sore in the spot where the dream tattoo had been. It turned out later that the leg was infected with a flesh-eating bacillus! The tattoo on the dreamer's leg implied engraving or drawing. 'Drawing', 'engraving', 'scribbling', 'doodling' and 'writing' are typical activities suggesting masturbation. The leg in a man's dream is an associative representation of the penis.

29. Clowning around with flute

'I dreamt of two clowns. One of them, the male in blue, was sitting on a chair while the female, in yellow, was perched on his thighs. The male clown looked like the flautist in Picasso's painting of 'The Three Musicians'. He wore a kind of monkish hood of a light blue colour. His face was snow-white and perfectly round like the full moon. Suddenly the female began to rock on her companion, moving her buttocks up and down. I felt quite embarrassed watching them. I thought: "At least they are wearing their clothes!"'

On the dream day this man took his family to an open-air festival in a park. He and his wife managed to find a seat on a park bench. A clown in a yellow and blue costume was some distance away. He had his back turned while fooling about with his drum. It was decorated with a blue ring on the white skin. Suddenly the dreamer's wife hopped on her husband's knees. She reached down into his pants and began to play unabashedly with his 'flute' inside his trousers. Because she was sitting on his knees the people around them could not quite see what was happening. Still, his wife's daring disregard of the public situation was an embarrassment to the husband. Yet to say 'no' to this was too hard for him. Music, musicians and musical instruments generally allude to 'making music' together. This metaphor is as popular in dreams as it is in every-day speech.

30. Cat-scan

'I dreamt this morning that the doctor came up to me holding a black cat whose paws were spread-eagled. It had lots of electric wires attached to its belly. They were all connected to some machine. The doctor moved the cat up and down over my belly and sideways.'

The day after this dream, the woman's mother-in-law phoned her and said that she would have to go to the hospital to have a cat-scan. Yes, dreams do have a sense of humour. Clearly this is where a joker's ideas come from. Despite the presence of the cat there was no sex to follow this dream.

31. Cat as child

'I dreamt that my girlfriend had two children who she needed to enrol at a suitable school. It wasn't difficult to find a class for the elder one. The problem was the younger one. She was a girl who turned out to be somewhat retarded. Mother was quite concerned about finding the right sort of placement for her.'

It soon became clear that the retarded child was the girlfriend's female cat. It was just before this dream that the boyfriend had installed a cat-door in his girlfriend's house. On the dream day the girlfriend tried to coax the cat through the door. It was all in vain. Ordinarily the cat displayed great intelligence, but now she failed to see the need for such a door. It took more than the usual training before the cat started to make use of this new convenience. The cat's reluctance to pass through the cat-door foresaw the girlfriend's reluctance to make love.

32. Boys and squelching pathways

'I was walking through the countryside with a young boy by my side. He chatted pleasantly with me. Then we came to a farmhouse with its stable attached to it like I had seen in Europe. We walked right through the stable where the aisle is also the guttering for the cow dung and urine. As I went along, my feet sank into the squelching path with cow dung coming up between my toes. Once we reached the hay barn we went past a young farm hand. It was a boy of about seventeen and bigger than my companion. He chipped into the conversation I was having with the younger boy. As I looked back at him he gave me a cheeky grin.'

This man was having an affair in the French Alps in his younger days. Now, as a mature male, his virility had begun to flag somewhat. But on the dream day he had sex with his new lady who was gradually restoring his potency and confidence in himself. The younger boy embodied his penis as lovemaking began. The older and stronger boy foreshadowed the dreamer's increasing virility.

33. Mushrooms between toes

'On my walk home I suddenly found it too difficult to move ahead. I took off my shoes to see what was holding me up. I found that there were little mushrooms growing between my toes.'

Two days after this dream this woman noticed that she was getting the thrush, which is the proliferation of a microbial fungus. Microbes in dreams are often portrayed in an exaggerated way. Instead of being represented in their true form they are vastly enlarged. In this way they make evident the connection between feet and the sexual organs. In his book, the 'Sacred Mushroom and the Cross', Allegro draws our attention to the structure of the mushroom. The stem is seen as the penis and the cap as the vulva. While on one level this symbolises human intercourse, on another level it pictures the sacred marriage or the divine union between heaven and earth, between the soul and the God-head.

It is not difficult to see that after this dream there would be a break in sexual interaction for this woman.

34. Cinderella's glass slipper

> 'I dreamt that I went to a department store to buy a pair of shoes for my wife. The goods on display were no ordinary footwear. The shoes looked more like the glass slippers Cinderella wore to the ball. They were encrusted with gold, silver, diamonds and other precious stones. They glittered and sparkled like the dew in the morning sun.'

In the evening of this dream day the dreamer sat in his lounge chair to take off his shoes and put on his slippers. While doing so his wife said: "By the way Peter Parsons tried to ring you today." "Oh yes, that reminds me, I was going to buy you a new wedding ring today to replace the one I threw into the creek!" The transient sparkle of the morning sun foreshadowed the impermanence of the dreamer's good intentions. The phrase, 'I was going to', underpins that. The atmosphere to making love evaporated as readily as the morning dew. Of interest here is that the dreamer chose to throw his wedding ring into a creek. Waterways in dreams represent the vagina ready for intercourse. When we remind ourselves of this, the disposal of the ring takes on two faces. One expresses the rejection of the present wife while the other cries out for a more suitable match.

35. Drowning in work

> 'I fell into the lake and was pulled down to the bottom. It was covered with a heap of papers.'

When I asked this student if she was 'drowning' in homework she heartily agreed. There are, of course, other ways of expressing an excessive workload. The dream chose to include water because it also foresaw intense emotions resulting from too much homework. A major part of them were sexual emotions. Dream interpreters often forget or ignore that aspect of water in dreams. It is always also a reference to a woman's reproductive system. So what was the erotic outcome of 'drowning in a lake'? A heap of papers pictures a static series. Repetition of one and the same movement.

36. Not dead, just missing

> 'I saw a black cat on the road. I thought it must have been run over because it was completely flattened. I went to pick it up. I was somewhat puzzled why I was not upset about this.'

Normally this dreamer would grieve over the death of any animal. That she was not concerned in her dream made her wonder about its meaning. It turned out that the dream had foreshadowed the disappearance of her cat. She didn't return for her usual meal. She stayed out all night. On the next day her absence started to worry the dreamer. She became anxious about the fate of her cat. She even drove along the road looking for her. She found nothing like a dead cat anywhere. Another night passed without the cat putting in an appearance. The dreamer began to resign herself to the fact that she might never see her again. Yet she did. The next morning her pet returned. This was foreshadowed by the dreamer's composure after having seen the flattened cat. Being puzzled exposes another reason for the dreamer's composure. This literary pheromone promised good sex. A run-over pussy-cat in a street underpins this. Here the dream delights in the violent aspect of intercourse.

37. Space invaders

> 'I am back in the house where I used to live before emigrating to this country. It is night and pitch dark outside. Suddenly there is a blue light flashing in the sky. I am terrified and rush to the window to pull down the blind. As I reach for the cord I see a space ship heading directly for the window. I thought: "Invaders from outer space!" Almost lame with panic I only just manage to close the blind. Then I wake up in a sweat.'

Freud rightly pointed out that windows often stand for the vagina. Window means wind-eye. The eye will also stand for the vagina. In view of this it is not difficult to see what it entails when a space ship heads straight for a window. Within this framework the blind becomes a contraceptive device. The police are a personification of the dreamer's watchfulness. They often stand also for the dreamer's conscience. Confirmation of this interpretation came from the husband of this dreamer. He said that his wife was looking for a new kind of prophylactic.

38. Drawing and petting

> 'I was drawing a reclining woman. The fingers of one of her hands were pointing upwards. I was dissatisfied with their appearance even though they looked very natural and relaxed. I rubbed them out and drew them again. This time they were no longer relaxed and natural, but stylised. My wife said to me that they looked very stiff. At that point I concentrated on the middle finger that now had swollen out of proportion. I decided to draw a little circle on the tip of it.'

It hardly needs explaining that this part of a longer dream was a classic figurative dramatisation of foreplay. The subject of the reclining woman set the scene. Without her it might have been just a case of plain masturbation. 'Natural' and 'relaxed', of course, referred to the flaccid penis. The fingers pointing upwards indicated the intended state of the penis. Quite generally it alluded to impending arousal. In this context 'stylised' foreshadowed an erection since it referred to the hardness of the 'stylus'. With that it not only alluded to an erection but also to 'drawing'. As always this is 'pulling' as in petting. Immediately after this the female partner spelled out what was implied in the previous sentence. After that the middle finger is completely 'denuded'. But the interesting thing is that this finger not only represented the penis. It also was the actual middle finger of the husband. The circular motion indicated by the circle on its tip was for the benefit of his wife. This fragment of a much longer dream is not only a classic representation of foreplay. It also is a splendid example of the condensed and allusive language of the dream.

39. Red-hot picnic

'My wife and I were at a picnic. I had made a large fire on the open ground that spawned lots of red-hot embers. My wife said that it would be a pity to let them just die there on the open ground and that I should shovel them into the fireplace. I got up to look for the spade, but our little boy had already found it and had begun to gather the embers. While doing this he stumbled and fell into the glowing heap of red-hot coals. I rushed forward to pull him out. But then I saw that he had protective gloves on and was burrowing in the coals for something. Here the dream broke off.'

This couple did go on a picnic. What happened at bedtime is more than obvious since fire is mostly passion. It can of course be an expression of violence and hatred. The open ground is speaking of the wife's receptivity to lovemaking. The passion of both partners finds expression in red-hot embers. Both the spade and the little boy who fell into the glowing heap of embers are easily identified. The dreamer rushing to 'pull him out' and 'protective gloves' are, of course, referring to precautions against pregnancy. The marker was a pair of garden gloves the dreamer had worn to gather firewood. They happened to be on the kitchen table while the lovers were engaged in tending their 'picnic fire' in bed.

40. Faceless

'I dreamt I was with a man at a party. After a while he kissed me. I felt that kiss as a warm tingling throughout my body. Although I could feel his stubble I was unable to see his face.'

The dreamer offered an enlightening comment about the lack of a face in a dream character: "When I dream of a man I don't know, he appears without a face." When this man of her dream appeared in reality six years later she wished to have sex with him. He was not interested. So the dreamer not only kissed an unknown man but also one she would never know in the biblical sense.

41. The proverbial mother-in-law

'I suddenly saw this huge bird crossing the yard. It looked like an emu but was much bigger. It came straight to the window with the passion-fruit vine in which a pair of doves had made their nest. When the bird got close the two doves flew from their nest and fluttered about anxiously. The big bird took little notice of them. It opened its broad and massive bill and started to chomp into the foliage of the vine. It wouldn't let up until the vine was totally bare.'

This newly-wed couple was living on the same block as the in-laws. The husband had converted the garage on the block to a bungalow. On the side facing the in-laws he had planted a thriving passion fruit vine. One day a serious argument arose between the mother-in-law and the young man. Living on the block with the in-laws became untenable. The couple moved away into a rented place. The dream aptly portrayed the young couple as lovebirds. The vine was, of course, symbolic of their passion for each other. But it also stood for life in general, much the same as the tree of life does in dream 3. The denuded vine dramatically expressed the end of their life in the bungalow. But it also signalled that on the dream day there would be no passion.

42. Sharks and polar bears

'I was swimming in the Artic waters. There were sharks everywhere. I could not understand that they were able to tolerate these freezing waters. I swam for my life towards an ice floe. I hauled myself onto it to escape the sharks. Suddenly three polar bears came trotting towards me. I woke up in terror!'

This dreamer learnt over time that whenever he dreamt of sharks there would be an almighty argument between him and his wife. And so it was on this day. In fact it was much worse. The appearance of the polar bears on the ice floe showed this. Here the 'terror' did not imply a sexual high. Instead it manifested as emotional upheaval, anger and despair.

43. Fire and mice

'My piano was on fire. The blaze started in a mouse's nest inside the piano. I was acutely aware that it was all my fault. I knew all along that the nest was there, yet I didn't do anything about it.'

The mouse nest inside the piano refers to the uterus. The piano is the womb while the fire in the nest of the mouse is the heat of ovulation. Normally this dreamer was rather 'cool' about having sex. On this day she was unable to resist it. Mice are typical representatives of the vagina. Not hard to guess is that the husband of the dreamer was a pianist. Music is a common indicator of love making. It is a common everyday metaphor for making love.

44. Snagging an octopus.

'I was fishing off the pier. Soon I hooked something that was so big and heavy it almost pulled me into the water. Eventually I managed to land it on the pier. To my shock and horror I had caught an octopus. It looked at me with a wry smile and then it started to move towards me in a threatening manner. I was terrified and began backing away from it. It followed me. I ran away into a cubby where I slammed the door and barricaded myself in.'

This young man had recently separated from his girlfriend. He went to visit her on the dream day in the hope that they would get together again. It got close. It seemed he had managed to win her back. Sometime after they had begun to make love things went inexplicably wrong. He hurriedly got up, dressed and left her flat without looking back. Once the relationship had broken down completely, a new girlfriend came the dreamer's way. This was indicated by the cubby hut and the 'feminine security' it provided. Was the dream playing with the word octopus/sy? Was the girlfriend a nymphomaniac? What is certain is that the girlfriend had complained on several occasions that the dreamer lacked passion.

45. Floods replenishing bank

'Lying on the edge of a steep embankment I look down to a dam which is almost dry. While peering down I hear a voice saying: "You can't imagine the floods that will swamp this dam soon." Immediately after these words, the thunder of water falling comes to my ears. Almost at the same time, that flood of water rushes into the dam, filling it up in no time.'

A dam is a reservoir and so is a bank account. (Em-bank-ment.) This dreamer was almost broke before this dream. Shortly after it he got a job. His bank account filled up more rapidly than ever before. This shows that water not only represents emotions and sexual fluids, but also monetary benefits. Just to confuse us, there was no sexual equivalent to follow this dream. On the other hand, a young woman who ordinarily never recalled any dreams confessed that there was one she did remember. It was a dream of a mighty waterfall. She had it the day before her honeymoon. This is why the Arab dream diviners always ascertained the dreamer's circumstances before they offered an interpretation.

46. House of relationships

> 'Something attracted my attention to the floor. It was on a drastic slope. When I looked up, I saw that the walls too were quite crooked. Wondering what would happen to the house I felt totally dreadful.'

When we remember that the floor most often refers to the woman of the house, we get an inkling of what to expect from this dream. On the dream day the partners had yet another soul-destroying argument. The relationship went from bad to worse. Eventually the bond between them fell apart. Here the house is obviously not just a representation of the woman. It also is a picture of the partnership.

47. Lounge as the womb

> 'I noticed a small hole in the lounge floor. When I had a closer look I saw water running through it into the lounge. It was like a small spring. As I wondered how I could stop the flow I saw that the water came from a hose under the house.'

Here the house and the body of the dreamer are identified in classical style. The floor of the house unmistakably points to the pelvic floor of the female body. The hose from underneath the floor can only be a reference to the ejaculating penis. The intention of the dreamer to stop the flow shows that she was concerned about getting pregnant. The water springing into the lounge represents insemination of the womb. Obviously the dreamer would forestall any intrusion if she could.

48. Lounge as the womb confirmed

> 'A burning log rolled out of the open fire into the living room. I was surprised that no one rushed to put it back into the fire place so it would not burn a hole in the carpet.'

While the open fire signals this woman's passion, there is a degree of anxiety mixed with it. She doesn't relish the idea that the fire should spread beyond its set bounds. This can only mean that she fears that the husband's 'burning log' might puncture the floor covering. It would mean that the protection against pregnancy would fail. The indifference of others towards this looming danger obviously shows that the husband believes that birth control is women's business.

49. Fruit and nuts

> 'Someone brought me a large consignment of goods. As I unpacked them they turned out to be corncobs, cantaloupes and chestnuts. I picked up two of the nuts and held them to my chest laughing: "Chest-nuts indeed!"'

It's easy to see that this dream was the precursor of a jolly romp. Laughter is particularly suggestive of happy sex. The chestnuts the husband found so delightful stood for the wife's breasts. When we look at the other name for cantaloupe, rock-melon, its significance is clearly spelt out for us. Its shape tells us that it was playing the feminine role in this fruity affair. Round objects always look toward the female. The corncob on the other hand was taking on the masculine role. Corncobs too may be peeled back to harvest their countless seeds. Let's not forget the word 'unpacking' which in this context explains itself. And speaking of context: The simplest way ever to uncover the sexual meaning of a dream is to think of it as an euphemistic description of our sexual disposition.

50. Unrequited love

> 'I dreamt that I had an exhibition of my paintings. An official came up to me saying I should come with him to look at this masterpiece in the main hall. When we got there I looked up at the wall which was full of paintings, yet I could see only one. It was several times larger than the others. It was a glorious landscape with shimmering water in the foreground. I was amazed at its beauty. There was a 'roundish' object on the left side I puzzled over. I was then told that this painting was done by my daughter and not by me. I was shocked. I thought all paintings were my work.'

When we encounter literary pheromones like 'amazed' and 'puzzled' we expect some kind of sexual interaction. The more so when the central object is a glorious landscape of great beauty displayed in the main hall. Since paintings are either of square or rectangular shape we can be sure that the target of desire in this case was feminine. This notion is supported by the presence of a mysterious round shape inside the landscape. Because there were lots of paintings on the wall we might be justified to see this as a static series suggesting repetitive action of a sexual nature. If this had been a woman's dream we would suspect a case of masturbation. But the dream came to a man. This meant that the desired object was a woman to whom he could expect to make love. But that didn't happen. The clue to this disappointment was the fact that the main painting was not done by the dreamer himself, but by his daughter. While thinking about this after waking up, it occurred to him that she was presently without a partner and missed her previously healthy sex life. This put him into the same category. It was obviously the bottom line of the dream's message.

51. Forgotten garden

> 'I went out into my garden. I was saddened that nothing grew there anymore. The vines were bare, the trees looked stunted and dry and the lawns were dead. I thought I must have forgotten to water it.'

It wasn't long after this dream that the dreamer's relationship with his wife dried up as well. Gardens are mostly a representation of the female's reproductive system. Once again the dream shows how much we identify with our surroundings. It testifies to the fact that the inner and the outer world are really one. Indeed, where would the landscape, the world, the universe be without the viewer? Because of this the mystics say that the ultimate experience on this plane of existence is the realisation that the knower and the known are one.

52. Strolling through the garden

> 'I took a leisurely stroll in my garden. I noticed that the crowns of the two mulberry trees had grown together. Before that they stood well apart. Now they formed a kind of natural arch. As I walked through it I felt elated.'

Shortly after this dream the dreamer found his love match. Just like landscapes, gardens represent the human anatomy. They mostly refer to the woman's reproductive system. Walking through the arch prefigured the dreamer's coming together with his new love. Here the dream reveals again how close its language is to that of poetry. In ancient Sumeria, ritual poetry repeatedly represented the female partner as the garden. This can easily be checked. Look up Solomon's Song of Songs in the Old Testament. It is a direct descendant of the Sumerian "Sacred Marriage Rite". For a garden example see Song of Songs chapter 4:12 and chapter 6:2-3.

53. Wrestling a giant

'I met a giant on the way to college. He was pale and totally naked. His skin glistened with oil. He would not let me go my way. Before I could pass him I had to wrestle with him. I tackled him. Because he was naked and oily he was too slippery for me. I could not get a proper grip on him. In the end I was thrown to the ground. I woke up quite depressed.'

On the dream day this student was called up at morning assembly and told to go to the principal's office. In the assembly hall was a mural of a giant naked figure with one knee on the ground. The principal told the student that his essay as such was first rate. But he had to submit a new one because he hadn't followed the expected criteria. He had gone against the art teacher's personal views. Clearly the giant was the authority of the institution represented by the principal and pictured by the giant on the fresco of the auditorium. From the sexual perspective the naked giant challenging the dreamer spells inevitable arousal. In that context the wrestling with the giant and his slippery nakedness becomes self-evident.

54. Lucky break

'I was driving a bus with young people along a winding mountain track. I came to a narrow part where the road had fallen partly away. I took the risk to pass there. The back of the bus didn't make it and we rolled down hill. We came to land on the roof among the rocks. We clambered out unhurt and walked away. The next day I returned to see if I could rescue the bus. When I got there the bus was being driven away by someone else. The rocks had all disappeared. Instead of them there was a beautiful field of lush, green grass.'

The bus and the young people in it indicate that this young man was a teacher. Driving a bus always indicates being involved in society at large. In the sexual context the presence of a large number of people indicates augmentation of feelings. This is parallel to the enlargement of buildings in which sex takes place. Soon after this dream the teacher was dismissed from his job. The condition of the road and the subsequent tumble indicate this. There was hope though. The hard rocks that were replaced by lush green grass betray this. The dreamer soon got a new job that was less stressful and paid more. Here again the colour green points to fresh hope and new life. Expressions like 'mountain track', 'narrow part', 'rolling downhill', and 'landing among rocks' make the sexual scenario more than evident. Mountains mostly refer to mounting. So the mountain track with its narrow part can only be an image of the Venusberg. The beautiful field of lush, green grass referred to the pubic area. Beautiful too is a literary pheromone. It alludes to the beautiful sensations during sexual intercourse. This indicates again that beauty in general is Venusian and always shadowed by Eros. Interesting in this context is that Hindu astrology sees Venus as the blind planet. This makes sense when we remember that love is blind. What is more curious is that it is said by the prude that self-love in form of masturbation causes blindness.

55. Haircuts

'Several of my friends and I were queuing up outside a bus to have our hair trimmed and shaped. I was last in line. My time came around to have my hair done. It was then that the hairdresser said that the bus was now too dirty to go on with his work. I had to wait till next time.'

Generally hair portrays our thoughts. In this case it also signified status. It turned out that the dream foresaw a time when the dreamer's official standing would change. This was not to happen at once. Some months were to pass yet before the dreamer was ready for it. What that was becomes evident when we know who those friends in front of the dreamer were. They were all separated from their partners. In short the dreamer would be single again. The fact that the dreamer lined up for this change to occur shows that her relationship was defunct. And so was her sex-life. Buses most often refer to society at large. Bus is short for omni-bus. 'Omni' is derived from the Latin word 'omnis' which means 'all'.

56. Joining hands

> After I parted from my husband I met a couple of dwarves in the street. I sat down with them to join hands with them.'

'Just one question cracked the mystery of 'joining hands with the dwarves': "Who comes to mind when you think of theses dwarves?" "Someone who has just suffered the tragedy of loosing a member of the family." The dreamer herself had only recently parted from her husband and now she was finding solace in joining hands with two people that were personifications of couples. It raises hopes of growing into a new relationship. This scene took place in the street because the dwarves were neither members of the dreamer's family nor close friends and acquaintances. They were members of the wider circle of society where a new partner might be waiting for her. The sexual scenario is revealed when we know that a street most often refers to the vulva. Thus dwarves in the street point to the clitoris. More than one dwarf suggest manipulation. Joining hands with the dwarves in the street points to self-pleasuring.

57. Reaching for the rhino

> 'I spotted some rhinos in a corral. One of them was close enough for me to reach through the timber fence. I wanted to pat it but it moved away from me so I couldn't touch it.'

We might expect that this dream of rhinos would explain itself. However it didn't make sense to the dreamer himself. Yet, upon taking a closer look, his circumstances might have given him a clue. What clues were available to him? He was living with his wife in the same house. They lived in separate wings. In 'separate corrals'. He reached out to her. She ignored him. Two months after this dream the husband left. Obviously there was no chance of sexual reconciliation with his wife. Wanting to pat the rhino involves the hands. Since the rhino moved away there was no masturbation either. There was just feeling 'horny'.

58. From fur cap to silk scarf

'I was walking along the beach in India. A peddler came along selling fur caps. I asked how much they were. The price was too dear. The peddler dropped the price to a mere $5 so I could afford it. I wanted to pay for it when another woman showed her interest in the cap. When I looked for my purse I found I didn't have it with me. So I let the other woman have the cap. I then moved further on into a large building. There were lots of silk scarves for headgear there. They looked very attractive. I finished up buying one even though it was very expensive. Strange to say I did find the money for this purchase. There was a label on it that said: "Blessings from Sri Bhagavan."'

Like hair, caps and hats indicate status. The essential message of this dream was giving up 'animal ways' for spiritual disciplines. The cost of the headgear showed which situation was more precious. Naturally it would exact a higher price. Part of that higher price was giving up sex for spiritual rewards. It also meant handing over the sexual privileges to the woman who had bewitched her husband. The dreamer was powerless to save her marriage. It is evident from the fact that she lacked the cash to buy the cap made from animal fur. Yet destiny magically provided the funds for the silk scarf. Some would see this as divine intervention. In reality it was all part of an integrated plan. Predestination.

59. Reflexology in dreams

'I dreamt that I had a kind of cancerous growth on the soles of both feet.'

After this dream no such growths developed. But something else did instead. It was sciatica and back pain in the area of the fourth and the fifth lumbar vertebrates. The dreamer checked out the areas of the dream cancer in a book of reflexology. It showed that these areas on the soles of the feet corresponded precisely with the lumbar area indicated. Injury in that spot will cause lumbar and also sciatic pains. Understandably these back pains forestalled all moves towards sex for the time being.

60. Neck and jaw

'While my chiropractor was manipulating my jaw she said: "The pain in your neck is caused by your jaw. Then she pressed the joint of the jaw and squeezed out a yellow fluid.'

The dreamer went to her chiropractor after this dream to have her neck manipulated. The jaw wasn't touched. Nor did the chiropractor say anything about the jaw. A day later she went to the dentist to have a filling done. In course of this work the dentist noticed that the woman's bite was out. He corrected it by grinding down certain teeth. He explained that this had to be done because it could cause a problem in the jaw. Moreover it might well affect the neck. Apparently women are particularly susceptible to such complaints because of hormonal factors. Interesting is here to see how the dream's first and second day manifestations combine to cover the dream story. It is quite usual to find many aspects of the second day manifestation to be surprisingly literal. Typical is the transference of some of the chiropractor's functions to the dentist.

The jaw is part of the mouth. The dream often represents the vagina as a mouth and the vulva as its lips. The yellow fluid is explained when we realise that the dream 'disguised' the husband as the chiropractor/ dentist.

61. Explicit sex as kindly love

> 'I was in bed with my son. We were both naked and I was lying on top of him. I started licking his throat and moved downwards very slowly. Gradually I moved closer and closer to his erection. The dream broke off before I reached the centre of attention.'

This dream came to a mother a day before she allowed her son to return to her home again. She had sent him away in anger. The purpose of the meeting was reconciliation. It is clear from the dream story which of the two would be the most loving and forgiving. This is yet another example of explicit sex portraying deep emotions away from sexual interaction.

62. Inverse projection

> 'In my dream a sawmill slowly moved towards my house.'

On the dream day a truck arrived to deliver a load of timber. It came directly from the sawmill. Such inversions happen quite frequently. Timber is feminine because it is harvested from living and growing trees. A load of timber arriving suggests that the woman in a partnership is welcoming sex. The fact that the dream brought the whole sawmill to the dreamer indicates unreserved participation.

63. Fish in pools

'My husband put the yolk of an egg into a warm pool fed by a spring. As he put it in the water the egg began to congeal. I told my husband he would kill it. He insisted that it would be all right. As I watched, the egg seemed to turn into a ball of water. At that moment six goldfish appeared. A larger, silvery one joined them. The larger fish began to swim around in wild circles. I said to my husband: "Well, that's it then. That fish will ruin the egg!" But my husband reached into the pool, caught the offending fish and threw it out of the pool.'

In the evening of that day the couple watched a documentary about an organism that killed masses of fish. Under the microscope this organism looked like a congealed egg. Later in the film there were three close-ups of a large, silvery fish. It was spinning around in the water as it died. Late in the evening the couple made love. A fish in a pool of water is often representative of this. The dreamer feared that she would conceive if the husband stayed on for the ejaculation, so he withdrew at the critical moment.

This shows how a sexual manifestation follows the dream plot. The husband 'threw the silvery fish out' before it could do any 'damage' to the ovum. The danger of getting pregnant was portrayed by the dream as something destructive and so it showed the fish as a danger to the egg. In reality it was the egg-like organism that 'killed' the fish. Yet another inversion so typical of dreams, but here it gets complicated. The fish as the penis was also killed in the sense that it could not get at the egg to cause a pregnancy 'disaster'. Actually, the dreamer was heading towards menstruation which destroys the ovum. That had to be built into the plot as well.

The next day the dreamer said to her husband that she had not seen their six goldfish in the garden pool. They seemed to have disappeared some days ago. The husband assured her that they must still be there since no predators were around the pool.

So they went out into the garden to the pool together to see if they could find them. The husband knelt down by the pool and lifted up the leaves of the water lilies. There they were, all six of them, hiding among the leaves and waterweeds. As mentioned before, such literality is fairly typical of the second day manifestation.

That a dream plot may manifest in the opposite way is most confusing. But such inversions usually happen only to a part of the waking manifestations.

64. Island of red roses.

> 'Then I saw that at the end of the stream was a big lake which had a small island of red roses on it.'

Lakes, streams, pools and oceans refer to the reproductive system of women. Life begins in the amniotic fluid. The island refers to the inside of the vulva; the base of the clitoris. The red roses allude to the clitoris itself. The plural is indicative of a static series alluding to manipulation. The dream knows its grammar and has a flair for puns. 'Rose' is the past tense of 'to rise'. To many it may come as a surprise that clitoris is derived from the Greek word kleitoris. It means divine, famous, goddess-like. The goddess leads us onwards to the jewel in the lotus of the well-known Tibetan mantra "Om Mani Padme Hum". 'Mani' is Sanskrit for 'jewel'. 'Padme' refers to the 'lotus'. In Roman times the rose was the emblem of Venus. She was the goddess of love and sex. Once Rome was Christianised the rose was transferred to Mary. Christianity repressed sex and with it the meaning of the rose as a reference to the vagina. The early botanists too were affected by this repression. They knew very well that flowers had all the same sexual organs as the human body. However they were not courageous enough to spell this out. They transformed the male organs to 'stamens' and code-named the female organs 'pistils'. Then they changed 'vulva' to 'stigma', 'penis' to 'filament', 'glans' to 'anther' and the 'vagina to 'style'.

65. Not measuring up to expectations

'I dreamt that my ex-husband had sent me some cartoons which his new wife had painted in the most appealing colours. I thought the drawings were really very good. The judge who was present while I looked at these little artworks disagreed. He took a ruler and laid it against the cartoons saying: "See, they don't measure up to expectations!"'

This dreamer's husband had left her for another woman. At first it looked as if there would be a threesome. But then things changed. The husband took his new wife to another place. She was pregnant by then. The dreamer was still hopeful that a threesome might be agreed upon. The colours of the cartoons reflected her feelings. Her readiness to accept the other woman as part of the family can be gleaned from her assessment of the rival's drawings. In the end her better judgement said that it wouldn't work. The cartoons with their appealing colours were, of course, a signal from the husband that his new love was more attractive to him than his wife. To start with the wife misread the message and hoped that she would not lose her husband. But then she realised that the 'ruler' was not for her, but for the new love. This triggered off the common defensive mechanism that follows the pattern of 'sour grapes'. Rulers, like all long and straight items, refer to the penis. Highly coloured works of art have intercourse in mind. Drawings, because the idea of 'pulling' is implied, may also refer to masturbation.

66. Jumping puddles with Princess Diana

'I was jumping into puddles with Princess Diane. We had such a lot of fun!'

This dreamer wondered why she suddenly should dream about Princess Diana when she had never dreamt about her while the tragic Princess was still alive. She understood that she was in a similar situation as Diana when it came to her love life. But that had been the case for three years. There would have been plenty of reasons to dream about the Princess long before this. The answer came when she went to her lover for the night. He had replaced his small single bed with a queen-sized bed.

67. Jumping from log to log

'I came to a swamp with lots of logs floating on the water. A childish desire overcame me to jump on the one nearest to me. When I landed on it I jumped immediately onto the next one to hold my balance. I thought this was fun and so I leaped from log to log.'

On the dream day this woman masturbated in a room with a poster showing birds of the swamps. The poster became the marker. Swampy ground has the same meaning as muddy paths. And the 'logs' in the female anatomy? The clitoris. 'Fun' is a typical pointer towards sexual sensations; sensations that are in fact divine and goddess-like. 'Holding balance' is of interest because it describes in physical terms the 'teetering on the brink of an orgasm'. It shows why tightrope walking and other circus acts cause such excitement with sexual undertones. Leaping and jumping might even be called 'gymnastic' or 'acrobatic pheromones'. When looking at dreams 66 and 67 side by side we notice that both include jumping in their story yet their sexual manifestations were different. It shows again how important the context and the dreamer's personal circumstances are. In short we cannot say in advance whether jumping in dreams is going to manifest as masturbation or as intercourse.

68. Olives and vertigo

'I dreamt that I was eating tiny olives from a glass jar. I fished them out of the clear liquid with my fingers. I puzzled over this since our olives are normally in dark-brown brine. They tasted delicious. Suddenly I found myself crawling on my knees along a narrow beam that bridged a big pool far below. It was so high up that I got dizzy when I looked down. Before I reached the other side I stumbled and almost slipped off the narrow beam.'

Jars are female. Because of this we might suspect that this dreamer was a woman. If it had been a woman's dream we might have concluded that fishing olives from a jar signalled masturbation. But the dreamer was a man which changes the scenario. Fishing for olives in that circumstance becomes foreplay. Caressing the vulva while at the same time sucking on a nipple. The olives are, of course, a reference to the clitoris. The clear brine is a reference to the font of urine which ultimately alludes to vaginal secretions. The appearance of the bridge indicates that foreplay changed to making love. This is clear from the dreamer being on his knees high up on a narrow beam over water. 'Narrow' mostly alludes to the vulva. 'Vertigo' is fear of heights. It betrays the intensity of the dreamer's orgasmic build-up. The near drop into the river indicates that the peak of the build-up has been reached. The slip and near fall show that the orgasm was withheld. The dreamer practised Taoist sex where the orgasm is suppressed.

The dreamer reported a second day manifestation. He noticed that a vine next to the house was growing into the spouting. He decided to cut it down. For this he needed a tall ladder. While standing high up there the splashing of the waterfall by the pond below attracted his attention. He realised that this was like being on that narrow bridge of the dream looking down to the pool of water far below.

69. Engulfed by floods of passion

> 'I dreamt I was waiting with some people in a bus shelter. A man came up to me. He kissed me and soon we began to cuddle and have sex in front of all the people. It was so passionate that a whole flood of water ran from us engulfing everybody in the shelter and in the street.'

This woman had no partner at the time of the dream. The first intercourse manifestation of the dream let the woman wait for two months (protracted manifestation). One of the signs that the dream was not likely to manifest on the dream day was the fact that the lovers made love in a place which is set aside for waiting. This dream is one of those rare examples that show explicit dream sex as the precursor of actual intercourse. It also foreshadowed not just one particular sexual act. It also looked towards a mighty love affair. This was made plain by the floodwaters that engulfed everything around the lovers.

Here we see again how sex in dreams is often a public act. It explains why a love affair creates so much social interest and why the law has its arm rather tightly around the matter. But it also works the other way round. Two new lovers exude powerful pheromones that attract the attention of those around them. Such lovers are happy about that; after all they themselves also wish to broadcast their new found happiness to the rest of the world.

70. Verger and Virgo

> 'I dreamt I was walking down the aisle on the arm of my father to the festive peal of the organ. But just as we step up to the priest, the verger appears and turns off the lights.'

This little drama ends in darkness signalling to the dreamer that it is time to look within. The case isn't as hopeless as it seems. The presence of the verger suggests that the status of the bride is on the verge of change.

But this dream is also an expression of a woman's longing for a sexual partner. The very phrase of the 'festive peal of the organ' is an allusion to the penis and its peel. Moreover, in times gone by, the verger used to bear a rod of office. It is a phallic object that was called 'virga'. It makes plain that the potential bride is still a 'virgo'. The two terms stand side by side like man and woman craving to be one flesh. This picture arises when we know that a Latin word ending in 'a' is feminine and one ending in 'o' is masculine. The intriguing thing here is that the phallic object, the virga, has a feminine ending while the female, the Virgo, has a masculine ending. This is very much like an ego-transference alluding to the essential unity between 'you and me', between 'bride and groom', between the 'inner and outer world', between 'mankind and the universe'.

71. Embracing fear of death

'I felt I was awake. I discovered some marks on the carpet near the heater. When I had a closer look, I realised that they were not dirt marks, but that something had happened to the floor under the carpet. It had lost its solidity and the carpet moved. It was no longer flat but wavy. The foundation had gone from under it. I wanted to run away and so I moved to the glass door of the lounge. I didn't feel secure any more in my own house. But just before I passed through it I said to myself: "Hey, this is only a dream, I am not going to run, I am going to face my fears!" I turned back and looked into the kitchen. There was a dead body of a woman on the floor. I went up to it and touched it. At that moment the corpse revived and got up and ran into the lounge where it threw itself on the floor. I caught up with it and reached out to touch it, to embrace it. But it got up again and escaped. The dream soon faded.'

This dream is mostly self-explanatory. It is worth noting the 'woman on the floor'. Under normal conditions this would refer to the pelvic floor of a woman in embrace showing womanhood as the basis of existence; as Mother Earth that sustains all life. The loss of the floor's usual solidity highlights the transience and frailty of life. The dreamer has come to the sudden realisation that she can't go on heedlessly any longer. By her willingness to embrace death she gains new life. She experiences a kind of awakening which is dreamatised by her move from ordinary dreaming to lucid dreaming. In the lucid state awareness is greatly enhanced and close to the sense of being fully awake. It offers a new kind of self-perception; a deeper and sharper sense of self-awareness. Interesting is, of course, that lucidity is caused by the sudden activation of the frontal lobe. It is this part of the brain that gives us the sense of self, of ego, of individuality; and of being in control.

This was clearly a 'big dream' which brought with it a temporary sublimation of the sexual instincts. In terms of Taoist philosophy, sex had become recessive to the point of non-existence, while the realm of spirituality took over most of the space on the yin and yang circle.

72. Books as the 'procreative word'

'I dreamt that someone gave me a lovely book of aquarelles. They were of a massive mountain range. On each page the range was shown somewhat extended. It created a three dimensional map of the range that was tinted with all the colours of the rainbow. The pages turned over magically. Unexpectedly the last three pages began to fall out.'

On the dream day this dreamer enjoyed a round of the most glorious lovemaking. The pages falling out signalled an ejaculation. If pages of a book turn by themselves intercourse follows. If pages are turned by hand, masturbation will manifest. The marker of it all was a post card the dreamer had received from the Austrian Alps earlier that day. High colours are pointing to high thrills. Mountains always spell mounting just as rocks always get us rocking. It is opportune here to remember that the leaves of books were originally made from leaves of trees such as palm leaves. The word paper comes from the Egyptian word papyrus which is a wetland sedge growing in the Nile Delta. Books hark back to living vegetation and have therefore much the same meaning in dreams as green twigs, branches and trees.

73. Broken and unbroken egg

> 'I dreamt that I had two eggs. One had lost its shell while the other was still intact.'

This puzzle was solved five days after the dream. The egg without the shell announced an impending period. The egg with the unbroken shell meant that 'there won't be any signs of the period yet. It will seem that it isn't coming.'

74. Sewn together

> 'I went to a seamstress to pick up my shirt that I had left there to be mended. At first I was given the wrong garment. I didn't realise this until I examined it more closely. I then saw that only the sleeves were like those of my shirt. The rest was really a parka. So I handed it back to the seamstress who then opened her bottom drawer where my shirt was. It had been taken apart ready for certain alterations. Its colour had also been changed from a blazing red to a gentle, soft pink. It looked so lovely I could hardly wait for it to be sewn together.'

On the day before this dream the dreamer had a blazing argument with his wife. By the dream day enough civility had returned to the household for the couple to go to the movies together. They had no idea what the film would be about. To their surprise it turned out to be the story of a couple about to separate. Their main manner of communication had become arguing and shouting at each other. The husband left to live on his own. Surprisingly the wife asked him some time later to come and get the two shirts she had picked up for him from the drycleaners. After the movie the dreamer and his partner went straight home to bed making love. The blazing red of anger of yesterday had turned to a gentle and loving pink. When reading the dream again it becomes apparent that the whole plot abounds with words of reconciliation. Even without considering the plot the dream interprets itself. We only need to examine phrases like 'at first wrong', 'examined more closely', 'to be mended', 'taken apart', 'certain alterations', 'colour changed', 'blazing red to soft pink', 'sewn together'.

75. Hippos in moat

'My lover came to my house which looked really grand. It had a moat with a bridge over it. I called my lover to come and see what was swimming in the moat. It was a huge hippopotamus. By the time my lover arrived the large hippo had disappeared. Instead there were lots of little ones swimming about. I put my toes into the water even though I was afraid that one of the little hippos might bite them.'

The hippopotamus reminded this dreamer of the mighty rhinoceros she saw as a four-year-old at the zoo. She was enthralled by it and her mother had trouble pulling her away from the animal. The rhino is an almost universal symbol of sexual prowess. Its horns are a prized aphrodisiac. "Come and see" in this plot is an invitation to sex. The large hippo cum rhino becoming little hippos in the dreamer's 'moat' is a dramatisation of an ejaculation into the dreamer's watered place.

Here again we meet a grand house. It is really the dreamer's ordinary house whose proportions have been boosted due to an impending emotional high. The rhino cum hippo is a reference to her lover. The dream features the qualities of the rhino by means of a hippopotamus because it is at home in water. And water is that hallmark of womanhood. Toes and feet in water are an associative projection of genital union.

There is something else in this dream which deserves special attention. It is the memory of the four-year-old girl of the encounter with a rhino. That experience had impressed and fascinated her at the time so powerfully that her mother could scarcely move her from the spot. Part of the reason for this might have been that the little girl darkly perceived what would happen to her in adulthood. While we see it as natural for memories to come back to us from the past, it is rarely considered that such childhood experiences might also foresee related future events.

Sceptics would dismiss such a suggestion vehemently. But since distance in time is irrelevant when it comes to making retrograde links to past memories, it should be equally plausible to make forward links with the future. This is most certainly so if it is the case that dreams can access future events.

The example of Sikorsky's dream and its manifestation demonstrates that dreams may look ahead as far as 30 years. This suggests that there is actually no limit to the years a dream can look ahead. As well as Sikorsky's case, we have learnt from the mysterium coniunctionis that in truth, past, present and future are all happening at once for all eternity. Therefore our memory must be able to move in either direction.

In other words, when the little girl came face to face with the rhino, she might also have come in contact with the grand dream house with the moat and the associated sexual high. I suggest that at the moment she set her eyes on the rhino, the little girl not only got in touch with the moat and grand house of the future, but also with her sex life of previous incarnations. In principle this can be seen as a mysterium coniunctionis moment such as Jung had. In the case of the four-year-old, however, it was a cryptomnesic coniunctionis. I believe we have many such moments throughout life, especially as children.

76. Bushed

'In a pack with others, I am running through a park which seems like a forest. As I run and run I feel all sorts of wild emotions.'

The translation of this dream goes something like this: I am running wild; my emotions are running away with me. I feel lost, bushed, abandoned. The sexual consequences are self-evident.

77. Poring over exam paper

'I dreamt that I was sitting in a deep trench poring over my exam paper. While frantically searching for answers, my examination paper mysteriously got all wet.'

While this student was sitting for his exam a trench was being dug nearby. Shortly after the jackhammers had started it began to pour with rain. It is of interest to note how the dreamer phrased his record of the dream: "I was 'poring' over my exam paper." Another point to be paid attention to is the fact that the examination paper got wet. When this student realised that he could not cope with the paper he panicked. The result was a spontaneous ejaculation.

78. Cello ablaze

'As I was playing my cello it suddenly caught on fire. I rang the fire brigade. The bloke at the other end said he couldn't come because their hose had a puncture.'

The young lady who had this dream was a cello player. She became amorous on the dream day and rang her ex-boyfriend in the hope that he would appease her passion. But like the fire brigade he was unable to help her.

Music of any kind has the same purpose as that of birdsong in spring. Beautiful music, like beautiful colours, pictures, vistas and landscapes etc. are all rooted in sex. Music in waking life is often aiming consciously at stirring the gonads.

79. Two arms on old record player

'I have a box of highly coloured Indian scarves and clothes. I am wondering whether to wear the orange or purple scarf. All the scarves have metallic threads through them. I wrap one of them around the knob of the second arm of my old fashioned record player. I have never seen this curious second arm before. Then I go ahead with playing a soppy Irish record I had bought for my ex-husband many years ago. My ex was not in the mood for this kind of music and lifted the arm with the needle off the record.'

This woman was in her second marriage. As is usual for dreams, the ex-husband is a stand-in or model for the new one. The latter is clearly represented by the second arm on the old record player. The arm is, of course, a representation of the penis while the knob and needle stand for the glans. The woman attended to it lovingly in foreplay. This is clearly signalled by the woman's handling of the knob. Notice the word 'wrap' becoming 'rapped' as it alludes to the husband's rapturous feelings. The old record was a reference to a sexually good time in the woman's marriage. It was now to be repeated in a new form. The dream makes this clear by having the ex-husband (who is a stand-in for the present husband) abandoning the old soppy tunes. The marker for this dream was the clothing in the open wardrobe that the dreamer could see while making love.

80. What's in a name?

> 'I dreamt of the German composer Schoenberg. I said to myself in the dream: "I know very little of his personal life. I must look in my book of biographies of famous artists and composers." I opened the pages where Schoenberg was listed and studied them carefully. In fact the pages opened by themselves. There was a strange picture among the text. I focused on it with particular attention.'

This dreamer had beautiful sex on the dream day. This was consistent with the composer's name, 'beautiful mountain'. Note the literary pheromones of 'focus', 'particular attention' and 'pondering' which all demand deep concentration. Here again we see the 'book' as the pivotal point of the action.

81. Pine hill

> 'I was walking with my wife up the hill on a farm, I noticed a huge Norfolk Pine which was laden with nuts. As I watched this mighty tree towering into the skyline my wife said to me: "The owner is a very secure man. He had plenty of foresight to plant this tree which gives him now so many riches."'

A pine endowed with nuts is the family tree in more sense than one. If we swap the places of the vowels in 'pines' we get 'penis'. Walking uphill is just another variation of climbing a mountain which most often turns to mounting. 'Secure' with 'many riches' expresses the husband's financial security as well as his confidence in his sexual prowess. Riches equate with virility and fertility.

82. Wingless angels

'I met an old lady in a field where I have been painting. She radiated a light blue light. I just knew that she was a higher being. After her appeared a man who also must have come from higher spheres. I asked him about destiny, wanting to know if it was fixed. At first he avoided meeting my eyes, responding in an evasive manner. In the end he looked at me directly and said simply: "Yes, it's fixed!"'

The word 'angel' is of Greek origin and simply means 'messenger'. At times birds of our dreams will have that function; after all they fly to and fro between heaven and earth. The wings of the angels as we know them were borrowed from birds by cultures that had left the wild in order to live in cities. Not all dream angels have wings as this example shows. The sign that points to a rarefied realm in this case is, of course, the blue light the old lady radiated. The same sign also indicates that this dreamer was looking towards a state beyond sex.

83. Garden of Eden

'I dreamt of going to the shed to find a piece of wallboard. After I found what I wanted, the board covered itself magically with blue paint.'

On the dream day this artist went to his studio and laid out one of the wallboards the renovators had pulled down. He then brushed it all over with a mixture of blue powder paint and paste. Later in the day he began to cover the blue panel with a wonderful scene of the Garden of Eden. His work glowed with a mysterious light and everybody commented on that. The wall-board stood here for the usual lounge floor or the lawn. A 'wall' often signifies the female partner. It has been so since ancient times. This can be checked by referring to chapter 8, verses 9&10 in the Song of Solomon which is an adaptation of the Sumerian 'Sacred Marriage Rite'. Intercourse followed since the dream showed the panel being covered magically. Cf. dream 6 and F7. Paste is starch. Semen is delivered in a starchy liquid. The painting was done at a time when the biggest hit was "Love is Blue".

84. Blood clots in my urine

> 'I dreamt that there were blood clots in my urine.'

On the surface this dream looks quite alarming. But it soon turned out that the woman's period was upon her. Two days earlier she had a dream that some fish were attacking a shell-less egg she possessed. This showed her that the blood in the urine was a sign that she soon would menstruate.

85. Murdered baby girl

> 'I dreamt that someone murdered their baby girl. I could not quite make out who that someone was. They had bashed her to death. Even though she was quite dead the baby would not lie down. It was a thoroughly disturbing situation.'

What followed this dream was for the dreamer disturbing indeed. Her period pangs started. She felt heavy in her belly and headaches began to plague her. This went on for six days. The dreamer became more and more anxious about this state of affairs. She began to think that she might be pregnant. Yet she was convinced that her period had somehow already started. All the symptoms were there except the bleeding. This state was akin to the part of the dream where the baby girl had been murdered but would not lie down. Eventually the bleeding started and everything took its normal course. There was no pregnancy.

Interesting is here that the dreamer 'could not quite make out who that someone was.' It was of course the natural process of shedding the broken down ovum or 'the murdered baby girl'. The dream spoke of a baby girl because before the dreamer gave birth to a boy she had had a miscarriage of a baby girl.

86. Creeping floods

> 'I dreamt that the floods had surrounded my house. When I went downstairs I saw that the water was creeping up the stumps. They all had become quite loose and wobbled when I touched them.'

Similar dreams usually appear about three days ahead of the menstruation period. They show again that the outer world and the inner state are really one.

87. Scarlet robe

> 'I saw my auntie sitting in a flowering gum. She was dressed in a scarlet robe.'

The colour scarlet is, of course, a reference to the blood of the menstrual period. It may be helpful to be reminded that the word 'flower' is derived from the verb 'to flow'. Of further interest in this connection is that the word 'blossom' is etymologically related to 'blood'. In Swiss German for instance there is no distinction between the words 'bleeding' and 'blossom'.

88. Laughing cousin

> 'I was with many girls. We were yapping like they do in the public service. Suddenly I saw my favourite cousin through the window. She was laughing her head off. She didn't say anything. She just kept laughing.'

Upon reflection it came to the dreamer's mind that this cousin was the first one of all the relations to get a job. Three days later the dreamer got the new job she had applied for. The sexual implications are spelt out by the 'window', but especially by 'laughter', which, like 'fun', is a ready bedfellow of sex.

89. Playing cards

'I dreamt that I was playing a game with this boy that I am currently seeing. It was a card game to do with Australian animals. Anyway there came a snake. The boy told me that it was a carpet snake and quite harmless. This snake became excessively huge as in fat. Then it became tiny and flew off into another part of the house. (We were in a courtyard) I wanted him to kill it but the boy said it was harmless and wouldn't return.'

Playing a game most probably refers to flirting and sexual playfulness. Animals refer to our 'animal ways'. Playing cards might be cuddling and petting since cards involve our hands.

A snake has many meanings. In this context it is clearly the penis. The dreamer's apprehension about it was based on her fear of getting pregnant. The carpet snake suggested that making love was to take place on the carpet. The carpet also alludes to prophylactics because it covers the (pelvic) floor.

The courtyard is the vagina since containers and enclosures are predominantly a reference to that part of the female anatomy. 'Court yard' sounds like 'caught in the yard'. The snake becoming tiny refers, of course, to the penis shrinking after an orgasm. Since it was flying away it signals the end of sex for the time being. Maybe forever since the boy said: "It is harmless and won't return." Wanting to kill the snake can mean that the dreamer was afraid of getting pregnant. It could also mean that she didn't want to have sex. Not long after this interpretation I got news from the dreamer that 'the snake' had flown off never to return.

90. Eloping with my brother

'I dreamt that I was eloping with my brother. We found a registry office and got married in secret.'

Such a dream may seem utterly ridiculous at first. But something like it could happen. And it did in this case. The lady met a man who was the same age as her brother. She fell in love with him and the two did elope. This highlights the fact that the dream is often a likeness rather than a literal prediction.

91. Christmas dinner

'I dreamt that a young woman took a little boy for a walk in his pusher. Everyone was waiting for her so the family could have dinner. She arrived very late. Because of this an older woman present asked her to stay the night.'

In reality the younger woman and the elder one were not present at this dinner as persons. They turned out to be merely two aspects of the dreamer herself. What is even more fascinating is that the dreamer is not at all present in the dream. Instead she is merely an observer of what is taking place.

On the dream day this woman visited her ex-husband and her grown son for some Christmas cheer. She prepared something for a modest dinner. But she also drank champagne. This raised her level of alcohol above .05. Because of this she was asked by her son and ex-husband to stay the night. But she only agreed to stay long enough to sober up enough for the drive home.

At this point we strike one of those typical inversions that are so much part of our dreams. Instead of the dreamer 'inviting' herself to stay the night as the dream seems to suggest, the dreamer was asked to stay. It inverts a part of the plot. This can be confusing if we are not familiar with this habit of the dream.

In order to sober up the dreamer had gone for a long walk with her son after dinner. On that stroll we see her in the role of the younger woman. This harks back to a time when she often did go for walks with her baby son in his pusher.

Here we notice yet another inversion. While the dream pictures the dreamer as the younger woman on a walk 'before dinner', in reality the stroll of mother and son took place 'after dinner'. This inversion is not altogether meaningless. While on their walk the dreamer felt uncomfortable because she was actually keeping her husband of the second marriage waiting at home.

There can hardly be a better example demonstrating that the dream is about the dreamer alone. Indeed, where are those others when we are dreaming? They are not separate from us. They are aspects of us.

If we take this a step further we find that this same rule applies when we are awake. All we see 'out there' is really 'in our head' just as it is when we are dreaming. The sense that the world is a separate creation is clearly illusory.

Hindus say that the world is Brahman's dream. There is nothing that could exemplify this better than our dream state. Those who cannot come to grips with the notion of God might consider substituting that idea with consciousness. From the point of view of consciousness the world is its dream.

92. Green twig and water pipe puppet

'I am pushing and pulling a green twig through a little stick figure that has been assembled from pieces of water pipe. The figure is lying on its back in a posture of self-abandonment.'

On the day before this dream (residue) the plumber had come to the dreamer's house to fix a burst water pipe. The dream then, like the creative artist, used the off-cuts left by the plumber in the backyard to form a human figure. On the dream day the dreamer trimmed a bush in front of the couple's bedroom window. The green trimmings became the marker of the sexual manifestation later on. The green twig was obviously representative of the penis. The burst water pipe signalled the impending ejaculation. Note that here 'pulling' did not manifest as masturbation because it was accompanied by 'pushing'.

93. Daughter rapes father

> 'My daughter suddenly sprang at me and tried to pull down my pants so she could rape me. I fought back as well as I could. I woke up with a fright.'

This was the dream of a father who had lent his daughter a considerable sum of money. The time came to repay the debt. The daughter denied that she ever had a loan. This denial came on the dream day. The father felt indeed raped. (Robbed) Fighting the rapist signals repression of sexual urges.

94. Raped in office

> 'I went to see my publisher when he suddenly pounced on me and raped me in his office by the computer.'

This dreamer was a writer. She went to see her publisher on the dream day. The latter had quoted her a certain amount for editing and printing. Instead of keeping his promise he charged her well over the agreed amount. Notice the rape happened by the computer. This device is the editor's main tool. But it also contains the word computation. Being robbed of the promised amount of money signalled being deprived of 'promised sex'.

95. Moon and three fried eggs

'I looked up to the sky and saw the moon disintegrating. Fragments scattered all over the sky and fell on the earth. As they splashed into the oceans, floods washed over the land. I heard sobbing everywhere and the waters turned red. Three pieces of the moon crashed down nearby. When I had a close look at them they turned to three fried eggs.'

Three days after this dream this woman's period began. On the same day she also heard the news of Princess Diana's death. She always regarded Diana as an incarnation of the Moon Goddess. What is quite startling here is that the breaking down of the ovum is seen by the dream as a cosmic event. It shows again that we are really at-one with the universe. It reminds us that seeing it as a separate creation is an illusion.

The connection between the moon and menstruation is well-known. The word menstruation (mensuration) is derived from the moon whose cycle is 28 days much like the average menstruation cycle. Moon and womb are closely linked. This can be gathered from the discovery of the two Balkan doctors Jonas and Miavec. They found out that if the birth data of a woman was known, her receptivity could be calculated. The calculation is based on the relationship between the Sun and the Moon. With this discovery it was possible for the two doctors to develop an astrological form of birth control. They also could predict and indeed "predetermine" the sex of a child.* (*See *"Astrology"* by Solange de Mailly Nesle; Inner Traditions International, pp 110-111)

96. Dry riverbed

'I am walking along in the bush searching for water. At last I come to a riverbed. To my great disappointment it is completely dry. I follow the bed upstream. It is heavy going because of the many rocks in my path. I wake up with an empty feeling.'

So what was the sexual manifestation of this dream? Did this man have sex on the dream day or perhaps later? It would seem so for he was 'looking for water'. Knowing what riverbeds stand for it should not be too difficult to determine what really happened. There is even the word 'bed' included in this term. But it also has rocks in it. In view of the fact that rocks will turn to rocking there can be little doubt about what had happened on that day. But there is something in this plot that looks difficult and hopeless. The dream said that the riverbed was dry. This suggests that the wife was too. Dry in more sense than one. It was the last time the couple had sex together. The two separated soon after.

97. Bed on roof

'As I was climbing into bed I suddenly realised that the stars were looking down on me. I was intensely puzzled by this. I looked around and found that my bed was on top of the roof of my house. Before I had time to wonder about this my attention was caught by something jutting out of the tiles. On closer inspection it turned out to be part of the plumbing of the house. It looked like a vent pipe leading down to the toilets.'

When the dream foresees an emotional high it places us on a high point. A common spot is on top of a mountain. It could also be high up on a cloud. Everyday language would express such a high as being 'on cloud nine'. The literary pheromones 'puzzled', 'my attention was caught' and 'on closer inspection' again express heightened sexual interest. The house in this case referred to the wife of the dreamer. Being on the roof of the house suggests being on top of his wife. The pipe jutting out of the roof and being connected to the toilet at the same time indicates sexual union.

98. Sliding down an icy slope

'I was leaving work which was situated on a mountaintop. As I stepped outside I could see that the landscape had turned wintry. Instead of walking down the steep slope I simply slid down on the icy snow. The ride was quite bumpy yet I didn't lose my balance and I enjoyed it tremendously!'

'Work' and 'sliding downhill' betray impending sex. 'Sliding' is an 'acrobatic pheromone' as it were. What is interesting here is that the sliding is happening on an icy slope. In reality there was no snow anywhere. The dreamer found the explanation for this when he woke. The night was cold and all the bedclothes had slipped off him.

99. Caught 'flat-footed'

'I dreamt that I had a flat tyre. I had no equipment to fix the flat, nor was I able to get help.'

After this dream the dreamer went to see his secret lover at her house. Unfortunately her husband was still at home. The two had expected him to be out. So that they could be close to each other they sat at the table opposite to each other. The husband joined them. After a while the dreamer started to play tootsies. But when the husband noticed the intimacies under the table this fell flat on its face. He stood up and angrily asked the dreamer to leave.

100. Conducting choir of girls

'I was teaching a choir of girls a new song. I began to sing it for them. But when I came to the refrain I could not remember it. I was stuck completely. Suddenly I could see the score close up. However the notes were missing. I could only see the lyrics. Mysteriously a Chinese writing brush got into my hand. With it I brushed over the text and the notes appeared magically. Now I could hear the tune and find the home key. I didn't even have to sing it for the choir. They sensed what I was hearing and they sang it effortlessly.'

In course of the day there were several non-sexual manifestations of this dream. Since songs are predominantly sexual, I shall report only the sexual interplay that followed on the dream day. Late in the evening the wife of the dreamer joined him in bed. She lay on top of him and started to rock gently. Soon they engaged in intercourse in reverse position. After a short while the husband found this too much of a constraint and tried to roll his wife off. But she pinned him down. He was stuck in that role. Gradually his excitement grew to an unbearable point. He threw his partner off and rolled her on her back. But before coupling with her again he 'brushed' over her pubic area teasing her into frenzy. In the end it was as difficult for him as for her to wait any longer to get into the 'home key'. There was no need for him to say anything. They managed to 'sing together' effortlessly. The 'home key' in this context shows again that 'home' in dreams alludes to sexual union. Here it is doubly clear since a 'key' in this context is the penis. Longing for home in dreams is mostly longing for sexual union. Ultimately it may stand for spiritual union such as that of the mystical marriage or the mysterium coniunctionis.

This shows again that the use of hands is about stimulating the genitals, but it also makes it clear that it need not always be of the self-indulging kind. The great number of people present during sex indicates intense feelings.

101. Rainbow bridge

'I dreamt that a shadowy figure was leading me towards the back of a temple in Colombo. When my companion opened the portal, a dimly lit room opened up. It was totally empty apart from a diminutive yogi sitting in Padmasana in the middle of the room. The moment I set eyes on him he stretched out his arm and touched my forehead with the tip of his finger. At the instant of contact I 'swooned'. I lost all awareness of my body and surroundings. Yet I retained a blissful sense of self. It expanded into an endless sea of gentle but radiant light. Time ceased to be. Imagery was lost. Thoughts were suspended until a new dream began. In it I found myself walking in strange robes through the thronging crowds of some kind of festivities. A small woman in a colourful sari came towards me. She placed a treasure chest at my feet and opened it. Unfortunately I was unable to see inside the chest because the half open lid obstructed my view. At that moment I woke from the dream.'

Right at the beginning of this book I discussed the three phases of human consciousness. There I said that deep sleep was seen by an observer of the EEG as quiet Delta waves. I also noted that for the sleeper this phase was a dreamless state of light and bliss. It is actually a foretaste of our true state of being. It is like being in the vestibules of heaven. At the start I promised to speak of my personal experience of this. The rainbow bridge dream describes it. It shows that during a dream we can actually 'wake up' to this state of bliss instead of to the usual waking experience. Western science is silent on this point. Dream researchers only report that deep sleep is a dreamless NREM phase.

Hinduism is far more awake to such inner states. Western researchers will have much to learn from Vedantic wisdom. There the state of light and bliss is well-known. It is generally referred to as Samadhi. Basically there are two Samadhis. One is called Kevala Samadhi, the other Sahaja Samadhi. When a devotee is in Samadhi his head does not drop as when he goes to sleep. This is because the senses are present although merged in a state of bliss. If we attached the EEG to the head of such a devotee sitting upright in Samadhi, we would see slow Delta waves.

Among mystics this state is referred to as divine ecstasy. The mystic burns with God's love. Indeed the French mathematician Pascal recorded his experience of the mystical union in one word only: 'Feu', or Fire! In Japanese Zen this fire is known as Satori.

When a devotee is in Kevala Samadhi he will return again to his ordinary senses and their activities. This contrasts with Sahaja Samadhi. Once in that state the devotee does not return to earth so to speak. He has reached Turya. This is the eternal substratum of existence. It is the supreme reality beyond all other realities. Then the devotee IS that state. He will know that he always was and always will be THAT.

Appendix

Dream Lecture to Melbourne's Society of Hypnotherapists 20th of February 2011

Introduction: The most common word we use when we retell a dream is 'weird'. Our dream stories almost always begin with: "I had this weird dream!" When we ask ourselves why most of us feel this way about our dreams, we soon realise that it is because dreams are so unlike our ordinary waking experience. Indeed, most of them come across as thoroughly absurd, preposterous, fantastic, and quite impossible.

But when we look for the underlying reasons for this, it soon becomes evident that our judgment is founded on the expectations that the dream ought to be like our waking experience. But it seldom is and so we declare it to be weird. This universal expectation shows that we instinctively regard the dream as an integral part of our waking self and not some arbitrary happening that is totally detached from our daily life.

So are dreaming and waking aspects of an integrated reality? Opinions vary widely. Indeed, the range of opinions in this matter stretches between assertions that there are no such things as dreams and the view that dreams are at least as real as waking, and, as within my own experience, more real than waking.

Since the advent of the computer it has become fashionable to compare dreaming to off-loading and reorganising data. In contrast to this, dreams in ancient times were thought to be messages from the gods. A vestige of this idea is contained in our term dream divining. Those that were divining dreams also believed that dreams were portents of things to come and their interpretations were made with that in mind. Some American Indians didn't just see their dreams as visions of things to come, but also attributed to them the same reality status as to waking. For this reason they were often considered by others to be consummate liars. On the other hand, in our own society, we have commentators like Phillip Adams who disparagingly labels his dreams as the wastepaper basket of his waking hours.

The most famous of dream diviners of our own culture is, of course, Joseph, son of Jacob, who got himself out of jail thanks to his gift of dream divining. Not only did he get himself a ticket to freedom because of his interpretative skills, but he was also promoted by a thoroughly impressed Pharaoh to the highest office of the land. "You shall preside over my house", said Pharaoh to Joseph, "and all my people shall be ruled in accordance with your word: only in the throne will I be greater than you."

Some promotion! No longer open to our modern dream diviners of course. The Age of Enlightenment saw to that. But then Freud came along and rescued the dream from total annihilation and installed it as the Royal Road to the Unconscious. Curiously enough he built his own skills of interpretation upon the foundation laid down in a book by the old Roman dream diviner Artemidorus of Daldis. Freud followed his every interpretative step except the last one. And what was this last and most crucial step the ancient dream diviner took? It was the transposing of the decoded dream plot to the future tense.

It is here where Freud broke with the ancient tradition of dream divining, making the interpretative task to what we now know as dream analysis. While still going along with the ancients in their belief that dreams were meaningful reflections of the dreamer, he rejected the idea that dreams were capable of looking into the future. For him the dream became a medical tool for the purpose of unravelling his patients' neuroses.

For him the dream no longer continued into the morrow as with the ancients who saw it as the blueprint of the future. For him it stopped in the dead of night. Dreams for him were, as everyone who has heard of Freud would know, the compensation for unrequited love.

There was however one form of continuity he could not deny. This was the fact that there was an indisputable continuation between yesterday's waking experience and the dream of the night that followed it. He discovered this during his analyses of his dreams and those of his patients. He found that there were always numerous features in the dream that undoubtedly harked back to the day before the dream. He called these items the 'residues' of yesterday.

But he also had to admit at one stage that not only was it quite common for these residues to actuate the dreams of the succeeding night, but that a great number of them could present themselves at that time. In short, they were clearly, as he said himself, a bridge between the day before and the dream of the night that followed. Moreover he was forced to admit that these residues at times usurped the plot of the dream, forcing it to maintain the story line of the day.

Whether he realised it or not, with this he admitted that there was manifest continuity between waking and dreaming. And if it was the case between waking and dreaming, it would seem unnatural if there was not also the same sort of continuity between dreaming and waking. In light of this, Freud's wish fulfilment theory annihilates itself. Indeed, there is no better epitaph for its liquidation than his recognition that 'the day's residue may just as easily be about something else than wishes'.

The role of the dream then, as I see it, is best summed up by regarding it as the will of the Master Hypnotist. The parallels between the dream and the posthypnotic suggestion are as parallel as parallels can be. As in the case of the posthypnotic suggestion, where the subjects execute the hypnotist's commands on time and with precision, so do the dreamers act out the suggestions of their dreams. And, just as the hypnotised subjects are unable to recall what has been suggested because that was part of the master's command, so the average dreamers won't recall any of their dreams. And last, but not least in any way, just as hypnotised subjects will give us good, yet wrong reasons, when asked why they did what they did, so will the general dreamers provide good, yet false reasons, for their daily decisions and actions.

DREAM of a Tonal Artist

"I had all these animals around me and the animals that I remember were mostly rabbits and cats. I especially remember a black cat and a beautiful, domesticated, brown and white English rabbit. I discovered them when I opened a door to a room. The rabbit had a white chest and white flash on the forehead and nose. He was very beautiful and I thought, "OMG - I don't remember shutting this rabbit in this room. I must get him some water and food QUICK!!! People will think that I have not cared for him!" I took 2 double food containers to the tap; one was plastic and the other stainless steel. The rabbit was there waiting along with the black cat and other rabbits and cats and other animals.

I looked over towards the left hand side where there was a very big poster, half the size of the studio wall. It was night and the poster was also dark. It portrayed a sombre landscape out of which emerged a man in a dark suit. I only could see his trousers at first, then his jacket, while his shoulders merged into the landscape. I could not see his face at all. I then heard his horrible, threatening voice. He said something like, "I will kill those animals, or I will hurt those animals!" I was very afraid at first and I almost wanted to run, but then something welled up inside me and I felt that I must fight for what is right whatever the cost even if it meant my own life; and the anger and revenge tugged at my heart. I hated this man and I wanted to kill him then and there. I grabbed a small but very sharp pointed object and I lunged at him with it and I said, "I will kill you!" This is when I woke myself making terrible sounds in the attempt to shout at the sinister figure in the dream."

Manifestations of the Dream on the same Day: After the dreamer returned from an outing in the afternoon, she went directly to her studio, opened the door and walked in. To her horror she discovered a dead rabbit on the floor near her easel where she had been working on a portrait of a person wearing trousers. As we saw, in her dream she "opened a door to a room where she discovered a cat and a very attractive, brown and white English domestic rabbit." In reality however the only thing that exactly tallied with her dream was the fact that she opened the door to a room which happened to be her studio. After that the first variations of the dream story begin to appear. In reality there was no cat and the rabbit of the corresponding waking event was not of the English domestic breed, but of the Australian wild variety, which moreover was cold and stiff.

Here we might be inclined to dismiss such a splintered resemblance to the dream plot as little more than fragmentary coincidences. But that would be too hasty, for dreams do seldom come true literally. This is because they are generated in a realm of a different dimension and time scale. It means that their condensed information will have to be unscrolled like the compressed content of a computer zip program before it becomes intelligible. If we were to view such a program in its compressed form, we would be nonplussed in the same way as when viewing our dreams in their pristine state. Yet when such a program is scrolled down the desktop, an intelligible text will gradually emerge. This is also the case with dreams. In short, before we are justified to dismiss the futuristic content of a dream, we need to unzip it first.

So, after having discovered the dead bunny, our dreamer jumped back in shock because she was sure that only her black cat could have killed this poor little baby rabbit. It was at this point that the black cat of the dream was making its appearance in real time. It was not in corporeal form, but in the shape of a firm and unassailable thought. Here we discover a common dream fact: thoughts of waking may present themselves in our dreams quite readily by means of living imagery. In short, the dream does not make the same hard and fast distinctions between things and 'thinks' as does our waking mind.

This is one of the reasons why dreams so often engender in us that sense of weirdness. While in waking we think certain things, the dream dramatises or rather dreamatises them by representing them as life-like experiences. An example of such dreamatisation away from our present plot might be this: the dream could place us on a little white cloud. After waking up we would consider this totally weird. But if we were told by someone that 'today he was on cloud nine', we would not find it extraordinary, fantastical, absurd, impossible or indeed 'weird', but would accept it in a perfectly matter of fact manner.

We can now appreciate why the waking manifestation of the rabbit dream was a mixture of literal fact and superimposed imagination. Perhaps one reason the dream had shown the dead rabbit in the studio as a live and attractive English bunny, could well have been that the dreamer had always had deep feelings for rabbits. This harked back to a time when she owned and cared for rabbits of the English variety.

Another difference between the dream and reality was that the dream actually featured several cats, while in waking there was only one imagined cat to be considered. The plurality of cats might well have been the dream's way of showing that the cat's action on that day would loom large in the dreamer's mind. This too is a rather typical dreamatisation of an emotional factor. To give another example: when lots of people appear in a dream, our emotions on the day of the dream will be on the happier side. In other words the dream uses our past experience of a crowd of people as a model for feelings that are engendered when there is much going on in our life.

It is not likely that our dreamer, when faced with the dead rabbit in her studio would rush off saying, "I must get him some water and food QUICK! So what is the dream trying to say here? For one thing, such a statement could express the dreamer's feelings for rabbits in general, but it also could foreshadow her anxiety about the impending encounter with the dead rabbit for whom fetching water was going to be all too late. Faced with the little corpse, she naturally blames herself for the death of the rabbit because it was her cat that killed it. So the phrase, "I have not cared for him", is an expression of guilt for not having prevented this death by confining the cat. But it is also an expression of her compassionate nature and her special empathy for animals. The question, if there could be even more to this, will always be in the back of an interpreter's mind. Indeed, the deeper we look into a dream, the more seems to come to the surface, just as in a zip program.

And there is more of course; but in light of the waking facts so far we cannot imagine why our artist "took 2 double food containers to the tap, one of which was plastic and the other stainless steel. Nor can we fully understand why she said in her dream: "The rabbit was there waiting along with the black cat and other rabbits and cats and other animals." Indeed, had she actually done so, we would have to have serious doubts about her sanity!

But when we realise that the painter's studio was also the cat's night quarters where an actual double water container for pets was kept, a more explicable connection between the dream and its corresponding waking scenario begins to emerge. Once again dreamatisation plays its usual part here. The dreamer had always thought she would have liked to change the actual plastic bowl for a stainless steel double bowl because it would feel and look much classier! And it might probably also be safer as well! Clearly the dreamatisation of the stainless steel bowl was meant to express her extra care for animals; her wish to give the animals the very best there is!

In the phrase "cared for him" and "2 double food containers" the dream reveals that the artist is indeed an animal lover who moreover participates in the "CARE 2" program on the Web, where she is actively fighting for animal rights and the prevention of cruelty to animals. Although the cat was not physically present when the dreamer encountered the dead rabbit in her studio, it was nevertheless there in spirit, for after all she was the cause of the rabbit 'waiting' there to be discovered by the dreamer. Interesting is of course that the dream said "waiting along with the black cat and other rabbits". In reality it was not only the rabbit that was 'waiting' to be discovered, but the cat was waiting for her mistress as well; waiting for her to discover the rabbit she had caught for her. The plurality of rabbits might be readily explained by the fact that the cat had caught several rabbits before this day. Here the dream states this fact of the past again by means of dreamatisation.

"I looked over towards the left hand side and there was a very big poster, half the size of the studio wall." In reality there was no such thing as a poster, let alone one half the size of the studio wall; so this has to be read in a metaphorical manner. Clearly a poster in a dream means much the same as what it means in waking: something needs to be made public for all to see. There is no doubt that the dream here announces that the matter posted on the wall is of prime importance. And because it takes up half of the room, which has turned out to be her studio, it threatens to take up half of the artist's painting time. So here we are face to face with the core of the dream, its central theme; its highlight. The highlight of a dream is also the summation of a dream, the climax just as it occurs in theatrical plots. Often a meaningful interpretation of a dream can be given by just looking at the dream's highlight. No less fortuitous is the fact that the highlight of a dream is not only the part that stands out above all else, but is also the part that is fading least and always last from our dream memory.

"It was night and the poster was also dark. It portrayed a dark landscape and out of it emerged a man in a dark suit. I only could see his trousers at first, then his jacket, but his shoulders merged into the landscape and I could not see his face at all."

There were, of course, many paintings in the studio, among them a great number of landscapes and also a portrait of a person in trousers in the making. The rabbit lay close to this portrait because the cat knew that her owner had been working there last. The rabbit was a trophy to be presented as a gift to her mistress. The portrait featured a figure standing upright wearing trousers. The night before, the artist had brought this portrait into the half light of the lounge (one of several night motifs) which shows up tonal faults in particular. She noticed that the trousers were too light in colour which forces the viewer to look at them before anything else. She realised that this would have to be rectified by bringing out one shoulder by means of lightening it and darkening the pants.

To a tonal painter this portrait presented extra challenges because the subject could not be lit up as is usual since it hurt the subject's eyes; for this reason she had to compromise and portray the face of the subject darker than what she would have preferred in this case. The dream exaggerated this by losing the upper part of the portrait in the dark of the landscape. Another darkness factor was of course her black cat that had killed the rabbit. In a way she was a part of the faceless man. That the cat was the culprit was only an assumption and thus also a faceless fact. At the time of the artist discovering the dead rabbit it was daylight. So the darkness in the dream was both an historical reference to the night before and to an emotional factor; but it was also a signal that it was by no means a proven fact that the rabbit was a victim of the cat. Darkness in the present context is also indicative of the fear of the unknown, the uncertain, and the threat of imponderables. In view of the poster being in the dark it is also pointing to a fear of public scrutiny. This would most certainly apply to the painter's art, but there could be much more to this.

"I then heard his horrible, threatening voice. He said something like, 'I will kill those animals, or I will hurt those animals'. I was very afraid at first and I almost wanted to run, but then something welled up inside me and I felt that I must fight for what is right whatever the cost even if it meant my own life; and the anger and revenge tugged at my heart."

At this point the dark cat that in the artist's mind had murdered the rabbit, (something which she really hated) merges with the faceless dark man who is a symbolical figure representing those faceless people who are in favour of the extermination and torture of all kinds of animals. They are faceless because they are people on the Web which the dreamer contacts by means of reproving emails, thus inviting aggressive responses.

"I hated this man and I wanted to kill him then and there. I grabbed a small, but very sharp pointed object and I lunged at him with it and I said, "I will kill you!' "

Here this man is clearly installed as the figurehead of those which the artist is actively fighting on the Web by endorsing petitions that attempt to abolish animal cruelty. "A small but very sharp pointed object" may well stand for the sharpness of the pen that is mightier than the sword. And the pen can easily be a stand-in for the keyboard on the computer. Her fear of the dark, faceless figure can readily be interpreted as an actual fear of being attacked personally via the faceless correspondents of the internet. At the same time her battle with the unusual lighting situation which the portrait of the trousered figure had brought about, mingles with this fear of the animal torturers, thus compounding her fear of the Web bloggers with the anxieties engendered by her creative struggle.

2nd Day Manifestation: There is of course more to this dream. I had long discovered that there is a distinct second day manifestation of every dream motif. These manifestations are always more literal than many of the first day manifestations. The artist was informed about this fact and she could report such a 2nd day manifestation.

It occurred when she was watching an episode of a crime thriller on TV. Towards the end there was a scene in which someone had broken into a shop at night. It was obviously dark in the room. Most interesting was that this someone actually remained invisible (!) to the viewer. This clearly became a more specific manifestation of the faceless man of the dream than the more metaphorical expression pertaining to the faceless public. While the intruder itself remained invisible, the silvery and sharp tip of the arrow he was to shoot at the owner of the shop was clearly manifest. In the dim light of the shop the owner was also an assumed presence, in this way augmenting the already intense apprehension and fear engendered. The arrow missed its target, penetrating instead the eye of a shop mannequin. So that small, sharp instrument of the dream, revealed itself on the second day as something more substantial than just a symbolical pen or keyboard. It showed itself as an actual weapon that could kill, which is in perfect keeping with the dream story.

Another motif of the dream that presented itself on the second day was the apposition of the two kinds of rabbits: the brown and white English rabbit next to the Australian wild rabbit. The latter was of course part of the first day manifestation. So where was the brown and white rabbit? It appeared in the next film the artist was watching. In that show a white rabbit was featured. While that was only 'half the English rabbit' so to speak, there appeared more colour in an associative manifestation. The astonishing thing was that this rabbit apposition actually anticipated another show the dreamer was to watch later. It was about the domestication of the dog. There the question of why and how our dogs that all had sprung from the wolf was examined. In a Russian breeding program of foxes over a 50 year span of research it was discovered that when the tamer animals were selected for breeding, they became not only more attuned to man, but they also changed their appearance; both their colour and physical features changed. Clearly the apposition of the English and the wild rabbit of Australia could only become fully meaningful in light of this program. This ultimately shows that the dream not only anticipates the waking phase subsequent to the dream, but also foresees features of the 2nd day. Further study would reveal an even greater spread of manifestations in time, for it has long been found that dreams can take weeks, months and indeed years before they manifest their main motif. One example would be Sikorsky's boyhood dream of a 'flying boat' which he remembered only again when it materialised in form of his 'American Clipper' he had built 30 years later.

But, believe it or not, there is more to the English rabbit and to what I call protracted manifestation. It will convince you that the associative manifestation of the fox breeding experiment examined earlier, (which the dream incidentally had anticipated by means of the dreamatisation of 'other animals among the cats and rabbits') was not a long bow, that it was not a contrived interpretation, but a 'legitimate' and typical, and indeed frequent kind of manifestation of a dream.

On the third day the dreamer was watching a current affairs program that featured a segment on live sheep export to the Middle East with its concomitant animal cruelty. After this report the dreamer went straight to her computer and called up 'Animals Australia' in order to join the association. To her surprise and delight she found that one of their main icons was the very beautiful, domesticated, brown and white English rabbit of her dream! Since joining the association obliges the members to distribute pamphlets against animal cruelty, the poster of the dream is more fully explained. The artist will have to go public and actually erect a bill board at the point of distribution. This will surely take up half her painting time, and if not that, it will most certainly encompass half of her emotional life. But it will also force her to face the dark and faceless 'man' directly; something to which this rather reserved artist is certainly not looking forward to. But her compassion for animals is sure to summon enough courage in her to face her fears head on.

Postscript: Twelve months later this artist is ever more involved in shielding and protecting animals from their mindless and sometimes deliberately cruel masters. As an active member of an animal protection group, she attends protest meetings against animal cruelty and live export. She collects signatures on a regular basis at a market where she displays her billboard with the plea against animal cruelty. This billboard takes up half the wall behind her stall, an unexpected literal manifestation of a part of her dream. As well as that, a new genre in her painting has emerged that is indeed taking up half her time as an artist. It is portraiture of animals in dire need of help.

In dream 75, "Hippos in Moat", I put forward the idea that the little girl must have experienced a cryptomnesic mysterium coniunctionis at the moment of coming face to face with the rhinoceros at the zoo. Something parallel to this also happened to our artist when she was a little girl of similar age. One day she was looking at a picture book which featured a matador being gored by a bull. Appalled at this sight she started hitting the picture crying: "Naughty, naughty, man hurting the poor bull!"

This apparently strange inversion of the facts was due, in part, to the little girl's general empathy towards animals, and not, as we might suspect, due to a misunderstanding of the picture. But it also was rooted in her future as an animal rights activist, the mission of which was launched by her cat and rabbit dream. The fact that she now carries out these activities under the insignia of a bull in a red square certainly strengthens this hypothesis.

It is worth noting the little girl's violent reaction at the sight of the picture. This corresponds with her violent reaction against animal abusers in her dream she had as the grown up artist. ("…and the anger and revenge tugged at my heart. I hated this man and I wanted to kill him then and there.")

Of no less interest is the fact that outwardly she is a very peaceable, always diplomatic, yet vigorous campaigner.

General Index

Part I
The Basics

Dream Index of Part I
Dreams A-T pages 4-45
A Thanksgiving Day
B Spilled briefcase
C Stopped too late
D Jetting to Africa
E Taking off with a jerk
F Suspended alligator
G "Sorry sir, I am closed!"
H To party in separate cars
I Grizzly bear at Central Station
J Stung by swarm of bees
K Restless canary
L Splashed into my eyes
M Leaf out of my book
N Looking for suitable box
O No fresh bread (bred)

Part II
The Freudian Interpretation

Dream Index of Part II
Dreams F1-F23 pages 71-118

Dream Index of Part III
One 101 Dreams
Dreams 1-101 pages 126-188

16. Hotfoot
17. Repressed urge
18. Lizard awaking
19. "Sorry, no screws!"
20. Convents and tractors
21. Sex kitten
22. Walking on water
23. Wrong focus
24. Driving without licence
25. Screwing as approval
26. The eyes have it
27. Fed-up
28. Tiger as flesh-eating bacillus
29. Clowning around with flute
30. Cat-scan
31. Cat as child
32. Boys and squelching pathways
33. Mushrooms between toes
34. Cinderella's glass slipper
35. Drowning in work
36. Not dead, just missing
37. Space invaders
38. Drawing and petting
39. Red-hot picnic
40. Faceless
41. The proverbial mother-in-law
42. Sharks and polar bears
43. Fire and mice
44. Snagging an octopus
45. Floods replenishing bank
46. House of relationships
47. Lounge as the womb
48. Lounge as the womb confirmed
49. Fruit and nuts

50. Unrequited love
51. Forgotten garden
52. Strolling through the garden
53. Wrestling a giant
54. Lucky break
55. Haircuts
56. Joining hands
57. Reaching for the rhino
58. From fur cap to silk scarf
59. Reflexology in dreams
60. Neck and jaw
61. Explicit sex as kindly love
62. Inverse projection
63. Fish in pools
64. Island of red roses
65. Not measuring up to expectations
66. Jumping puddles with Princess Diana
67. Jumping from log to log
68. Olives and vertigo
69. Engulfed by floods of passion
70. Verger and Virgo
71. Embracing fear of death
72. Books as the 'procreative word'
73. Broken and unbroken egg
74. Sewn together
75. Hippos in moat
76. Bushed
77. Poring over exam paper
78. Cello ablaze
79. Two arms on old record player
80. What's in a name?
81. Pine hill
82. Wingless angels
83. Garden of Eden

Index/Glossary for all Dreams

Amazed: dream 50
Amazement: literary pheromone: dreams F13, F14, P
Amniotic fluid: dream 64
Amorous: dreams 78, F12
Angels, wingless: dream 82
Anger: deep red: dream; 42, 61, 74
Animal cards: signifying animal nature: dream 89
Animation: lifeless objects dramatising/dreamatising
sexual acts: dream F18
Announcement: dream F22

Index/Glossary for all Dreams

Acrobatics: dream 2

Acrobatic pheromone: dream 67

Acrobatics in dreams: sexual agility, often a sign of impending sexual interaction; dream 2

Actors, colourful: dream F21

Acts and scenes of dreams integrated: dream F20

Advice, incomprehensible: dream 16C

Advisor, spiritual: dream F17

Africa: dream D

Alarming symptoms: blood in urine; dream 84

Allegories, dreams are mostly: dream F23, comments

Alligator: almost always an impending betrayal; dreams 3 & F

Alligators: dream 3

Alterations of garment: as expression of making amends; dream 74

Alter ego: mystery companion: dream H

Amazed: dream 50

Amazement: literary pheromone; dreams F13, F14, P

Amniotic fluid: dream 64

Amorous: dreams 78, F12

Angels, wingless: dream 82

Anger: deep red; dream; 42, 61, 74

Animal cards: signifying animal nature; dream 89

Animation: lifeless objects dramatising/dreamatising sexual acts: dream F18

Announcement: dream F22

Antiques as dead relationship: dream 5

Antiques: past events and bygone relationships; dream 5

Anxieties: dream H

Anxiety: While it is mostly a literary pheromone, here it is also anxiety in the sense of being afraid; dreams 24 & 48

Anxiety, rise of: dream F21

Apartment, modern: dream 16B

Aphrodisiac: rhino's horns, by extension rhinos signal sexual desire; dreams 57, 75

Appealing colours: sexual attraction or sexual highs; dream 65

Approval: screwing as nonsexual approval; dream 25.

Arab diviners: ascertained dreamer's circumstances before interpreting; dream 45

Argument: sharks and polar bears; dreams 15, 41, 42, 46. Blazing argument as red colour; dream 74

Armful of dolls: dream F8

Arm on record player: representative of penis and ultimately of husband/s; dream 79

Arousal: dreams F13, F15, 38 & 53

Artemidorus: Roman dream diviner of the 2n century CE. Freud learnt the steps of interpretation from him and adopted all of them except the last one: the transposition of the interpretation into the future tense. Also see dream 23; Part II Point 3, paragraph 2; Point 6 paragraph 1; Point 7 paragraph 2

Artic waters: shows that love is in deep freeze; dream 42

Artistry of dreams: dream F23

Artist/s: dreams 80, 83

Artists' Society: dream 16C

Ashram: things started to go wrong; dream F16

Associated manifestation: dream 16A

Associations as clue to dream's meaning: dream 50

Associative characteristics: dream F2

Associative factor: dream F2

Associative identification: dream T

Associative language: dream F2

Associative representation: dream F3

Astrological birth control: dream 95

Atmosphere of great love and spiritual satisfaction: dream F17

Attendant at liquor shop: dreams G & F2

Attention, attracting: attention drawn to; dream F6. Unwanted attention; dream 16B. Focus on the sexual state between partners; dream 46. Particular attention; dream 80.

Augmentation of feelings: frequently indicated by an enlargement of a room, building or panorama and so on; dream 21

Awaking: arousal, erection; dream 18

Awareness lost: dream F21

Axes: striking without hands as sign of intercourse; dream 6

Baby girl: the vagina; dream 8

Backing away: withdrawing from lovemaking; dream 44

Back pain: indicated by points on sole of foot; dream 59

Back to snow: dream 14

Bag, striped: dream 1. Bags, handbags are always also a reference to the vagina

Balance, holding: teetering on the brink of an orgasm; dreams 67, 98

Banging: colliding in intercourse; dreams 10, 13, F9

Banners centre stage: dream F21

Barren landscape: suggesting barren womb; dream 16F

Barren womb as barren landscape: dream 16F

Basement: dream Q

Bashed to death, baby girl: dream 85

Bashing: dream F9

Bear, grizzly: dream I

Beautiful: mostly a literary pheromone; dream 54

Beautiful colours/light: dream F14

Beauty: promise of sexual high, importance of grammar of dream language; dream 50

Bed on roof: dream 97

Bee sting: injection: dream J

Bees, swarm of: dream J

Belt through eyelet: dream F18

Betrayal: in guise of alligator; dream 3

Between inner and outer world: dream 70

Between mankind and universe: dream 70

Beyond sex: dream 82

Bhagavan: spiritual guidance, guru; dream 58

Bike ride: as sexual intercourse; dream F19

Birds of prey: dream K

Birdsong in spring: dream 78

Birth control: astrological; dream 95

Biting: signals passion; dream 75

Bittersweet syrup: spiritual healing effected through spermatic medication; F16

Black robe: dream S

Blazing argument: expressed as red colour; dream 74

Blazing fire: dream F15

Bleeding, a long time coming: difficult menstruation; dream 85

Blind drunk: dream L

Blindness: dream L

Blinds: pulling down blinds refers to prophylactics; dream 37

Bliss: dream 101

Blood clots in my urine: announcing menstruation; dream 84

Blossoms - related to blood: dream 87

Blue light, radiating: dream 82

Blue paint magically covering wallboard: dream 83

Blurred speech: dream 16C

Boards: dream F3

Books: as the procreative word; dream 72. Signifying intercourse when pages turn by themselves; signifying masturbation when pages are turned by hand; dream 72. Book opening up by itself; dream 80

Book, tear leaf out of: dream M

Bottle and glass: dream F10

Bottle as male: dream F10

Bottle, long, green: F11

Bottle of bittersweet syrup: dream F16

Bottle of curious shape: dream F10

Bottle of gin: dreams G & F2

Bottle, unusually elongated: F11

Bottom drawer: reference to the dreamer's readiness to have change of heart and welcome sex; the dreamer is identified with the seamstress; dream 74

Box, inability to find one: waiting for resolution; dream N

Box: vagina; dream 79; the womb, secrets, hiding things; dream N

Boxes, lots of: dream 16A

Boy, little, running towards the entrance: dream F22

Boys and squelching pathways: dream 32

Boys, two in play: dream F21

Boys, younger, older, little: penis in various states of virility; dream 32, 39

Brahman dreaming the world: dream 91

Braking too late: dream C

Branch as fulcrum: dream F12

Branch as penis: dreams F12, F19

Branch, snapping off: dream F19

Brand name: dream F5

Bread, fresh: new start; dream O

Breaking: often breaking up orgasmically; dream F7. In dream 11 it is breaking up of a relationship. It includes emotional breaking up and also sexual disconnection.

Breaking away: dream F7

Breaking communication: dream 11. Inability to communicate as a sign of no sex.

Breaking through: dream F7

Breasts: nurture. In dream 12 it is erotic self-indulgence as well as emotional nurture.

Bride: dreams A & 70

Bridging: change from foreplay to intercourse; dream 68

Briefcase: spilled effects, ineffectiveness; dream B

Broken relationship: dream 44, 56

Brother's age: the same as that of lover; dream 90

Brush/brushing: over pubic area; dream 100

Buildings: the dreamer's body; dreams 8 and Q. Hall-like building; dream F14

Bull, bullying: dream 15

Bullying bull: dream 15

Bumping: sexual intercourse; dream 13.

Burning: dream 16

Burrowing in embers: fervent intercourse; dream 39

Burst water pipe: as ejaculation; dream 92. Burst hoses; dream F15

Bushed: dream 76

Bush, holiday in: dream F15

Bus, omnibus: public domain; dream 20. Driving it is being in charge of sections of society; in charge of students; dream 54. Travelling by bus to change to a smaller vehicle as it goes uphill on rocky road. Dream 16D

Bus shelter: place for waiting; dream 69

Busy people: dream F13

Buttocks, up and down: dream 29

Camp, in charge of children's: dream F22

Canary, restless: longing for freedom; dream K

Cancerous growth on feet: indicates sciatica and back pain; dream 59

Cantaloupes: reference to the vagina, as rock melon it signals rocking; dream 49

Cap, fur: indicates sexually active person; inability to purchase fur cap alludes to giving up sex; dream 58;

Car parts, corresponding with body parts: dream 19

Carpet, covered with: dream 16C

Carpet, green: dream 16C

Carpet, swept under: dream 16C

Car represented by kangaroo: dream C

Carry phone to spring: dream 16A

Cars, in separate: dream H

Cartoons: dream 65

Case, packing: dream F3

Cat: dream 30. Flattened cat on the road; dream 36

Catapulted into the air: an orgasmic high/shock; dream 20

Cat as child: dream 31

Cat door: the vagina; dream 31

Cat-scan: dream 30

Cat-scan: dream humour; dream 30

Caught flatfooted: dream 99. Caught between rungs; dream F9

Cello on fire: dream 78

Celluloid: dream F5

Cemetery: dream E

Central corridor: reproductive passage to the womb; dream 8

Central Station: dream I

Centre stage, banners: dream F21

Chalk: dream F3

Challenging destiny: dream 1

Changing nappy: faeces flying into mouth signifying being fed-up; dream 27

Changing to smaller vehicle: dream 16D

Charades: dream M

Chestnuts: referring to the breasts; dream 49

Child, four-year old: at the zoo, memories of past lives and future episode; dream 75

Childish desire: dream 67

Children: one child as cat; dream 31

Children's camp, in charge of: dream F22

Child, retarded: as cat of the house; dream 31.

Chiropractor: alluding to sexual manipulation; dream 60

Chiselling: dream F7

Christmas dinner: dream 91

Church: dream A

Cinderella's glass slippers: attempt at a new start in relationship; dream 34

Circle: indicative of circular motion in foreplay; dream 38

Clay, soft: dream F6

Cliff: disruption of life, sudden change; dream D

Climbing a mountain: the mountain is almost always the Venusberg; dream 81

Climbing into bed: climbing sexual partner; dream 97

Climb up: dream F5

Clinton: dream F5

Clitoral erection: tree in volcano; static series (in association with dream F3)

Clitoris: dreams 64, 67, 68; static series

Clocks, departure: dream I

Closer sitting together: more intimate; dream 16D

Clowning around: daring fondling in public; dream 29

Clowning around with flute: dream 29

Clowns: dream 29

Clutch: the vagina; dream 19

Coals, red-hot: as in red-hot embers; dream 39

Coitus: from Latin 'coming together'; dream 20

Colleague, alligator-like: dream F

Collision: sexually bumping into partner; no collision no sex; dream 24

Colour change: change of state of mind; red to pink, anger to love; dream 74. Black to red indicating arousal; dream F18

Coloured, highly: intense sexual feelings; dream 79

Colourful actors: dream F21

Colours, appealing: Sexual attraction or sexual high; dream 65; high colours signify high feelings; dreams 72, 78, F14

Colour scarlet: colour of menstrual blood; dream 87

Come and see: invitation to sex; dream 75, dream F15

Communication: this is often portrayed by the phone; dream 11. Lack of phone connection means inability to have intercourse.

Course, wrong: dream 16F

Court, royal: dream F21

Courtyard: vagina, play on words; dream 89

Cousin, laughing: dream 88

Covered with carpet: dream 16C

Crack: often a reference to the vulva. In dream 11 it is a metaphor for splitting up.

Crafts, practising: dream F13

Crashing: most often an orgasm due to intercourse; dream 10

Creativity of dream: assembling pipe off-cuts to form a human figure; dream 92

Creek: the vagina; dream 34

Creeping floods: announcing menstruation; dream 86

Crowded: expresses closeness of bodies in sexual interaction; dream F20

Crowded cafeteria: dream F20

Crowded stage: dream F21

Crows: dream K

Crystals, pinned to hat: cooling head; dream P

Cubby hut: secure retreat, at the same time a new woman. Cubbies are especially expressive of the intimacies and securities of the womb; dream 44

Cupboard, kitchen: dream F5

Cycle of life: dream 71

Dam as bank account: dream 45

Dark: dream Q

Dark corner: dream F3

Darkness: as looking within; dream 70

Dark tunnel: dream F 21

Daughter association: as catalyst to the dream's meaning; dream 50

Daughter rapes father: dream 93

Daughter's house: dream F3

Dead body: of a woman; dream 71

Delivering timber: carried by the sawmill itself instead of by truck; expressive of wholehearted participation; dream 62

Dental filling: Sexual intercourse; dream 60

Dentist, as husband: dream 60

Depression: being thrown to the ground by greater force; dream 53

Desire, childish: sexual desire gratified without a partner; dream 67

Destiny, challenged: dream 1. Submitting to destiny; dream 58. Fixed; dream 82

Dew in morning sun: transience of proposal; dream 34

Diary of dreams necessary: dream 16C

Dipping fingers into wine: dream F10

Dipstick: the penis; dream 19

Disappointed: dream F7

Disturbing period: drawn out menstruation; dream 85

Divine: referring to clitoris; dream 64

Dizzy: orgasmic high; dream 68

DNA/RNA: dream J

Doctor of family: dream F16

Dodging oncoming traffic: avoiding mishaps; dream 24.

Dog: often representing one's libido; dream 4

Doing little: as ejaculation, dream F22

Dollars: dream F10

Dolls, taken away/getting back: dream F8

Doodling: dream 28

Door, inserting key into lock: F1

Door, opened: dream F4. Doors flung open; dream F22

Downstairs: reference to reproductive system; dream 86

Drag: being drawn into sexual intercourse; dream 20

Drawer: vagina. Half open drawer; dream 13

Drawing and petting: dream 38

Drawing, as in petting: dream 38.

Drawing as masturbation: dream 28

Dream as creative artist: dream 92

Dreamatise: dreams M & F18 (animate/dreamatise)

Dream diary a necessity: dream 16C

Dreamer as observer of self: dream 91

Dreams are about the dreamer: dream 91

Dreams as theatre with acts and scenes integrated: dream F20

Dreams, many per night: dream F20

Drifting: letting go, disregarding the needs of oneself; dream 12

Driver of car: dream F13

Driving along with boys: dream C

Driving: being in charge; dream 24

Driving without licence: dream 24

Drowning in work: as for everyday metaphor; dream 35

Dry riverbed: signalling vaginal dryness; dream 96

Dwarves in street: reference to the clitoris; dream 56

Eating bacillus: life threatening; dream 28. Eating olives as sexual pleasures; dream 68

Economy of language: dream 16E

Ecstatic feeling: spiritual ecstasy likened to sexual ecstasy; dream F16

EEG: dream 101

Effects: effective/ineffective: dream B

Egg, without and with shell: impending period/no signs of the period yet: dream 73

Egg yolk: ovum; dream 63

Ego-transference: dream 70; dream T

Ejaculation: dream 47. Spontaneous; dream 77. As burst water pipe; dream 92. Shower of rain; dream F6. Wood breaking away/through, orgasmic 'breaking up'; dream F7

Electric wires: dream 30

Elephant, lifting onto back: dream Q

Elephants and guru Ganesha: dream 4. Bull elephant; dream R

Elephants: power, strength, helping force as in Ganesha; dream 4; danger of being squashed by; dream R. As sexual potency; dream F18

Elongated bottle: F11

Eloping with my brother: dream 90

Em-bank-ment: play on words pointing to a bank account; dream 45

Embarrassed: dream 29

Embers: dream 39

Embracing fear of death: dream 71

Emotions: water; dream 22. Emotions expressed by means of explicit sex; dream 61

Empty feeling: before marital breakdown; dream 96

Endless, passage seemingly: dream Q

End of life: dream 71

Engine parts: dream 19

Engraving: dream 28

Engulfed by floods of passion: dream 69

Enthralled: literary pheromone; dream 75

Entrance, going towards: dream F21

Erection: in act of explicit sex expressing non-sexual love; dream 61

Eros: Greek god of love, son of Aphrodite, goddess of love; dream 54

Examination, medical: dream F16

Examine: self-assessment, dream 74

Excitement: dream 16B

Excrements, into mouth: fed-up; dream 27

Exhibition of paintings: dream 50

Ex-husband: stand-in for new husband; dream 79; visit from; dream O

Expectations: not measuring up to; dream 65

Explicit sex, as kindly love: dream 61. As expression of spiritual healing; dream F16

Exquisite taste: dream F10

Eye: representing vagina; dream 26

Eyelet for pulling belt through: dream F18

Eyes, splashed with: dream L

Faceless: dream 40

Faceless man: person unknown; dream 40

Facial shapes: dream 16C

Faint haze: dream F14

Falling into red-hot embers/coal: as for falling in love; dream 39

Fallopian tubes: dream 16F

Fame and fortune: referring to clitoris; dream F13

Family doctor: F16

Famous: referring to clitoris; dream 64

Farmhouse: reference to female lover; dream 32

Fascinated: Sexual arousal, literary pheromone; dream 18; dream F13

Fascinating, etymology of: dream F13

Fear of pregnancy: dreams 27, 39, 47, 63, 89

Fed-up: dream 27

Feeler gauge: the penis; dream 19

Feeling ecstatic: due to insertion of ten fingers into vagina, spiritual ecstasy likened to sexual ecstasy; F16

Feeling empty: precursor of marital breakdown; dream 96

Feet: dreams 16 & 75

Female body: dream 47

Female partner as wall board: dream 83. Usually the lounge floor or lawn/ground.

Fertility: dream 81

Festive peal of the organ: dream 70

Festive scene: dream 21

Field: the ground, the earth, the floor, the pelvic floor, the woman; dream 20. Field of beautiful, green grass; dream 54

Fight, mock: representation of sexual intercourse: dream F 18

Filleting: dream 22

Filling dam: as replenishing bank account; dream 45

Fingers: representing the penis and general arousal; dream 38. Middle finger; dream 38; fingers in foreplay; dream 68. Ten fingers inserted into vagina; dream F16

Fire: intense passion; dreams 6, 39. Fire in mouse nest inside piano signifying ovulation; dream 43. Fear of fire not contained; dream 48. Open fire as receptive female partner; dream 48, dreams 78. Blazing fire; dream F15

Fire and mice: dream 43

Fire brigade: dream 78

Fire, caught on: dream 78

Fire on horizon: arousal, erection; dream F15

Fireplace: vagina; dream 39. Picnic type fireplace: F12

First lover: dream 16B

Fish attacking egg: precursor of menstruation; dream 84

Fishing out olives from a glass jar: foreplay; dream 68

Fish in pools: dream 63

Fish, vagina, penis: dream 22. Fish in pool alludes to intercourse or pregnancy; dream 63. Gold fish; dream 63. silvery fish; dream 63. Throwing fish out of pool; dream 63.

Flattened cat: dream 36

Flautist: dream 29

Flesh-eating bacillus: dream 28

Flight to Europe: dream N

Floods replenishing a dam/bank account; dream 45. Threatening house, impending menstruation; dream 86

Floods replenishing bank: dream 45

Floor as foundation of life: Mother Earth, dream 71

Floor in danger of dropping onto pylon in water: before orgasm; dream F13

Floor, pelvic floor: refers to women, often the womb; dreams 2, 6, 13, 46, 83

Flowering gum: dream 87

Flowers – the word is rooted in 'flowing': dream 87

Flue: the penis; dream 6

Fluid, sexual: emission; dream 60

Flute as penis: dream 29

Fly, opened: dream F22

Focus, wrong: dream 23

Focused with particular attention: dream 80

Follow: a male dreamer following his son mean following his penis; dream 13

Foot: dream 16. Foot on grassy ground; dream F13

Football field: dream F20

Football ladder: dream F20

Football, literal manifestation as question if boy could rejoin football: dream F21

Football match played: dream F20

Foreplay: dreams 21, 38, 68, 79, F3, F9

Forgotten garden: dream 51

Forgotten lines: dream F21

Fortune, hoping for: sexual arousal, orgasmic high, clitoral excitation; dream F13

Fossilised rain: as ejaculation; dream F6

Foundation lost: dream 71

Fried eggs and the moon: dream 95

From fur cap to silk scarf: dream 58

Frontal lobe: gives sense of control; is activated in lucid stage; dream 71

Front door: dream F1, F4

Fruit and nuts: dream 49

Fruit: as genitals; dream 49

Fruits of the earth: dream A

Fulcrum, as pivot for branch: intercourse; dream F12

Fun: ready bedfellow of sex; dreams 66, 67, 88, F12

Fungus: dream 33

Furniture, same as: dream 16B

Future in dreams proven: dream 16G

Garage with door open: dream F14

Garden, forgotten: dying relationship; dream 51. Garden as new and thriving relationship; dream 52.

Garden of Eden: dream 83

Garment, wrong: returned to mend relationship, for reconciliation; dream 74

Geyser: dream 16A

Giant, to be wrestled: authority that has the last word; sexual arousal that is stronger than resistance to it; dream 53. Giant as erection; dream 53

Gin, bottle of: dreams G & F2

Girl, little: dream 7, dream 26

Girlfriend: dream H

Glans: dream 79

Glass as female: dream F10, F11

Glass slipper: fragility of the attempted new start; dream 34

Glorious landscape: dream 50

Gloves: prophylactic; dream 39

God as consciousness: dream 91

God as dreamer of the world: dream 91

Goddess-like: referring to clitoris; dream 64

Grammar: dream J. Of dream language; dream 50

Grandchild, as waning sexuality; dream 27

Grass around the house: pubic hair; dream F15

Grass: often pubic hair; dream 13, 54

Grassy ground: dream F13

Great love: F 17

Green: growth, fertility, hope; dreams 6, 13, 54, 92

Green twig and water pipe puppet: dream 92

Green twig as penis: dream 92

Grin, cheeky: sleazy allusion; dream 32

Grooming hair: masturbation; hair refers to pubic hair; dream 9

Grooming the body as honing speech: dream 9

Ground, open: woman open to sex; dream 39

Ground: refers to women much like the floor; dreams 2, 39

Ground, thrown to: the ground here refers to being at lowest point/ depressed instead of to a woman; dream 53

Growth, arrested: dying relationship; dream 51. Growth on feet corresponds with sciatica and lumbar pain; dream 59

Guru: spiritual guidance; dream 22

Gushing spring: dream 16A

Guttering: vulva; dream 32

Gymnastics: an 'acrobatic' pheromone; dream 67

Hair: often thoughts, but also status. In dream 9 it also has pubic hair in sight

Haircut: change of status; in dream 55 becoming single again.

Haircuts: dream 55

Hall-like building: as for hall-like room; dream F14.

Hall-like room: enlarged spaces indicate augmented feelings; dreams 21, F20

Hammer: dream F7

Handbag: dream 1. Always also a reference to the vagina.

Hands: magic appearance of axe in hands; dream 6. Striking without being conscious of hands foresees intercourse; with clear awareness of using hands it refers mostly to masturbation or petting in foreplay. Hands pointing upwards indicating state before arousal and penile erection; dream 38. Joining hands, finding solace/self-pleasuring; dream 56. Absence of hands yet chiselling; dream F7

H A P P Y X M A S: dream F3

Hat, Tibetan monk's: dream P

Hawks: dream K

Haze, faint: dream F14

Head, cooled by crystals: dream P

Head on erection: intellectual intimacies, spiritual intercourse: dream F17

Heap of papers: static series; dream 35

Hearts, Ten of: success in love and sexual/reproductive matters; dream 16F

Heat: passion; dream 6

Higher being: dream 82

Higher spheres: dream 82

Highlight: dream F5

Hinduism: dream 101

Hips: associated with pelvic floor; dream 8

Hippos in moat: dream 75

Hit, hitting: reference to sexual colliding; 20

Hole in floor: vagina; dream 47. Hole in carpet, concern about pregnancy; dream 48

Holiday in bush: dream F15

Home key: finding it is sexual union; also represents spiritual union, the mystical marriage; dream 100

Honeymoon: dream 45

Hooked: dream 44

Horny, feeling: dream 57

Horse race: dream 16F

Hoses burst: male orgasm/ejaculation; dream F15

Hoses, place of: Man's erogenous zone, specifically reference to penis; dream F15

Hoses ready: arousal, erection; dream F15

Hose under house: penis; dream 47

Hose with nozzle: penis; static series (in association with dream F3)

Hose without nozzle: clitoris, static series (in association with dream F3)

Hot: dream 16

Hotfoot: dream 16

Hotfoot: speedster. Excessive speed is often a sign of a surplus of testosterone; dream 16

Hot, red-: sexual heat, dream 39

House: dreams 6, 8, 20, 31, 32, 37, 46, grand 75

House: house-wife, the wife; dream 97

House of relationships: dream 46

House partly on water and partly on land: woman sexually aroused; dream F13

House surrounded by floods: impending menstruation; dream 86

House surrounded by grass: reference to woman's pubic hair; dream F15

Huge hall: when normal size dwellings are enlarged by the dream it indicates emotional intensity; dream F20

Hugging tall, skinny man: dream T

Humour, sense of: dream 30. The dream often plays with words and ideas. It frequently makes puns.

Hurry: dream B

Ice-floe: in arctic surroundings promising safety, but with polar bears on it, it accelerates fear and desperation; dream 42

'If-clause': dream 50

Impressions of rain drops: traces of ejaculation; dream F6

Incomprehensible advice: dream 16C

Infected: dream 28

Inner and outer world, essential unity of: dream 70

Insemination: dream 47

Inserting key: dream F1 & F4

Intercourse as mock fight: F18

Intercourse, last before separation: dream 96

Intercourse, sexual: 1, 3, 6, 10, 13, 20, 32, 36, 39, 54, 60, 63, 65, 68, 69, 72, 96, F1, F4, F5, F6, F7, F8, F9, F10, F11, F12, F13, F14, F15, F18, F19, F20, F21, F22, F23

Intercourse, spiritual: head on penis; dream F17

In touch physically: greater intimacy; dream 16D

Inverse projection: dream 62

Inverse projection: timber is brought by the sawmill instead of by truck; dream 62

Inversion: right to left; dream J

Inversions, brain wiring: dream J

Inversions in dreams: dream 91. Inversions of part of the plot; dream 91. Of 'before and after'; dream 91

Island of red roses: clitoris; dream 64

Island of red roses: dream 64

Jar: refers to vagina; dream 68

Jaw, dental work: grinding down teeth to avoid problems; dream 60. Mouth association leading to vulva, vagina; dream 60

Jerking take-off: impatience, hurry; dream E

Jet: fast movement, quick decisions: dream D

Jewel: Mani, Sanskrit; dream 64

Job, getting: dream 88

Joining hands: finding solace/self-pleasuring; dream 56

Judge: dream 65

Jumping from log to log: clitoral stimulation; dream 67

Jumping in front of car: dream C

Jumping puddles: 'jumping' is an acrobatic/gymnastic pheromone. Puddles, like all watery places, refer to women; dream 66. Jumping from log to log; dream 67.

Jumping puddles with Princess Diana: dream 66

Junior: refers to penis like all boys; dream 2

Kangaroos as cars: dream C

Key, home-: sexual union; dream 100

Key: the penis; dreams 100, F1, F4

Kids, getting together: dream F22

Kiln: like ovens refers to the womb; dream 6

King on throne: dream F21

Kiss: dream T

Kissing: as prelude to sex; dream 69

Kissing decision left to me: dream F17

Kitchen cupboard: dream F5

Kitchen utensils: dream 16A

Kitten: the vulva; dream 21. Euphemism for 'pussy'; dream F8

Knees, on my: indicates intercourse; dream 68

Knob: glans/head of penis: dream 79

Knower and the known are one: dream 51

Knowing: carnal knowing; dream F13

Knowledge: often 'carnal knowledge', 'biblical knowing'; dream 21

Know someone in the biblical sense: dream 40

Kundalini cure by means of spermatic medication: 'Kunda' is a pit for sacred fires. Kunda is etymologically related to 'cunt' F16.

Ladder: dreams 68, F9. Football ladder; dream F20. On top of ladder; dream F20

Ladder of emotions: dream F21

Ladder of success: dream F21

Ladder, on top of: dreams F20, F21

Lady cloaked in black: Lady Death; dream S

Lake: vagina, reproductive system; dream 63

Land it: bringing in to land where land refers to the bed and ultimately the female partner; dream 44

Landscapes: dreams 50, 52, 78, 98. Barren; dream 16F

Language, economy of: dream 16E

Large rooms: augmented feelings engendered in ordinary rooms/bedrooms; dreams 21

Latin endings a & o: dream 70

Laughing cousin: dream 88

Laughter: signals sexual interaction; dreams 49. As ready bedfellow of sex; dream 88

Lawns, dead: dying relationship; dream 51

Lawns: dream 83. Lawn sods; dream 6

Leaping: an acrobatic/gymnastic pheromone; dream 67

Leaves, of book: referring to greening, to life; dream 72

Leg as penis: dream 28.

Lever, as penis: dream F12. Lever catching fire; dream F12

License, without one: sign of inexperience; dream 24

Licking: as reconciliation; dream 61

Lift, getting a: obtaining a (sexual) high, getting high on something; dream 20

Light: dream F12, 83, 83, 101

Light, blue: dream 37

Light shaft: skyward, heavenward, lifted up, uplifted: dream D

Likeness projected in dreams: dream 90

Lines, forgotten: dream F21

Lines, trying to remember: dream F21

Liquorice: dream F5

Liquor shop: dreams G & F2

Literal manifestations are rarer: dream 90

Literary pheromones: dreams 36, 50, 80, 97, F12, F13

Little, as urination symbolising ejaculation: dream F22

Little boy: dream F22

Little girl: dream 7, dream 26

Little hippos from big hippo: ejaculation; dream 75

Lizard awaking: dream 18

Lizards: most often the penis; dreams 3, 18. Lizard wrapped around tree as intercourse; dream 3; as thwarting livelihood; dream 3

Lock: dream F1 & F4

Lock, inserting key in: dream F1 & F4

Log as clitoris: dream 67

Log, burning: penis aroused; dream 48;

Log of firewood: as penis; dream F12

Lollies: dream F5

Lost awareness: dream F21

Lost only one game: dream F20

Lots to offer: dream 16C

Lounge: (Appropriately called living room) refers to women, especially the womb; dreams 5, 13, 47

Lounge as womb: dream 48

Lounge as womb confirmed: dream 48

Love affairs: creating public interest; dream 69; exudes powerful pheromones; dream 69

Love, great: dream F17

Love is Blue: dream 83

Love match: dream 52

Lover, first: dream 16B

Lucid stage: dream 71

Lucky break: dream 54

Lucky break: saved from disaster but also separated from old job; dream 54

Lucy: attendant in liquor shop; dreams G & F2

Machine: dream 30

Main hall as womb of woman; dream 50

Main Street: Important task; dream 24

Making love: colour pink; dream 74

Making music, everyday metaphor: dream 29

Making out, unable to do so; dream 23

Mani: Sanskrit for jewel; dream 64

Manifestation, mixed: dream A. Multiple manifestations; dream F23

Manipulation of neck: sexual allusion; dream 60

Many dreams per night: dream F20

Mantra, Om Mani Padme Hum: dream 64

Map of Africa: dream D

Marker animation: dream F18

Markers, examples: objects/situations that mark sexual activity; dreams 13, 20, 25, 39, 92. Vicarious; dream F5. F6, F7. Of literal manifestation: F11. Sex in the dark; dream F12. Serial markers; dream F14. Potting bonsais; dream F19. Dream F23

Marriage, mystical: dream 100

Marriage proposal rejected: dream 16B

Married in secret: dream 90

Masterpiece: dream 50

Masturbation: dreams 1, 5, 8, 9, 15, 28, 72. Not masturbation; dream F7. Suspected; dream 50.

Measuring up to: not doing so; dream 65

Medical examination: dream F16

Membrum virile: virile penis; dream F13

Memory, retrograde and forward looking: dream 75

Menstruation: dream 63, 84, 95

Menstruation is rooted in mensuration of lunar phases: dream 95

Metaphor, every day: dream 29, 43

Mexican cowhand: dream 16F

Mice: referring to vagina; dream 43

Microbes; enlarged: dream 33

Mid-air: suspense suspended; dream D; dream F

Middle: often the middle of the body, the sexual organs; dream 21

Middle finger: the penis; dream 38. Swollen, stiff; dream 38

Minds, being of two: dream H

Miracle, hoping for: dream F21

Miscarriage: dream 85

Missing screw: dream 19

Missing sex life: dream 50

Mixed manifestation: dream A

Moat: like all water it refers to women's reproductive system; dream 75

Mock fight: representation of sexual intercourse; dream F18

Modern apartment: dream 16B

Monk, Buddhist: dream P

Moon and womb linked: dream 95

Moon fragments turn to fried eggs: dream 95

Moon's disintegration as breakdown of ovum: dream 95

Mortise hole: dream F7

Mother-in-law: dream F8

Mother of All/Universe: dream F16

Mother's grave: dream E

Mountain range: signifying mounting in intercourse; dream 72

Mountain: feeling high, most often 'mounting'; dream 2

Mountain top: dream 98

Mountain track: Venusberg, vulva; dream 54

Mouse nest inside piano: uterus; dream 43

Mouth, excrements into; dream 27

Mouths, moving: dream 16C

Moving mouths: dream 16C

Mud, buried in: latent sex; dream 18

Multiple dreams per night: dream F20

Multiple marker: dream F16

Murdered baby girl: impending menstruation; dream 85

Mushrooms between toes: dream 33

Mushrooms, between toes: signs of oncoming thrush; dream 33

Music: dream 29, 43; 78

Musical Instruments: dream 29

Musicians: dreams 29, 43, 78

Mysterium coniunctionis: past, present and future are all one; dreams 75, 100

Mystical marriage: dream 100

Nails, large: dream F9

Nails, sticking out: dream F9

Nakedness: being exposed and defenceless but also stripped of clothing due to sexual arousal; dream 53

Narrow part: precarious passage; sexual reference to vulva/vagina; dream 54

Narrow track: vagina; dream F19. Narrow, steep and rocky uphill road; dream 16D

Narrow waterfront: vagina; dream F13

Natural, fingers appearing: indicates time before general arousal; specifically before penile erection; dream 38.

Navigator's seat: in control, knowing where to go and what to do; dream D

Necessity of dream diary: dream 16C

Neck and jaw: dream 60

Neck, connection with jaw: dream 60

Nest, mouse: dream 43

Night: dream S

Nine months later: protracted manifestation; dream C

Nipples: dream 68

Not dead, just missing: dream 36

Notes, no such: dream 16G

Not measuring up to expectations: dream 65

NREM: dream 101; Non-REM as dreamless Delta state; also see dream phases

Nurture: often indicated by breasts; dream 12

Nurturing breast: dream 12

Nuts: as for testes; dream 49

Oceans: mostly a reference to women since they carry the amniotic fluid. All life rose from the oceans, hence a classic image of Mother of All. If the oceans die the earth will follow soon. Dream 64

Octopus: possibly a play on words, an oversexed female in this case; dream 44

Offer, lots to: dream 16C

Official, officer: dream 50

Oil on slippery giant: signifies inability to come to grips but also alludes to ejaculation; dream 53

Old lady: dream 82

Olives and vertigo: dream 68

Olives: reference to clitoris and nipples; dream 68

Om: sacred syllable: dream F16

Omnibus: public domain, the outside world. 'Omnis' is Latin for 'all'; dream 20, 55

Only a dream: lucid stage; dream 71

Open discussion: travelling in open vehicle; dream 16D

Opening door: dream F4.

Open, wide; dream F14

Operation of fallopian tubes successful: dream 16F

Oral sex: dream F19

Orgasm: dream F14

Orgasmic high: catapulted into the air, getting a lift; dream 20. Also dreams 9, 10, 68

Orgasm, spontaneous: dream 8

Orgasm withheld: dream 68

Oven: the womb; dream 6

Ovulation: dream 43

Ovum: destruction of; dream 63

Owl crashing against window: dream 10

Owl: nocturnal inspiration, wisdom; dream 10

Packet: dream F5

Packing: dream F3

Padme: Sanskrit for lotus; dream 64

Pages: leaves of books which ultimately were leaves of trees; dream 72

Paint, blue: dream 83

Painting as intercourse: dream 83

Painting is not my work: changing the meaning of the dream from possible sexual interaction to wishful thinking; dream 50

Paintings: dream 50

Painting, talent for: dream 16C

Panic: dream I, F21, intensifies; F21

Panicked: dream 77

Pansies: 'remember me?' dream E

Pantomime: dream M

Papyrus: origin of the word paper; reed growing in the Nile Delta; dream 72

Participation in sex, unreserved: dream 62

Partly literal manifestation: dream F16

Partnership: dream 46

Party, went to: dream H

Past referencing: dream F3

Pathway, squelching: vagina secreting sexual fluids; dream 32

Pat the rhino: desiring sex; initiating sex by petting; dream 57

Paste: starchy substance; dream 83

Peal/peel of the organ: allusion to both church organ and male sexual organ; dream 70

Pearly Gate: dream F1

Pellet: dream F3

Penis as phallus: channel between heaven and earth, bearer of spiritual light; dream F17

Penis: as tree in dream 20; as leg in dream 28; as boys in dreams 32 & 39. As spade and shovel in dream 39. Penis as hose under house: dream 47. As arm of record player; dream 79. Pines with vowels reversed spells penis; dream 81. As green twig; dream 92

Perfect shot: dream F9

Performance of teams: dream F20

Period: dream 84. Announced three days ahead; dream 86

Period pangs: dream 85

Peter, St.: dream F1

Petting: dream 38.

Phallus: dreams 26, F17

Pheromones, literary, suggesting masturbation: dream 28

Phone: always an icon of communication. Inability to phone is inability to communicate both sexually and non-sexually; dream 11. Phone rings; dream 16A. Phone carried to spring; dream 16A

Photos: memories; dream 5. Interaction with photos refers to sexual intercourse or masturbation. The deciding factor is the role of the hands.

Piano: as womb but at the same time referring to 'making music'; a signal that ovulation is upon the dreamer; dream 43

Picket fence: protection against sexual advances; dream 15. As a static series it can suggested male masturbation. This shows again that the context of a dream is of paramount importance.

Picnic, red-hot: dream 39. Picnic type fireplace; dream F12

Pictures: dream 78

Pine hill: dream 81

Pine nuts: dream 81

Pines with vowels reversed: spells penis; dream 81

Pine, treated: F9

Pipe above roof connecting with toilet: sexual union; dream 97

Pipe: penis; dream 97

Plane: fast travel/motion; dream E

Platform, fireplace: F12

Playing cards: petting, cuddling; dream 89

Play on stage: dream F21

Ploughing, the fields: metaphor for sexual intercourse; dream 20

Plural: of roses, indicating static series; dream 64

Pockmarks: dream F6

Poem of Mother of All/Universe: dream F16

Poetry, close to dream language: dream 52

Polar bears: fear of domestic upheaval; dream 42

Pole, leaning against: dream F21.

Police: alertness, watchfulness, moral guardians, often a sign of wrong doing; dream 37

Pond below: dream 68

Pondering: dream 80

Poring over exam papers: dream 77

Potting bonsais: dream F19

Pouring with rain: dream 77

Predestination/destiny: dream 58

Predetermination predetermined: dream 95

Pregnancy, fear of: dream 47; not predicting 27; precautions 39; prevention 63; drawn out period 85

Pricing: dream F10

Princess Diana: dream 66

Proof that dreams are of the future: dream 16G

Proposal of marriage rejected: dream 16B

Protracted manifestation: dream 69; dream C

Public sex: dream 69

Pulling: often the same as in every day metaphors; dreams 13, 38, 65

Pulling and pushing: dream 92; here pulling did not manifest as masturbation because it was part of a pushing action

Pulling out: prophylactic precautions; dream 39

Put it where it belongs: dream 13

Puzzled: typical literary pheromone; dreams 36, 50, 68

Pylons: penis, promise of new sexual relationship; dream Q. Pylons in water as erection; dream F13

Queen-sized bed: dream 66

Race, completed and won: dream 16F

Race, horse: dream 16F

Radiating blue light: dream 82

Rainbow bridge: dream 101

Rape: betrayal; dream 7

Raped as robbed of promise: dream 94. Robbed in both the financial as well as in the sexual sphere; dream 94

Reproductive system: garden; dream 51, 52. Lake; dream 64

Rescue: salvage job; dream 54

Residue: dream ingredients from the day before the dream; dream 6, F7, 92

Retrieve an armful of dolls: dream F8

Returned handbag: dream 1

Rhinoceros: classic expression of sexual prowess; dreams 57, 75

Riches: as virility/fertility; dream 81

Ride, bumpy: sexual intercourse; dream 98

Ride to work: sexual intercourse; F19

Ring, wedding, disposing of: as rejection of the sexual aspect of the marriage; dream 34

Risk: both precarious move and sexual excitement; dream 54

Riverbed, dry: as dry vagina; dream 96

River flat: dream F`19

Road, rocky: dream 16D

Robbing of money as rape: dream 93

Robe, black: dream S

Rock on companion: dream 29

Rocks: both hitting rock bottom and rocking in the sexual sense; dream 54. Foreseeing rocking but with difficulties; dream 96

Rocky road uphill: dream 16D

Rod of office: dream 70

Rolling downhill: a sexual tumble and also failing to progress safely and retain status quo; dream 54

Roof of the house: top of wife; dream 97

Roof, on top of: parallels on top of wife; dream 97

Room: the womb; dreams 5, 10, 21, 48

Roses, red: dream 64

Round objects: referring to females; dreams 49, 50

Royal court: dream F21

Rubbing out drawing: repetitive motion for sexual stimulation; dream 38

Ruler: reference to penis; dream 65

Running wild: dream 76

Run-over: as intercourse; dream 36

Rust, rusty: sign of lengthy inactivity; dream 6

Sacred Marriage Rite: dream 52

Same furniture as: dream 16B

Satisfaction: dream F20

Scarf, silk: spiritual aspirations; dream 58

Scarlet robe: sign of menstruation; dream 87

Scene, festive: dream F21

Schoenberg, composer: dream 80

School, placement of children: dream 31

Sciatica: indicated by growth on sole of foot; dream 59

Science: knowledge, often a reference to 'biblical knowing'; dream 21

Screwing as approval of job contender: dream 25

Screws, no: dream 19

Scrubbing: most often intercourse. Masturbation; dream 9

Sculptures, soft: dream 16C

Sea: dream D

Seamstress: dream 74

Searching for water: desiring sex; dream 96

Second arm of record player: penis of second husband; dream 79

Second day manifestation: always more literal; dream 63; 68

Security: dream 81

Semen: delivered in starchy liquid; dream 83

Separate ways: dream H

Separation between self and world is an illusion: dream 91

Serial manifestation: multiple manifestations of a single dream theme; dreams 6 and F23 –three manifestations

Serial marker: dream F16

Sewn together: reconciliation; dream 74

Sex, beyond: looking towards transcending sex; dream 82

Sex decision left to me: dream F17

Sex, explicit: as reconciliation and kindly love; dream 61. Explicit dream sex becoming actual sex; dream 69. As spiritual interaction; dream F17

Sex in dark as marker: dream F12

Sex in public: dream 69.

Sex kitten: dream 21

Sex kitten: the vagina; dream 21

Sex life, defunct: dream 55

Sex life, missed: dream 50

Sex, looking beyond: dream 82

Sex not wanted: dream F17

Sex of dreamer: dream F2

Sexual fluids, not just: dream 45.

Sexual frustrations: dream 50

Sexual organs: names for the sexual organs of flowers; dream 64

Shadowy, familiar figure: alter ego, the dreamer herself at another time: dream 16F

Shapes, facial: dream 16C

Sharks and polar bears: dream 42

Sharks: sign of an oncoming argument, fear of domestic upheaval; dream 42

Shirt: to be mended; dream 74

Shoes: new ones; an attempt at renewing the sexual aspect of marriage; dream 34

Shopping centre: dream 16B

Shovelling: penis in action; dream 39

Shower of rain: ejaculation; dream F6

Sikorsky: one of his dreams manifested 30 years later; dream 75

Singing: dream 100

Sister-in-law: dream 16A

Sisters: the vagina, the female partner; dream 20

Sitting closer together: greater intimacy; dream 16D

Slamming the door: emphatic end to a relationship; dream 44

Sleeping under bus, son and friend: dream 16E

Sliding downhill: 'sliding' on female partner; dream 98

Slippers: casual attempt at new sexual relationship; dream 34

Slippery giant: Unassailable authority, unassailable sexual urge; dream 53

Slipping through the hand: shortening of foreplay; dream 21

Slope, foundations of the house: dream 46

Slow rise: impatience: dream E

Smile, wry: forecasting an unexpected turn of events; dream 44

Snagging an octopus: dream 44

Snagging: catching something unexpected and worthless or annoying; dream 44

Snake: Penis; dream 89. Fat one, indicating an erection; dream 89. Snake to be killed, prophylactic precautions; dream 89. Shrinking snake; penis after ejaculation; dream 89

Snapping branch off: dream F19

Snow: dream 14

Sobbing everywhere: as precursor of Princess Diana's death; dream 95. (Abraham Lincoln heard sobbing in his death dream)

Society of artists: dream 16C

Soft sculptures: dream 16C

Son and friend sleep under bus: dream 16E

Son: the penis; dreams 8, 13. Son as actual person; dream 61

Song of Songs: dream 52

Sorry, no screws: dream 19

Space invaders: dream 37

Spade: dream 39

Spare parts for engines: Dream 19

Spectacle: erotic excitement; dream F15

Speech blurred: dream 16C

Speech: refers to the procreative word; dream 9

Spheres, higher: dream 82

Spiders caught in hair: dream F19

Spiders popped by squeezing them: dream F19

Spiders, two: dream F19

Spirits: dreams G & F2

Spiritual advisor: dream F17

Spiritual ecstasy expressed in terms of sexual ecstasy: dream F16

Spiritual matters talked of: dream 16A

Spontaneous ejaculation: dream 77

Spring, gushing: dream 16A

Square shapes: feminine objects; dream 50

Squeezing spiders: dream F19

Stage, bravely stepping on: dream F21

Stage, crowded: dream F21.

Stairs, steps, upstairs: regular motions as in intercourse or masturbation; dreams 2, 8

Static series: representation of repetitive motions in sexual activity; depending on the context either intercourse or masturbation; masturbation in dream 35. Possible female masturbation; dream 50. Plural of rose as static series; dream 64

Steep and narrow uphill road: dream 16D

Stiletto as penis: dream F18

Stop saying 'yes': dream 16B

Stop, too late: dream C

Stream: vagina; dream 64

Street/Road: as street; dream S. As vulva; dream 20. Wider circle of society; dream 56

Striped bag lost: dream 1

Stroking: sexual stimulation; dreams 18, 21

Strolling through the garden: dream 52

Strong residue and serial manifestation: dream 6

Studio: dream F6

Stylised drawing: indicative of an erection; dream 38.

Subconscious as dream memory: dream 22

Success/ful: in the sexual context it is an orgasm; dream 9

Successful operation of fallopian tubes: dream 16F

Sumeria: referring to the woman as garden in love poetry; dream 52

Surprised: literary pheromone but also 'ordinary' surprise; dream 48; dream F13

Surprisingly: literary pheromone/sudden arousal F18

Survey of wine: dream F10

Swamp: the same meaning as muddy tracks; dream 67

Sweets: sexual delights; dream F5

Swimming: usually this indicates sexual intercourse. Swimming in arctic waters means that sex won't be available. It foretells domestic trouble instead; dream 42. Hippos swimming in moat indicates sexual intercourse; dream 75. Swimming in pool; dream F23. Swimming with clothes on; dream F23

Syntax: dream J

Table: often a reference to the woman's body; dream 21

Talent for painting: dream 16C

Taoist sex: dream 68

Tape measure: classic image of the extendable penis; dream 13

Tasting/eating: as sexual pleasure; dream 68

Tattoo, drawing, engraving, writing, doodling: dream 28

Teeth flashing: threat; dream F

Ten fingers inserted into vagina: as typing a poem with ten fingers; dream F16

Ten of Hearts: success in love and sexual/reproductive matters; dream 16F

Terrified: fear of the non-sexual kind; dream 44

Thanksgiving: dream A

Thank you for choosing me: dream 16B

Theatre of dreams: dream F20

The eyes have it: dream 26

The proverbial mother-in-law: dream 41

Thighs: dream 29

Third dimension, mountain range: intense feelings through mounting; dream 72

Thousand dollar/lira note: dream 16G

Three fried eggs as three days to the period: dream 95

Throne: dream F21

Ticket box: dream I

Tiger as flesh-eating bacillus: dream 28

Tiger, life threatening: dream 28

Timber: reference to the female of the species because it is harvested from living and growing plant life; dream 62. Timber sticking out: dream F9

Time foreshadowed by three pieces of the moon turned to three fried eggs: dream 95

Toes, cow dung between: male and female sexual organs at intercourse; dream 32. Mushroom between toes as sign of oncoming thrush; dream 33. Toes in water: sexual contact; dream 75

Toilet, inability to find one: repression of sexual urge; dream 17. There are also toilet dreams which simply project the need to go to the toilet. However that need may also stand for associated needs.

Toilets: associative projection of genitals; dream 2

Tootsies: secret lovers playing tootsies under the table; dream 99

Top of ladder: dream F20

Tossing up high: dream F9

Touching physically: greater intimacy; dream 16D

Track, narrow: vulva/vagina; dream F19

Tractor: derived from Latin tractus/trahere, 'to drag'; dream 20

Train, to catch, missed: dream B

Transient sparkle: dream 34

Travelling by bus with colleagues: dream 16D. Travelling across Europe; dream 1

Treated pine: dream F9

Tree in volcano: clitoral erection; static series (in association with dream F3)

Tree, little: dream F19

Tree, lizard wrapped around: dream 3

Trees: life, livelihood, the body of the dreamer , the penis; dreams 3, 20

Trees, stunted: dying relationship; dream 51. Crowns of trees grown together as new relationship and sexual union; dream 52

Tubes: the penis; dream 6

Tunnel, dark: dream F21

Two arms on the old record player: dream 79

Undifferentiated reality: dream 16A

Unfulfilled desires: dream 50

Unhurt in accidents: Accidents like landing on rocks or cars bumping together often mean sexual bumping and rocking; as in dream 54

Union: sexual, spiritual; dream 100

Unity of inner and outer world: dream 51, 70, 86

Unpacking: undressing; dream 49

Urine: font of urine ultimately alluding to vaginal secretions by association; dream 68

Utensils, kitchen: dream 16A

Vagina, inserting ten finger into: dream F16

Vedantic wisdom: dream 101

Vegetation as foundation of books; dream 72

Vehicle, changing from bus to smaller open vehicle; dream 16D

Venus: the blind planet; dream 54

Venusberg: dream 54, Venus + Berg which adds up to 'Mount Venus'. 'Berg' is German for mountain. Also dream 81

Venusian: refers to Venus, goddess of love and sex and beauty; dream 54

Verger and Virgo: dream 70. Verger alludes to being 'on the verge' of

Vertigo: feeling dizzy as orgasmic high; dream 68

Vicarious marker: dream F5

Vines, bare: dying relationship; dream 51

Virility: dream 81

Virgo: dream 70

Vistas: dream 78

Vulgarism: dream F6

Vulva: dream 64; dream 68

Waiting for sex: indicated by waiting rooms, bus shelters and so on; dream 69

Walking on water: dream 22

Walking: sexual activity, intercourse or masturbation, depending on the context; dream 8. Non-sexually it means moving ahead but may ultimately lead to new sexual relationship; dream 14. Walking on water: expecting miracles with the hope of getting into a new sexual relationship; dream 22. Walking through tree arch as love bond leading to new sex life; dream 52. Walking down the isle establishing a regular sexual relationship; dream 70. Walking uphill as climbing the Venusberg; dream 81

Walking upstairs with baby on hip: masturbation; dream 8

Wall: ancient reference to female partner in sex; dream 83

Wallboard: dream 83

Wallboard magically covered with blue: dream 83; compare with dream 6 and F7

Walls, crooked: dream 46

Watch, not waterproof: 'watch out', indicating danger of getting pregnant: dream F23

Water: emotions, 'subconscious'; dream 22. Walking on water spiritual aspirations; dream 22. Water as 'strong water' or semen; dream 47 and in the introduction to Part III; almost pulled into; dream 44; swimming in arctic waters; dream 42; drowning in; dream 35. Forgotten to water as dying relationship; dream 51. Hallmark of womanhood; dream 75

Waterfall: money pouring into bank account; dream 45. It can also herald exceeding vaginal secretion; dream 45

Waterfront, narrow: vagina, dream F13

Water, lifting arm out of: prophylactic precautions: dream F23

Water pipe, burst: as ejaculation; dream 92

Water, searching for: desiring sex; dream 96

Water, shimmering: as definite indicator of female presence; dream 50

Waterways: the vagina; dream 34

Wedding: dream A

Welding: dream F14

What's in a name: dream 80

Wide open: F14

Windows: the vagina, the vulva; dreams 10, 26, 37, 88

Wine survey: F10

Wingless angels: dream 82

Wish fulfilment, not a: dream F4

Wishful thinking: dream 50

Withdrawal, prophylactic: indicated by lifting arm out of water; dream F23

Withdraw the offer: dream 16B

Woman: dreams F11, 38, 58, 71, 91, 101

Woman reclining: foreshadowing intercourse; dream 38

Womb: dream 13, barren; dreams 16F, 47, 48

Wooden frame: vagina; dream F6

Workbench: place of sex; dream F6; dream F13

Working area: place of sex; dream F13

Work/job: reference to sexual intercourse; dreams 6, 98

Work, preparing for: dream F19

Workshop: dream 16D

Work, wife's advice: dream F19

World as Brahman's (God's) dream: dream 91

World seen as separate from self is an illusion: dream 91

Wrapped – rapped – rapturous: dream 79

Wrestling a giant: dream 53

Wrestling, giant: futile defence of submitted work, but also wrestling with sexual arousal, defeated on both fronts; dream 53

Writing: dream 28

Wrong course: dream 16F

Wrong focus: dream 23

"Yes, stop saying": dream 16B

Zip program: dream F3

Bibliography

Allegro, John M, *'The Sacred Mushroom and the Cross'*, Hodder and Stroughton, 1970. ISBN 0 340 12875 5

Artemidorus, 'Oneirocritica'. *Translation and Commentary* by R.J. White. Noyes Press, Park Ridge, N.J., 1975

Brennan, J. H., *'Discover Astral Projection, How To Achieve Out-Of-Body Experiences'*, Aquarian/Thorson, An Imprint of Harper Collins Publishers. 77-85 Fulham Palace Road, Hammersmith, London W6 8JB, 1991, ISBN 1 85538 107 9

Cartwright, Rosalind, *'Night Life'*. 1977, Prentice Hall, Inc., Englewood Cliffs, New Jersey 07632.

Combs, Allan, and Holland, Mark, *'Synchronicity, Science, Myth, and the Trickster'*, Paragon House, New York, 1990. ISBN 1-55778-304-7

Cowan, James, *'Mysteries of the Dreaming'*, *The Spiritual Life of Australian Aborigines.* Brandl & Schlesinger Pty Ltd, 24 Wilberforce Avenue, Rose Bay N.S.W. 2029, 2001. ISBN 1 876040 28 9.

Dunne, J.W., 'An Experiment with Time'. Faber and Faber Ltd., 3 Queen Square, London, W.C.1. First published 1927, third Edition 1934, 1973 Reprint.

Faraday, Anne, *'Dream Power'*. Hodder and Stroughton, St. Paul's House, Warwick Lane, London EC4P4AH, 1972

Frazer, Sir James, *'The Golden Bough'*. A Study in Magic and Religion. Abridged Edition in one Volume. 1960, Macmillan & Co Ltd., London.

Freud, Sigmund, *'The Interpretation of Dreams'*. The Pelican Freud Library, Volume 4. Translated by James Strachey, edited by James

Strachey, assisted by Alan Tyson. Revised Edition, Angela Richards. Penguin Books 1976, 1977 reprint.

Gazzaniga, Michael S. *'The Social Brain'.* Psychology Today, November 1985

Grant, John, *'Dreamers, A Geography of Dreamland'.* Grafton Books. A Division of Collins Publishing Group, 8 Grafton Street, London W1X 3LA, 1986 ISBN 0-586-06500-8

Inglis, Brian, *'The Power of Dreams'.* Grafton Books, a Division of the Collins Publishing Group, 8 Grafton Street, London WIX 3LA, 1987

Jung, Carl Gustav, *'Memories, Dreams, Reflections'.* Recorded and edited by Aniela Jaffe. Translated from the German by Richard and Clara Winston. Collins. The Fontana Library 1967. Ninth impression Nov. 1975

Jung, Carl Gustav, *'The Practice of Psychology. Essays on the Psychology of Transference and other Subjects'.* Translated by R.F.C. Hull. Bollingen Series XX, Pantheon Books.

Jung, Carl Gustav, *'The Structure and Dynamics of the Psyche'.* Second Edition. Translated by R.F.C. Hull. Bollingen Series XX. Princeton University Press.

Koestler, Arthur, *'The Roots of Coincidence'.* Picador, Pan Books Limited, 1974

Kramer, Samuel Noah, *'The Sacred Marriage Rite'.* Aspects of Faith, Myth, and Ritual in Ancient Sumer. Bloomington, Indiana University Press, London; Jan. 1969. ISBN 025 3350 352.

Maharshi, Sri Ramana, *'Talks with Sri Ramana Maharshi',* Vols. I to III, Second Edition, Published by T.N. Venkataraman, Sri Ramanasramam, Tiruvannamalai, s. India, 1958.

Mannoni, Octave, *'Sigmund Freud, In Selbstzeugnissen und Bilddokumenten'.* 1975, Rohwolt Taschenbuchverlag GmbH, Reinbek bei Hamburg.

Sabom, Michael, M.D., *'Light & Death'*, Zondervan Publishing House, Grand Rapids, Michigan, 1998. ISBN 0-310-21992-2.

Sannella, Lee, M.D., *'The Kundalini Experience'*, Integral Publishing, 1987).

Schiffman, Richard, *'Mother of All'*. Blue Dove Press, San Diego, California 2001. ISBN 1-884997-28-7

Solange de Mailly Nesle; *'Astrology. History, Symbols and Signs. Inner Traditions International'*. Rochester, Vermont, 1985

Springer/Deutsch, *'Left Brain Right Brain'*, 1981, W.H. Freeman and Co., San Francisco.

Thornton, E. M., *'The Freudian Fallacy';* Freud and Cocaine. Paladin Grafton Books, 8 Grafton Street, London W1X 3LA. Revised Edition 1986. ISBN 0-586-08533-5

Underhill, Evelyn, *'Mysticism'*. University Paperback, Methuen London. Twelfth Edition, revised, 1930

Walker, Barbara G., *'The Woman's Encyclopedia Of Myths And Secrets'*. Harper and Row, San Francisco, 1983.

Wilder Penfield, *'The Mystery of the Mind'*. A Critical Study of Consciousness and the Human Brain. 1975, Princeton University Press, Princeton, New Jersey.

A big thank you to the four friends who vetted my MS: Jerry Dickman, Jo Starkie, Indra and Lyndel

www.ingramcontent.com/pod-product-compliance
Lightning Source LLC
Chambersburg PA
CBHW050125030726
47505CB00007B/2045